MW01518948

Supervillain Rehabilitation Project #2

H. L. Burke

For information about H. L. Burke's latest novels, to sign up for the author's monthly newsletter, or to contact the writer, go to

www.hlburkeauthor.com

Author's Note:

The Supervillain Rehabilitation Project (AKA
SVR-Verse or DOSA-Verse) is a multi-series
superhero universe (currently) consisting of four
separate series.

**Series One: Supervillain Rehabilitation
Project**
The first series from a timeline perspective, this
series follows superheroine, Prism, as she
attempts to redeem her late father's legacy by
helping his disgraced protege get back on the
hero path.
Relapsed (Short Story Prequel)
Reformed
Redeemed
Reborn
Refined
Reunion

Series Two: Supervillain Rescue Project
This Young Adult spin-off takes place after the
main series when Prism and Fade start a camp
for at risk superpowered teens and follows three
new superpowered characters, Jake, Laleh, and
Marco.
Power On
Power Play
Power Through
Power Up

Series Three: Supervillain Romance Project
This series follows the Park family, a separate superhero clan, as they fight villains—and sometimes date them. This series can be read independently, though later books feature crossover characters from the YA and Original Series.
Blind Date with a Supervillain
On the Run with a Supervillain
Captured by a Supervillain
Engaged to a Supervillain
Accidentally a Supervillain

Series Four: Superhero Romance Project
While there are some cameos from other series, this is a series of standalone romantic comedies featuring other superpowered characters from the universe and can be read independently.
A Superhero for Christmas
A Superhero Ever After
Coming Soon:
Second Chance Superhero

To Goose the Cat. We're destined to be together.
—Heidi

Chapter One

Prism hung onto the straps in the helicopter, waiting as they approached the drop zone. Next to her, two of her team members, Fade and Keeper, sat, ready for anything. The blue expanse of the Pacific Ocean stretched out below them, dotted with whitecaps beneath the morning marine layer of fog.

She tapped on her earpiece. "Forte, check in. Do you have eyes on the target?"

"Got 'em, Pris," Forte, AKA Tanvi Anand, said through their communication channel. Ahead a shape zoomed out of the fog towards the water, a human figure clad in white and hot pink exo-armor with blazing rockets on the back, feet, and outstretched arms. "No one on deck. I don't think they're onto us. Let me get a closer look, though."

"Careful!" Prism cautioned. "If you go into the water—"

"Easy, boss, I've had four months of training in this thing."

Prism bit her lip. It was supposed to be six months, but Tanvi tended to be competitive. She had somehow managed to condense the training to pass her exo-armor flight qualification course into a DOSA—Department of Super-Abled—record.

Fade reached over and squeezed Prism's hand, drawing her attention to his dark eyes. "She's got this, Lucia," he soothed.

Her heart warmed to him, and her nerves eased.

She glanced down at his brown fingers intertwined with her much paler ones. He had a way of calming her which she always appreciated. Still, if Tanvi got herself hurt —

"I just feel she needs reminders not to get carried away," she said.

"Thanks, Mom," Tanvi intoned. "Okay, there's a single man at the helm. Want me to disable him before we go in?"

"Let's time this carefully." Prism glanced at the Marine pilot flying their bird. "Bring us into position, please, Lieutenant," she said. "We're going to do a jump."

"Yes, ma'am." The pilot nodded.

The helicopter dipped closer to the water.

"Keeper, Fade, you good to go?"

"Aye, as always, Luce," Keeper replied, his Scottish accent flavoring his words. He scanned the water beneath them. As an animal charmer, he'd be staying with their ride, ready to call in an assist from either marine life or seabirds if needed.

Fade's powers radiated an intense, tingling energy, signaling his readiness to ghost out of the helicopter at a moment's notice.

"Now, Tanvi!" Prism ordered.

Tanvi dove from the mist towards the boat bobbing on the horizon. She crashed into the crew member. In a blur of movement, she had him down with his hands zip tied behind his back.

"Got him!" she crowed.

The helicopter swooped over the waves, the water stilling beneath it.

Fade's hold on Prism's hand tightened.

"Say when?" he prompted.

Prism waited until they were right over the deck of the small vessel. "Now."

Fade's energy crackled through her, and they sank through the helicopter. Fade's power made them light as air as they floated down towards the deck, landing softly.

As soon as they stood on the deck, he released her hand, and her body returned to its natural density.

Tanvi landed beside them, beaming. Of Indian descent, she had dark skin, long black hair, and sparkling dark eyes, though those were now obscured by a tinted flight visor.

"Keeper, you got a lead on the cargo?" Prism asked over the channel.

"Aye, I can sense them. They're frantic. Let me know if you need them calmed."

An idea struck Prism. "Tanvi, Fade, what would you say to a distraction?"

Fade smirked, and Tanvi nodded.

"The exact opposite," Prism continued, addressing Keeper. "Can you rile them up?"

"On your count."

"Thanks, Bob." She motioned towards the other two members of her team. "Places."

Fade moved to one end of the deck while Tanvi hurried to the hatch to the cargo hold below."

Prism activated the lasers on her wristlets, ready to cut through the deck. "Now!"

The chaotic cries of dozens of tropical birds rang out from below them. Someone shouted. Prism sliced through the deck. A strength sable—super-abled—Tanvi tore the hatch from its hinges. Fade dropped into the hold, and the three sables landed together.

Prism threw out her hands, and a burst of light lit the cargo hold. Men cried out in panic, the sound barely audible over the cacophony of bird cries.

Tanvi tackled an armed man. Prism blinded another with a second flash then kicked him into the wall of the hold. In less than a minute, it was over. Four smugglers sat, bound with zip ties, in the corner of the hold while Prism examined a cage filled with colorful, exotic birds, still chattering anxiously.

"We've got it, Keeper," she said. "You want to get down here and make sure they're well?"

"Aye. The coast guard is coming in with a tow. I'll drop down as soon as they've got it secured."

The oldest member of the team by nearly two decades, Keeper, sometimes known by his birth name, Bob McCabe, had the strength and healing factor inherent to most sables, but in his mid-fifties, he didn't like to strain himself with jumping out of helicopters if he didn't have to. Especially since his powers were better served observing and directing from a distance.

"How much do you think these birds are worth on the black market?" Fade slipped his arm around Prism's waist as they considered the cargo.

"No idea." She put on an exaggerated stern-face. "You thinking about getting into the game?"

He chuckled. "If I were to get back into the supervillain life, I'd go with something a little less noisy and messy than bird smuggling."

"Well, behave yourself." Prism returned his embrace. "If you crossed over to the wrong side of the law again, I'd have to take you down, and that'd just be sad."

He swept her off her feet. "I don't know. I'd like to see you take me down—"

"Ew, get a room, you two." Tanvi rolled her eyes. "I'm heading up to the deck for some fresh air. Between this tub bobbing up and down and you two flirting, I'm about to hurl."

Prism pried herself away from Fade. "Someone needs to take the helm until the Guard gets here, anyway. Do any of us have boating experience?"

She started towards the ladder leading to the upper deck, her hand still wrapped around Fade's.

When Fade had joined their team roughly nine months before, as a former supervillain looking to make things right, she hadn't anticipated falling in love with him, or how essential he'd make himself to both her life and the team's dynamic. Originally, he was supposed to be the first of many subjects entering the Super Villain Rehabilitation Project. However, when a supervillain had targeted the team, costing them a valuable member—Prism's brother, Aiden—she'd opted to put the project on hold and focus on rebuilding their existing team rather than incorporating yet another member. Over the last few months, they'd learned to work together to the point where fighting alongside Fade was a highlight of her life.

She climbed up the ladder onto the open deck. The fresh sea breeze ruffled through her short blond hair, dyed blue at the tips. Fade followed close behind, his tall, athletically built frame overshadowing her for a moment.

Another job well done. Time to head back to HQ and debrief.

***

Prism's team was stationed in a repurposed Naval hospital on Marine Corp Base Camp Pendleton. They were a smaller DOSA team who covered a section between the areas overseen by the larger San Diego and LA sable teams. Prism liked the assignment. Laid back enough to allow for some days spent hiking and beach combing, but essential enough that she felt she had purpose.

After a successful mission, it was always good to come home.

"Second floor conference room in fifteen minutes," she told her team. "I want to get everything on paper so we can file reports."

"Aye aye, Captain." Tanvi gave a mock salute.

Prism clicked her tongue at her friend before they divided up, each heading to their own destination. Fade, however, stuck close to Prism.

"Good mission," he commented. "Are we doing a group dinner tonight?"

She shrugged as she approached the elevator. "It's tradition, so probably. Why?" She punched the "up" button.

Fade leaned against the wall, watching her. "I was thinking tonight we could do something just the two of us. It's been busy lately, and we haven't had a real date in a while."

Delight flared within her followed swiftly by doubt. "I would love to, but Tanvi and Keeper might be disappointed."

"They'll get over it." He smiled, that charming smile that always made her stomach do backflips. "I haven't had you to myself for almost a week, and I feel like being selfish."

The elevator dinged, and the doors opened.

"Maybe a compromise?" Prism suggested. "We order pizza for the team then slip out and go get drinks somewhere? Maybe that margarita hut on the beach— though I know you don't like margaritas."

"They serve other things." They entered the elevator together. "It's the company I'm interested in. Not the menu."

Her face heated but in a pleasant way. Yeah, an evening sipping brightly colored beverages on the beach with Fade sounded perfect.

"It's a date. Let's hurry through this debriefing—" They arrived at their floor and walked to the conference room. She opened the door, and her mouth fell open.

A man in a hooded cowl sat at the head of the table.

"Adjudicator?" Prism swallowed. "What are you doing here?

The DOSA committee member stood. "Is that how you always greet your superiors, Ms. Powell?"

Prism's jaw clenched. Proper sable etiquette was to address another sable by their hero-handle in a professional setting, but as one of the three committee members leading DOSA, the Adjudicator never missed an opportunity to pull rank.

"Only when they show up unannounced in my team's headquarters." She crossed her arms, determined not to let him throw her. "Honestly, you're lucky I didn't lead with a light blast, assuming this was some sort of villain incursion."

Fade came to her side, his powers flickering. She felt stronger knowing he was ready to back her up if needed.

The Adjudicator stood from his chair. "I have important matters to discuss with you and—"

"Hey, Pris!" Tanvi marched into the room. "I know you're busy with reports, but I wanted to talk about dinner —" She stopped short, blinked, then glared at the Adjudicator. "What's he doing here?"

The Adjudicator's lips curled. "As always, I'm impressed by the professionalism of your team, Ms. Powell."

Prism returned his stare, daggers for daggers. "My team is one of the most successful DOSA teams on the west coast. We've taken down multiple villain incursions, including one caused by a rogue member of your own committee. I don't think we need to go out of our way to prove our professionalism to you, or anyone else for that matter."

At her side, Fade made a gentle humming noise in his

throat. She stood a little straighter.

"I'm sure you didn't come down here just to criticize my team's decorum or lack thereof. Perhaps it's best for all parties if we get to the point." She pulled a chair out from under the conference table and sat to face her unwanted guest. Tanvi and Fade positioned themselves behind her like bodyguards.

"The committee has decided that the SVR should take on a new subject." The Adjudicator reached under the table and pulled out an electronic tablet.

Prism stiffened. "The committee or you?"

"It was a two to one decision, but either way, there was a majority, and it is decided." He tapped the screen bringing up a file with a list of names. "We gave you your first choice of subjects last time. This time, we've limited your options to five potential candidates. All villains with histories that lead us to believe they could be rehabilitated, but also powers that would be of great use to DOSA if harnessed for the right side of the law." He slid the tablet across the table.

Prism angled away from it. "If I may remind you, sir, after the Cosmic/Mymic event and the loss of ... Counsel," it was easier not to get emotional if she referred to her brother by his rarely used hero-handle rather than his actual name, "I requested some time before the SVR started up again, so I could focus on rebuilding my team after the trauma."

The Adjudicator smiled condescendingly. "It's been six months, Ms. Powell. If you haven't gotten things together by this point, you should hand in your resignation and pass the SVR Project to a more resilient sable."

Fade's powers flickered. Prism reached back and touched his arm.

"I've got this," she murmured.

His posture relaxed slightly, though he continued to glare at the Adjudicator

"The team has mostly recovered, but we're nearly at full capacity. The Oceanside zone isn't hot enough to justify a team of more than five. If we take on another, they'll be the last member we can fit in. Rehabilitation is a precarious job in the first place, but if we're going to cycle through villains, rehabilitating them, then transferring them out, it will further destabilize the situation." She tapped her fingers against the tabletop. "So maybe you're right that the SVR should pass to another sable, not because I can't handle it but because a villain would be better served with a team that could support them long term, rather than temporarily."

The Adjudicator's jaw hardened. A quiver cut through Prism. *He didn't expect me to call his bluff about passing the SVR onto new hands.*

"The committee would not approve of that. Training another team to integrate a villain adds an extra element of risk."

"But you suggested it! Like thirty seconds ago!" Tanvi protested.

"If your team needs more room, we can always transfer out one of your existing members." The Adjudicator leaned forward.

Prism's chest tightened. "My team works best together."

"You say that now, but I have it on good authority that there are personal entanglements that could cause, shall we say, drama down the line." He eyed Fade who crossed his arms and drew himself up taller.

Prism scowled. "DOSA does not have an official policy against fraternization within teams. My relationship with Fade is, simply put, not the department's business."

The Adjudicator stood. "Maybe so, but Fade is an in demand sable." He switched his focus to Fade. "With your power base, you could have your pick of DOSA teams. Maybe even one where you could eventually move into a leadership position in spite of your past." His eyes narrowed through the slits in his cowl. "If your team needs space to take on another villain, and you want to advance your career, I could arrange your transfer."

"I like where I am, thank you very much," Fade said dryly.

"For now you have a choice. If your team leader isn't willing to stretch the team for a fifth member, it might be necessary to transfer you whether you like it or not." The Adjudicator strode around the table. He paused at the door, pointing a finger at Prism. "Your brother's death, while tragic, left a hole in this team, so don't give me any nonsense about you not having space for another sable. Either you open your team up to a new SVR subject before the end of the month, or I'll find a way to break your team to pieces so you can prioritize the SVR. Trust me, Ms. Powell, as much as I hate to make you lose another team member, I will do what I have to for the good of DOSA."

Rage ignited beneath Prism's skin, and she shot to her feet. "I think you should go."

Tanvi strode forward. "I'll see you out." She gripped the Adjudicator by the arm and tugged him through the door, slamming it behind him before the man had a chance to protest.

Prism's shoulders slumped. She sat, this time on the table itself instead of in her chair, and sank her face in her hands.

"You all right?" Fade sat in the chair in front of her and placed his hands on her knees.

"I ... I wasn't expecting to have to think about replacing Aiden so soon." She moved her hands to rest on top of his. "I know we have an opening, technically, but it's Aiden's place. Giving it to some stranger feels wrong."

"I know, and I wanted to punch that jackass for suggesting it." His fingers pressed into her legs. "You're right. The SVR could easily pass to another team. He's trying to bully you, is all."

"But what if he really does have the power to transfer you?" She swallowed.

"I won't let him. I'd leave DOSA before I accepted a transfer." He leaned forward and kissed her forehead. "They employ me; they don't own me. I'm not going anywhere, Luce. I promise." He stood and drew her against his chest.

Prism nestled into him. She still missed Aiden every day, but having her friends and Fade with her kept her sane. If any of them were to be transferred—especially Fade, but the loss of Tanvi or Keeper would hurt almost as much—it would rip another hole in the life she'd only recently pieced together again.

He continued to kiss the top of her head, massaging her back and shoulders. His strong hands worked into her muscles, easing her tension and melting away her stress. She smiled and wrapped her arms around his waist.

"I hope you're right. I kind of like having you around." She ran her hand up his back to the base of his neck and pulled him in for a deep kiss.

Their lips melded together, his body swaying with her. Heat flushed through her. She squeezed his bottom lip between her teeth. A tremor shivered through him. His hands sneaked beneath her jacket and shirt, skating up her back.

Prism jerked away as his fingers found her bra clasp. "Stop!"

He froze then released her. They stared at each other. Shame rippled through Prism. Confusion crossed his face, followed swiftly by disappointment.

"Sorry, got carried away." He stepped back and rubbed at his forehead.

Prism's gaze dropped to the floor. "We were supposed

to be debriefing. Would you tell Keeper that we're rescheduling? We'll start the meeting whenever the pizza gets here."

Her phone weighed heavily in her pocket. She could easily text Bob, but she needed a moment to catch her breath.

"Sure. I'll see you at the meeting, then?"

She nodded.

He hesitated, stepped forward, and kissed her cheek before heading out the door.

Prism hid her face in her hands once more.

Well, went smoothly.

Tanvi strolled into the room, giving Prism a once over that further flustered her.

"Got rid of our unwanted pest." Tanvi hopped up to sit on the conference table beside Prism. "Saw Fade beating a hasty retreat. Trouble in paradise?"

Prism flushed. "No ... yes. Maybe?" She inhaled then let all her thoughts escape on the exhale. "I don't know what to do, Tanvi. He wants ... things I'm not ready to give him, and I don't blame him for wanting them, and he's not pressuring me or anything, I can just tell, and I hate saying no to him, but I can't say yes, and I know I should talk to him about it directly, but I can't figure out a way to bring it up that doesn't sound like I'm a religious nut or that I'm accusing him of being a bad person—" She paused for breath.

Tanvi arched one eyebrow. "You're talking about sex, right?"

Prism's cheeks heated to inferno levels. "Yeah."

"Ah. Does he know you still have your v-card?" Tanvi coughed.

"I think he does."

"Meaning you've never brought it up, but he's not an idiot, and he's probably reading the signs?"

Prism groaned, nodded, and pressed her hand into her forehead. "I thought this would be so much easier. When I was a teen, I assumed I'd meet a nice boy at church who was just as naive as me and we'd stumble through this together. Now here I am, twenty-six, only having kissed two boys, including the one I'm currently dating, and the one I *am* with is a former supervillain who's way more experienced than me, and I have no idea how to talk to him about it."

"Fade's kind of far along on his path. He's not likely to change who he is at this point, no matter how much he likes you." Tanvi bit her bottom lip. "If you don't mind me saying so, Prism, maybe he should take the transfer?"

Prism recoiled. "I thought you liked Fade!"

"I do. He's a fun guy, a kickass sable, and I like how he's loosened you up a little. That said, if what you want is that perfect fairytale white wedding, he's probably not your guy. Maybe you should let him off easy now and go find your chaste church boy."

Prism's throat tightened. "But I love him."

"Love is great, but it doesn't bridge all gaps. Like I said, I like him, but I love you. You're my best friend, my team leader, and a weird mix between my big sister and a second mom. Which is why I know you know I'm not saying this to hurt you, but if you and him are heading for a crash because you can't work this out, for the sake of the team, you need to let him go."

Prism's shoulders slumped. What if Tanvi were right? What if Prism was trying to make Fade into something he wasn't and would never be? They'd worked out so many things. He was open minded towards her beliefs, had even gone to church with her a few times. They worked together well professionally. Time spent with Fade was the best time, and she didn't want to give it up.

But if it was doomed, was she being unfair to him and

the team by dragging it out? She could use some wisdom. Another opinion to help her decide whether to follow Tanvi's common sense or the part of her soul that sang whenever Fade entered a room or touched her hand.

"I wish Aiden were here," she whispered.

Grief creased the corners of Tanvi's eyes. "So do I." She patted Prism's back. "Look, whatever you decide with Fade, I know you'll do the right thing. Maybe you're right. Maybe you're his one true love and he'll be willing to put his sex drive in park until whatever time you think is proper. You're right that he isn't being aggressive or entitled about it. Actually, I'm kind of impressed by how patient and respectful he's being."

"Yeah, so am I. He's a prince." Something fluttered within Prism. She really did love him, and he deserved it. Still, maybe he deserved better than her. Maybe he deserved a partner who was brave enough to be honest with him rather than skirt around potential conflict.

But what if I bring it up, and we can't agree?

Her insides roiled. Things were supposed to be getting easier, but between her relationships and the Adjudicator's ultimatum, it was anything but easy.

How am I going to hold this team together?

Chapter Two

Fourteen-year-old Alma sat in the booth table of Handler's trailer staring at the single laptop she and the other two kids under Handler's "care" had access to. Shaina had tuned into a gaming livestream of the latest battle royale FPS. Alma watched for a little while then rested her head into her arms with a moan.

"I don't get how you can watch that for so long. Play it, sure, but watch other people playing?"

"Shh, it's my turn to pick." Shaina waved her off.

Across the booth, Jackson tapped his pen against the side of his notepad. "I got it!" he crowed triumphantly.

"Huh?" Both girls looked up at him.

The skinny red head grinned. "My professional name. How about Columbus?"

Alma tilted her head to one side. "Why not Hitler? You know how many indigenous people that jerk killed."

Jackson's cheeks flushed. "He can't be so bad if they gave him his own holiday. I'm just looking for a famous navigator."

"Dude, Columbus is famous for *accidentally* stumbling into America." Shaina rolled her eyes. "All those old white dudes are problematic, though. Think modern. Maybe Earhart or something."

"Like the girl?" Jackson's brow furrowed. "I think that would be confusing. Besides, I don't fly. It would make more sense for Alma to be Earhart."

"Nah, that's not me." Alma wrinkled her nose.

Jackson had gone through a dozen or more potential handles since Handler had plucked him out of a Nevada foster home four months prior. Alma, who had been the first teen sable Handler had discovered, let Jackson have his fun even though she knew it didn't matter. No, DOSA registered sables, heroes, needed handles so they could look fancy in the press and start fan clubs. Villains—well, they had them for essentially the same reason. Handler's team, though, their business was to stay out of the news.

Still, the search for the perfect name kept Jackson busy and was slightly less annoying than Shaina's livestreams. Alma crossed to the double bed in the corner of the trailer. She shared this with Shaina—Jackson taking the bed that you could make by folding down the table while Handler had the last bed, the bunk over the couch. Getting into the cupboard, she took out her backpack with her few personal items and glanced around the cabin. Handler was still out on his errand, and the other two kids were too busy with their own distractions to notice her.

Slowly, she pulled away a section of the backpack lining that she'd carefully ripped then secured with double-sided tape. Behind this lay a strip of photographs from a boardwalk photo booth showing her and her sister Lupita. Her heart lightened. Every day she was a little closer to bringing their family together again. She reached further into the lining and found the resealable bag filled with worn bills.

Handler kept most of their take for himself, but the kids got a little here and there, depending on how well they did on the various jobs they were assigned.

How much do I need to have a chance? A few hundred for bus tickets, if I want to get far enough away that he'll never find us, but then more to give us a start.

Alma wasn't naive enough to think a fourteen-year-old and an eleven-year-old could live on their own with any sense of normalcy—no one would hire her, and getting Lupita into a school meant explaining why they didn't have parents. However, with enough cash and Alma's powers to protect them, they could make some sort of a life … as long as they could keep away from Handler.

The door burst open, shaking the whole trailer. Alma's muscles seized. Her brain screamed at her to close the pocket, to hide the backpack, to do something—but it was too late.

A bedraggled, middle-aged man in a ratty T-shirt and khaki shorts stomped inside. Handler's dark gaze fell upon Alma. His yellow teeth bared, and he darted down the narrow aisle way between the dinette and the kitchenette, straight for her.

He grabbed her at the pressure point between her neck and shoulder and pinched. Pain rocketed through her.

"You stupid, careless brat!" he hissed. "Did you think I wouldn't find out?"

She jerked away. "I didn't do anything! Let me go!"

"Oh, didn't you?" He thrust a phone in her face.

Her brain short circuited.

There on the screen was a social media post from some random person, a blue Californian sky with a distant figure zipping across it—flying across it. The post accompanying it read, "#SableSighting #SuperSpotter Saw a #Flyer today. Do you think it's @Glint or maybe a new one? Too far away to be sure. #DOSAFanGirl."

Her face heated. It was her, but at that distance, Handler couldn't be sure … could he?

"That's not me."

"Liar!" he hissed. "This was exactly when I couldn't find you the other day. What were you thinking? Flying about in broad daylight? Do you realize what danger you put yourself in? Your whole family in?" He grabbed her backpack and turned it over. She winced as her baggy of money fell onto the mattress along with her few treasured personal items. "You need to learn that your family comes first. Your stupidity cost us our safety which costs us time, which costs *me* money." He snatched up the baggy and shoved it into a pocket in his shorts.

"That's mine!" she protested.

"No, it's mine. You owe it to me for the delays and inconvenience your stupid stunt has caused." He held up his hand, extended index finger quivering. "Do I need to teach you a lesson, niña?"

Her heart pounded. "No, sir," she said through clenched teeth.

Behind him, the other two teens stared, wide-eyed. Anger flared in Shaina's gaze, but Jackson showed nothing but pure terror.

Handler gave a satisfied nod and turned away.

Alma collapsed, head against her knees. Her money was gone, but it could've been worse. It could've been so much —

Handler spun towards Shaina and jabbed his finger at her. Shaina gave a cry of pain, then with a jerking motion threw her hand out towards the laptop. An electric bolt— Shaina's power—slammed from her hand into the screen. The laptop exploded in a shower of sparks.

Alma squeaked, and Jackson dove for cover.

Handler's eyes glinted. "A shame. You kids won't have any entertainment for the foreseeable future, and all because Alma couldn't obey a few simple rules." He sneered at Alma. "We have a mission to plan for. I'm not letting your idiocy cost me good money. Be ready girl."

He exited the trailer, slamming the door behind him. The teens stared at the ruined laptop as if it were the corpse of an old friend.

Alma scooted into the furthest corner of her bed possible. She had known she shouldn't risk leaving, but at the same time had needed to get away. She hadn't seen Lupita in too long, needed to get to a place she could call her without Handler knowing what she was up to ... oh, but it had cost her all her money and possibly her friends—

I need to get out of here. I need to escape, but without money, and with Handler watching my every move—Oh Dios mio ... I'm doomed.

Alma drew a deep breath, forcing her body to stop shaking, her mind to clear. She couldn't live like this any more, but she needed money to escape. However, every time she got close to saving enough, Handler found a reason to take it from her. No, she couldn't get it in bits and pieces any more. She needed a score that provided it all in one lump sum, a score just for her.

After all, if Handler had taught her anything, it was how to be a supervillain. Time to use those skills for her own benefit.

Chapter Three

Fade motioned to the last slice of barbeque chicken and bacon pizza as the team sat around the conference table. "Anyone want to fight me for it?"

"Nah. I'm feeling like I should've opted for a salad." Tanvi patted her stomach and leaned back in her chair. "We should get pizza for every meeting."

"Not in the budget." Prism dipped a piece of crust into a side of garlic butter.

Fade considered her. Her eyes were far away, her voice lacking the usual pep it had when Tanvi tempted her to get off track and banter instead of continuing the meeting. In fact, the meeting had mostly been off track. A half hour in, most of the pizza was gone, but other than informing the team of the Adjudicator's demands and passing around dossiers for the villains he'd suggested should join the SVR, they really hadn't done any business.

He placed the pizza on his paper plate, wiped his hand on a napkin, then leaned over to touch her wrist. "You doing all right?"

"I'll be fine." She sat up straighter. "There isn't really anything to talk about. I saw you all filed your reports, and the mission went smoothly—in fact, I'm proud of all of you." She widened her focus to include the other two team members. "After everything that has happened, it's good to know I'm surrounded by such competent and exemplary sables." She let out a long breath. "We might have some hard choices to make in the near future, and by we, I mean me. I'm the team leader. I need to make the final call on whether or not we open up the SVR again. I'm not trying to pass that responsibility off to any of you. However, I am open to your input."

Tanvi and Keeper exchanged a glance.

"Whatever you decide, lass, we'll support ya," Keeper put in. His black cat—and secretly his shape-shifter wife, Yui—hopped up on the table and pawed a loose bit of sausage out of a pizza box.

Fade shifted uncomfortably in his chair. The rest of the team, other than Keeper, of course, didn't know that Yui was, in fact, a human who chose to use her powers to live as a feline, and while he respected her right to her secrets, he always got anxious when she was especially "catty" around him. It weirded him out knowing that there was a middle-aged Japanese woman sitting on their conference table licking sausage grease off her paws.

Keeper ran his hand down Yui's back, smoothing her dark fur. "Our team has gone through worse than the Adjudicator can throw at us."

"I mean, a new team member wouldn't be the worst thing, even a villain." Tanvi picked up a piece of cheese pizza, apparently changing her mind about the salad thing. "Fade turned out all right—mostly." She winked at him.

A thought struck Fade. "I wasn't the only villain in the original SVR, but it had a high dropout rate. Of the original six recruits, more than half ended up back in holding cells, but Allay also took on a couple new subjects. I think at the end of the program it was me, Manifest, She-Tiger, the Catch, and Mountain Man." He leaned forward. "What happened to them after the project dissolved?"

Prism sighed. "Since they'd all received official pardons due to their participation in the SVR and hadn't violated their terms, the way you were accused of doing, DOSA was in an awkward position where they couldn't arrest them but also didn't want to work with them. They were released under supervision. Last I heard, Manifest and She-Tiger opened a catering business together outside of Pittsburgh.

The Catch relapsed after a year of going straight. Died attempting to rob a bank in Atlanta a couple years ago. Mountain Man?" She shrugged. "Went off the grid. No one knows exactly where he ended up."

"He was always more of a weird, antisocial type than a true villain, anyway." Fade tried to remember ever interacting with Mountain Man, but even when Mountain Man was a full-fledged SVR recruit, the guy had never had his heart in the game. Fade hoped he had found a cabin somewhere and was living in a way that suited his name. Even knowing that the fall of the original SVR hadn't been his fault, that he'd been framed for the crime that had discredited the program and led to its cancellation, he couldn't help feeling a little guilty that his former comrades had lost their DOSA jobs. At least Manifest and She-Tiger had apparently made a life for themselves.

"It's not like there's a shortage of villains running around. While pulling Fade from the original project worked out, if we really want to add a villain to our roster, there are prisons full of them," Tanvi pointed out. "It's up to you, Pris. New villain or stand your ground. Either way, I'm with you."

Fade chuckled. "And you know I have your back, Lucia."

She smiled. "Thanks, all of you. I think we can end the meeting for now. I didn't mean to keep you guys so far into the evening in the first place."

"So we're excused then?" Tanvi sprang out of her chair, still gripping her pizza.

"Sure, go have fun." Prism smiled wearily.

Tanvi nodded to Keeper, her eyes darting meaningfully towards the door. The older man picked up Yui and left the room. Tanvi started to follow but paused with her hand on the knob. "Hey, Fade, can we talk for a minute?"

"Give me a second." He scooted his chair closer to

Prism's.

"Okay. I'll be in the hall." Tanvi closed the door, leaving Fade and Prism alone.

Prism toyed with her phone. "I put in a call to both Talon and Shepherd. After all, the Adjudicator is only one third of the committee. One-fourth if DOSA gets off their butts about replacing Cosmic—which I should've brought up to him today. If they can drag their feet about bringing on a new member, so can we."

"Hypocrisy and government kind of go hand in hand."

"Yeah. Still, if I can get either or both of the other members on my side, we might be able to sidestep the Adjudicator altogether."

"Is that really what you want, though?" He took her hand. "You heard the team. They have your back if you decide we should rehabilitate another villain. I have to think you had greater ambitions than just bringing me back into the fold when you started the project."

"I did, but I wasn't expecting to lose Aiden or fall in love with you—everything changed so quickly." She rested her forehead in her hands. "Honestly, Fade, I'm not sure what I want any more other than that I don't want to lose anybody else, especially you. I'm not usually afraid of change, I swear, but so much over such a short period of time … I was just starting to feel I'd found some normalcy again."

"I know." He squeezed his fingers around hers. "You don't have to decide anything tonight." He glanced at his own phone. "This is later than I wanted to get started. We're probably too late to catch the sunset, but we can still get a drink."

She smiled. "That sounds—" Her phone went off. Her smile faded as she glanced at the screen. "Nevermind. It's Talon. This might take a while. I'm sorry, Fade. Maybe tomorrow."

"Yeah, tomorrow." He kissed her cheek.

"I'm a terrible girlfriend, aren't I?" She gave him her best puppy dog eyes.

He smirked. "The worst. It's a wonder I put up with you."

She laughed and answered the phone. "Prism speaking."

He stood. Probably a good time to see what Tanvi wanted.

Fade stepped out into the hallway and stopped short. Tanvi and Keeper stood, side by side, waiting for him.

He swallowed. "Uh, hi, guys. Tanvi, you, um, wanted to talk?"

"You want to go get a beer?" Tanvi asked.

Fade glanced back at the door that had already swung shut behind him. "Prism says she'll be a little while. On the phone with Talon right now."

"That suits us just fine, lad." Keeper crossed his arms. "It's you we're interested in chatting with."

Fade's powers flickered to life within his body in a way that usually only happened when he was experiencing a fight or flight rush. "I don't know. I don't want Prism to feel like we all abandoned her."

"Trust me, this is as much for her good as yours. We need to talk about your intentions towards my sister from another mister." Tanvi stuck her finger in his face.

Fade flinched. "That does not make me more eager to come."

"We want the best for you as well as her, Fade." Keeper gave a fatherly smile. "Just askin' you to hear us out is all."

Fade shifted from foot to foot. "I'm not sure—"

"Keeper and I will pay for your drinks," Tanvi interrupted. "Prism will be fine. I'll text her and let her know we're borrowing you for our own devices but will return you unharmed at the end of the night."

Fade's shoulders slumped. As much as he hated to go

over his private business with anyone, Tanvi and Keeper were Prism's family. If he wanted to be with her, he was kind of stuck with them.

"All right, but I'm not a cheap date. I'm expecting craft beer, on tap. None of that canned crap."

"We know just the place." Tanvi beamed.

***

A little later the trio sat around a small, round table at a local restaurant and bar. Classic rock played over the sound of people talking and laughing. The waiter brought them drinks and an order of nachos.

Fade sipped at his second IPA, all too conscious of the other two watching his every move. The small talk they had made so far was obviously leading up to whatever it was they really wanted to talk about.

He cleared his throat. "Thanks for buying, by the way. It took DOSA nearly three months to figure out my paycheck situation. I guess they didn't have a precedence in their system for a single-named sable, so it kept getting kicked back by the computers when I left the forms blank. I finally got it accepted by filling it out as 'first name F, last name Ade' instead of just Fade, but I still haven't gotten my back pay." He shook his head. "With so many sables going by their hero-handles, you'd think they would have sorted that by now."

Tanvi snorted. "Most of us don't use our hero-handles on official documents. You're kind of a special snowflake that way, F-Ade."

"Maybe but it's the only name I've got, and I'm sort of attached to it." He laughed.

Keeper swirled his whiskey around his tumbler. "Seems like you need an extra name, lad. What if you have children someday? You'll want something to pass on."

Fade shrugged. "I've always assumed that the chances of anyone wanting to have kids with me were pretty low, so

I've never given it much thought."

"Prism's going to want kids. You know that, right?" Tanvi hid behind her massive margarita.

Fade's powers flickered in and out again. So they were going to jump right into it. "I guess it fits with what I know of her personality." He focused on the nachos, trying to get one that had a little bit of everything on it. Weirdly, the idea of kids didn't worry him much. "She's awkwardly brought up whether I like kids or not in passing once or twice. I do, though not a lot of people are clamoring for former supervillains to babysit, you know?" He crunched down on the tortilla chip, savoring the salty cheese, the smooth guacamole, and the bite of a jalapeno.

Yeah, he liked kids, even if he had no idea how he'd be as a father. Prism would know what to do, though. Prism had practically raised her little brother after their mother had passed away. The team always joked about how she was the team mom. If she could mother-hen a group of misfit sables, she could handle kids.

"Lucia would make a great mom," he allowed the thought to slip out, avoiding his friends' faces in favor of the nachos.

"Aye, she would." Keeper leaned across the table. "And that's related to the reason we wanted to talk to you. How are things going between you and your lass?"

"Good, great even." Fade took another chip ... and it wasn't a lie. He loved Prism. He was happy with Prism. Still ...

"There's a but, though, isn't there?" Tanvi prodded. "Out with it, dude. We're all friends here."

"It's not any one specific thing." Sort of a lie, but that one specific thing had a lot of baggage it dragged along with it. Tanvi was Prism's protective best friend. Keeper might as well be her second father. He needed to choose his words carefully. "It's just that certain things are progressing slower than I would prefer." That seemed safe.

"Meaning she hasn't let you score yet." Tanvi apparently wasn't in the mood for safe, carefully chosen words.

Fade thought about protesting. He could tell Tanvi it wasn't her business, but he was tired. He was stressed and confused, and he could use a moment to vent. "To put it bluntly. I know I've been out of the game for a long time, but it seems like six months in, we should be a little more intimate. Am I wrong about that?"

"It's just Prism," Tanvi said. "You know she's religious, right?"

"Yeah, we've talked about it." He settled into his chair. This conversation might be awkward, but maybe less awkward than going directly to Prism about it. "I'm still trying to work out how I feel about the finer points of her faith, but I'm at least theistic. I realized a while ago that if I had to make a conscious decision between being a villain or being a hero, I wanted more moral authority behind it than, 'this is what feels right to me' because I've been in positions where I very much wanted to do something illegal or immoral. I don't always feel like doing the right thing, if that makes sense. I need something beyond myself to hold me accountable, and DOSA, with its bureaucracy and hypocrisy, isn't going to cut it."

"Sure, nothing wrong with that if it keeps you on the path." Tanvi nodded. "That said, Prism isn't vaguely spiritual, philosophically theistic, or anything halfway like that. She's full on Christian including the part where she's hoping to save herself for marriage."

"The Christian part I knew. The saving herself explains a lot."

"Is that going to be a problem for you?" Tanvi leaned further across the table until her chest threatened to dip into the nachos.

Keeper slid the basket a little to the side so she didn't get a shirt full of guacamole. "Ease off the lad, Tanvi."

"I need to know he's going to do right by my girl." Tanvi frowned.

"I guess it depends on what you mean by a problem." Fade took a drink of beer, washing the salty chip residue down his throat. "I won't lie. Every time she's pulled away, it's been a struggle for me not to take it personally, but from what you're saying, it has nothing to do with me and everything to do with her."

"And trust me, as her college roommate who was on team 'loosen up and live a little, girl', you're not going to talk her out of her convictions," Tanvi waved the little umbrella from the top of her drink at him. "She's held that belief for her whole life, and as much as she cares about you, she cares about being true to it just as much."

"Yeah, I can't really expect her to rewrite her rules for me." Though it would've been nice to be an exception. It would've been very nice.

Fade ran his finger through the condensation bubbles forming on the outside of his mug. It wasn't as if Prism had been dishonest with him, nor was it as if he were entitled to her physical affection. Still, he wanted it.

"So, what do you suggest?" He eyed his girlfriend's best friend.

Tanvi exchanged a glance with Keeper.

"We're torn about that." Tanvi sipped at her margarita. "We both agree, though, that if you two are going to break up—" She cleared her throat.

"If you two aren't going to work it out, for the good of the team, you should probably take the transfer to another DOSA region," Keeper spoke quickly, as if the words brought him physical pain.

"And here I thought you two liked me." Fade laughed wryly.

"We do, lad, we do." Keeper reached across the table and clapped him on the shoulder. "However, this is Prism's team. If things get ugly between you, she's not going anywhere, and as much as I like you, I've known Lucia since she was a wee bairn."

"And she's my best friend," Tanvi agreed. "Do you really think you two could go back to being just friends without it being hella awkward?"

"Probably not." Fade rubbed his forehead. He didn't want to. He liked being with Prism romantically. Even if he wasn't getting everything he wanted out of the situation, he was still getting quite a lot. "So what if I want it to work?"

"I think you should whisk her off to Vegas and be done with it." Keeper winked. "Nothing dissolves moral objections quite so well as making it legal."

Fade choked on his beer.

"I'm a little more cautious." Tanvi frowned. "I know she loves you, but if you're only marrying her so you can get her in bed, are you really going to be able to last long term? I'd rather you leave her now than after she's gotten in that deep, if those are the two options."

"I'd like an option that doesn't involve leaving her at all." Fade grimaced. He wiped his mouth with the back of his hand. "I've been taking this one day at a time since we started seeing each other. Everything seemed so uncertain at the beginning, with my DOSA position being tenuous. No point in making long term plans with there being a high chance I could screw up and end up in a holding cell."

"That's not going to happen." Keeper shook his head. "You're a quality hero, lad. Whatever your past, DOSA is lucky to have you, and if you keep to the path, you'll be able to stick it out, both with DOSA and Lucia."

Fade ghosted his fingers in and out of his mug. When he faded into liquids, it was almost like he could taste them in his skin, a novel sensation, presuming the liquid wasn't something unpleasant. "Six months together is a decent trial period. Other than the sex thing, it's gone way better than I'd expected it to."

If he were honest with himself, while Prism was inexperienced on the physical side of things, the relationship half of love was as foreign to Fade as bedroom activities were to her. Life as a supervillain was hardly conducive to romantic commitment. He'd had flings, but other than Lucia, he couldn't think of a time he'd said, "I love you," and actually meant it.

"Then maybe you need to ask yourself what you want out of life," Keeper said.

"And how Prism fits into that," Tanvi quickly added.

"Makes sense." Fade finished his beer in a single long gulp.

Keeper held up his hand, flagging down the passing waiter. "Would you mind topping my pal off, please?"

The waiter smiled and took Fade's empty glass.

Fade hesitated. "I feel like I should get back. Lucia wasn't in a great place when we left."

"One more round so we can end the night on a happier note?" Keeper urged.

"Or we could text her and have her join us now that the awkward conversation is done with!" Tanvi's whole visage brightened. She pulled out her phone and started tapping away before anyone could comment. A moment later her phone buzzed. Tanvi's brow furrowed. "Meh, she says she's feeling tired and doesn't want to change back out of her pajama bottoms." Her lips pursed. "That's not great. Prism loves hanging out with me. Maybe you're right. Maybe we should check on her. Let me see how long the wait is for an Uber."

The waiter returned with another beer. Fade drank it quickly while Tanvi messed with her rideshare app.

"We've got maybe fifteen minutes. I think I'd like to

wait outside." She slipped from her chair and knocked back the dregs of her margarita. "How about you two?"

"You go ahead. I'm going to the lavvy real quick." Keeper started in the direction of the restaurant's bathrooms.

"Fresh air sounds good." Fade pulled on his jacket and followed Tanvi out.

The restaurant and bar Tanvi had chosen was right on the harbor. Even from the parking lot, the dark expanse of the Pacific Ocean was clearly visible. The reflection of the lights danced upon the waves.

Tanvi stopped and stared out over the water. The sound of the pounding surf washed over them, drowning out the muffled music from the bar and the distant buzz of motorists. Fade turned to scan the parking lot, wondering when the Uber would get there.

A sniffle from Tanvi turned him around again. A tear glimmered on her cheek.

Fade snapped to attention. "Are you all right?"

"I miss surfing," she said.

Astute enough to realize surfing was probably Tanvi-code for something else, he eased closer to her. "I kind of forgot you surfed, actually. I don't think you've mentioned it since—" He stopped as his mind put the timeline together.

"You can say it. Since Aiden." Her gaze dropped to her feet. "We used to go together. It was our thing. Neither of the other team members were into it, but I'm not the kind of person who would surf alone. Replacing him as my surf-buddy … I don't like to think about it, but the idea of replacing him on the team makes me wonder if maybe it's time."

Fade cautiously placed his hand on her shoulder. "After Aiden died, I was so wrapped up in making sure Prism was all right that I kind of forgot how much a part of your life he was too. I never asked if you were okay. I'm sorry."

"He was Prism's little brother. In the hierarchy of grief, that's a bigger deal than even a good friend. You were right to make her the focus. Don't worry about me." Tanvi gave an unconvincing smile.

Fade kept his hand on his shoulder but shifted his focus to the horizon. "You know the kid had a thing for you."

Tanvi gave a hoarse laugh. "You call him a kid, but you do realize he was only a year younger than me, don't you, old man?"

Fade smiled. "I'm just saying Aiden wore his adolescent angst more openly than you do."

"But yeah, the whole team knew. Prism thought she was subtle about teasing him about me, but Prism and 'subtlety' have never been more than passing acquaintances. He never would've acted on it, though. Aiden was far too 'virtuous' to ask me out. You think Prism has hang ups? Aiden was one big overthinking hang up." She shook her head. "I used to joke that he'd never date. He'd just somehow show up one day full-on married, and we'd have to accept it."

They fell silent again. Fade scratched the back of his neck, wishing the Uber would arrive and save him from having to think of something comforting to say. Thankfully, Tanvi broke the silence first.

"I would've said yes, you know," she whispered. "Not to marriage, obviously. I need a little more build up than that, but a date? Multiple dates? Even a relationship, I would've been up for it. It's weird, mourning something that never was. It's like an imaginary loss. The idea that maybe if things had gone differently, instead of teasing Prism about her celibacy, I'd be tempting Aiden to violate his or … I don't know, maybe even agreeing to a period of chastity to see if we could work things out. More than anything, though, I just miss that snarky little jackass's face."

"We all do," Fade murmured.

Keeper emerged from the bar behind them. "Cab here yet?"

"Nope." Tanvi checked her phone. "Actually, I think I want to take a walk. You two can head home without me. I'll call another ride later."

The men exchanged a look.

"We can stay with you," Fade volunteered. "Safety in numbers and all that."

She scoffed. "The only thing either of you would do if I got into trouble would be to slow me down. You realize, I'm the brawn of the group, right? Your best skill is essentially to not get hit, Fade, and what's Bob gonna do? Call in bats as backup? No offense, Bob."

"None taken, but I could use a breather too. Let me walk with you." The older man smiled. "Not for the protection, but for the company?"

"You are good company." Tanvi eased out of her defensive posture. "Not you, though, Fade. Take the ride and make sure Pris is okay."

Fade checked the time on his phone. Almost midnight. "She's probably asleep ... but yeah, if she is awake, I'd like to talk with her. She had a rough afternoon."

"Be a gentleman." Tanvi winked at him. "I'd hate to break that pretty nose of yours." She jabbed a punch at his gut. Fade instinctively accessed his powers, and her blow cut through him as if he'd been mist.

He laughed. "Yeah, good luck with that. I promise, though, only honorable intentions tonight. You two have given me a lot to think about, but even before that, I already knew I didn't want to hurt Lucia. I think I'd never forgive myself if I did."

"Good lad," Keeper's voice practically hummed.

Headlights turned into the parking lot. Fade nodded to his friends. "I think that's my ride. I'll see you back at HQ.

Don't stay out too late."

A short while later, Fade's Uber pulled into the parking lot of their headquarters.

"Thanks for the ride, man." He held out a bill to the rideshare driver as he climbed out of the car.

The man took it, smiled, and gave a quick, "Stay safe," before Fade shut the car door and he drove off into the night.

Fade stood beneath one of the overhead lights for a long moment. He breathed in the cool night air, letting it clear his mind from the slight stupor one too many beers had left him in.

What do I even want?

The question from his talk with Tanvi and Keeper latched onto his brain and wouldn't let go.

Striding out of the pool of golden light, he focused on the dark night sky.

Short term, I want her.

He'd been with women before. He knew the pleasures of it, the dance of it. He hadn't experienced that with Lucia yet, and the lack ached within him like a hunger. To feel her against him, to watch her eyes in the throes of passion, to hear her breathing sync with his.

He longed for it. In the short term, it was all consuming, frustrating and unrelenting ... but that short term desire meant pressuring her to give up something long term, a value she'd apparently held for years before he came into her life, her commitment to hold that for something sacred, something permanent that they hadn't yet reached.

So short term, I'm screwed ... or more accurately, I'm not. With a wry chuckle he started towards the doors.

Keying in his access code, he waited for the sliding doors to open before striding into the empty lobby. A weak light shone up ahead, from the entertainment room. Unzipping his jacket, he ambled in that direction.

But long term, what do I want? I can't live day to day anymore. I'm not a villain on the run with no idea when I'll get caught and lose it all. Also, as much as I don't like to admit it, I'm also not a kid anymore either. Half of my thirties gone, forties coming quick. Is what I am now what I want to be forever? And where does Lucia fit into this?

He strode through the entertainment room door and stopped short. Gentle, electronic music swelled to meet him from a farming simulator's loading screen, paused on the TV, but that wasn't what drew his attention.

Prism lay on one of the couches, a knit throw over her body, her face relaxed in slumber. His whole being softened. She was beautiful, but more than that, she was her. Her features, so familiar and beloved, her hair disheveled, a partial smile on her resting lips. The very essence of her sang to him.

Long term I want to spend my life with her—which as a long term goal fits ridiculously well with my short term one. Like puzzle pieces ... no, like a connect the dots where one thing leads to another. Oh, man, am I thinking what I'm thinking?

He stepped around the couch and sat on the coffee table in front of her. He stroked her hair.

Her breath hitched, then her eyes fluttered open. She gave him a groggy smile. "Hi."

"Hey." He laughed before bending down to kiss her lips. "You didn't wait up for me, did you?"

"No ..." She sat up. The blanket fell away revealing a navy blue sweatshirt with an EMT logo over the heart. His stomach twisted as he recognized the garment as one formerly belonging to her brother. She usually only wore that when she was missing Aiden. She motioned towards the screen. "I'm trying to gather enough resources to build a grain silo for my virtual cows, which I know is a stupid reason to stay up so late, but they're really cute virtual cows."

Fade sat beside her. "You're a cute virtual … never mind." He shook his head. He must be drunker than he thought if he had hoped even for a second that that line would land.

She giggled before reaching for the remote and turning off the TV. "How'd your night go?"

"Good." He considered her. "Would've been more fun if you were there."

"Why didn't they want me there?" She avoided eye contact. Prism wasn't an idiot. Chances were she had some idea what her friends were up to.

"Nothing to worry about." He slipped his hand onto her knee. "We can talk about it tomorrow, if you'd like, but I'm kind of tired and blurry right now."

Tired and blurry wasn't the time to make major life decisions, even if everything within him was screaming that now that he knew what he wanted, it was time to act. No, he'd take one night to sleep on it at least. In the morning, if he felt the same way, then it was a sure thing.

"Of course." She rubbed her eyes. "I should get to bed too. I need to look over the villains the Adjudicator picked for me in case we do have to choose another SVR candidate or face him transferring one of us out of here." Her shoulders hitched towards her ears. "I should've started tonight, but I couldn't bring myself to consider it yet."

His hold on her leg tightened. "I'm sorry the Adjudicator is putting you through this. You shouldn't have to think about replacing Aiden."

Prism sighed. "As much as I miss him, I can't hold still forever, and I know that. Maybe it's time." The sadness in her eyes drove another nail into the coffin of his bachelorhood. He wasn't sure he'd mourn it. No, he needed to make plans for them now, not just him.

He kissed her forehead. "You can deal with it in the

morning. Though one thing before you go, we never had those drinks on the beach we were talking about. How about a full on, respectable date tomorrow evening? I'll even make a reservation at that cheesy little Italian place with the grape vines painted on the walls."

She grinned. "That sounds amazing."

He leaned in for a kiss, intentionally keeping it light and chaste. Even so, he lingered close to her, wanting to stay forever. Not now, though. For her, he was going to do this the old fashioned way. "Can I walk you to your door?" He offered her his hand.

She laughed and took it. "You know, for a villain, you're kind of a gentleman."

"Shh." He put his finger to his lips. "You'll ruin my reputation."

Her eyes lit up in the way that filled his chest with pure bliss.

Yeah, RIP, bachelorhood. May we never meet again.

Chapter Four

Tanvi ran the bow slowly across her violin's strings, swaying to the strains of "My Immortal" by Evanescence. She closed her eyes and sank into the melancholy melody.

The tramp of footsteps followed by the patter of dog claws on tile entered the room.

"You all right?" Keeper asked.

"Of course." She continued to play, but opened her eyes to watch as Keeper settled into a chair on the other side of the entertainment room, Houdini, his border collie, at his side.

"It just seems to me you only play that particular tune when you're a wee bit sad." He scratched at the dog's silky black ears. Houdini's pink tongue lolled appreciatively out of his ever-smiling mouth.

"Just thoughtful." She managed to shrug without missing a note. Tanvi's ideal career had been in hip-hop violin performance art, before she'd met Prism in her dance class and got pulled into "the life." She ended on a high note, letting it linger in the air for a long moment before carefully putting her instrument on the table. "Fade and Prism left for their date yet?"

"I think about fifteen minutes ago." Keeper nodded.

Tanvi played with her ponytail. "You think she's mad at me?"

"Nay, lass, why would she be?"

"Oh, I don't know, maybe because I meddled in her personal life and suggested she break up with her first and only love." Tanvi plopped onto the couch.

"She knows you meant well—besides, I don't think that story is going to end the way you think it will." Keeper winked at her. "Fade's not a brash young lad apt to throw away his long term happiness for short term fun."

Tanvi twitched her fingers as if still working the strings of her violin. "You're probably right. I just know Prism has never had a serious relationship before now, and she's all in with Fade. What if he hurts her?" Her insides roiled at the thought.

Keeper tilted his head to one side. "You want to let me know why you care?"

Tanvi started. "She's my best friend, our team leader, and just a good person. Why wouldn't I care?"

"Ach, if she got hurt, I'm sure you'd care. I'm sure you'd want to rip Fade's head off and use it as a football." Keeper laughed. "What I mean is why are you suddenly imagining the worst case scenarios for a friend I know you've repeatedly tried to force out of her comfort zone to take more risks?"

"Someone has to." Tanvi's throat closed in on itself.

"But why you, lass? That's never been your place before." Keeper's gaze remained unwaveringly upon her.

Tanvi concentrated on the lights glistening off the polished surface of her violin. "I mean, usually Pris and I ... I mean, I did want her to lighten up, have more fun, live a little more, but there was always—" She swallowed.

"Aye? Go on?" Keeper's bushy eyebrows arched.

"Aiden was always there to put the brakes on when we needed it," Tanvi let it burst from her. "Prism is all ethics and heart and I'm all impulse and adrenaline. Those are both great, but someone needs to be the common sense and caution."

"And now that he's gone, do you really think you're going to fill that gap?" Keeper reached over and grasped Tanvi's shoulder. "My girl, we all miss the boy, but you can't be the boy. That's not what you're cut out for."

Her vision blurred. "I just don't want anyone else I love

to get hurt."

Pity creased Keeper's face. "That's all of us, lass. We had our hearts broken when we lost Aiden, and in some ways we've healed. We've put our family together again, but we're not exactly in a line of work that lets us bubble wrap each other."

Tanvi's jaw clenched and unclenched. Aiden's sharp gray eyes and sardonic smile burst into her memory like a slap of cold water, and she hopped from the couch.

"I'm going for a run."

Keeper nodded. "I'd offer to go with you, but I know I'd never be able to keep up. Stay safe, lass. I'll see you when you get back."

Tanvi jogged up the stairs to the floor with their sleeping quarters. Once there she kicked off her flip flops and replaced them with barefoot running sandals. Tanvi always had a tendency to wear activewear as her default— it had gotten her in trouble at her cousin's graduation party —and tonight was no different. Because of this, all she had to do was secure her long, black hair back with the trusty hair tie she'd left around her wrist, shove her phone into her best waterproof (and sweat-proof) armband, and do some quick stretches to be ready to go. Before she left her room, however, her gaze fell on the compact telescoping version of her exo-armor that she'd asked to have designed specifically to wear out in public without drawing attention. The device was attached to a comfortable waistband and looked, for better or worse, like a fanny pack.

She paused. It wasn't like she needed it, but it would be nice to have it on hand. Deciding, she snatched it up and strapped it around her waist. She adjusted her T-shirt to fall over it then headed down the stairs, through the lobby, and out the door.

The sun had already sunk below the hills between

headquarters and the ocean leaving the sky in a pale twilight with only a few first stars. Her hand strayed to the exo-armor's activation button. While a quick run through the winding back roads of Camp Pendleton would be nice, a run along the Pacific Ocean would be nicer. If she used her exo-armor, she could be at the beach in five minutes.

No reason not to.

She pushed the button.

With a series of pleasing clicks and whirs, the exo-armor slid over her body as easily as cat's claws leaving their sheaths. The helmet visor snapped over her eyes, and gauntlets grew over her hands, still leaving her fingertips and palms free. A smile crossed her face. After her parents had paid for the genetic "upgrade" that granted her superpowers, she'd hoped and prayed she'd develop flying as well as speed, agility, and strength. Several attempts had proven that she'd missed out on that one, but she'd never stopped envying flying type sables and the freedom they had in the open skies. When Prism had approached the team asking for volunteers to go through the flight training program, Tanvi threatened to fight anyone if they tried to stop her from being the "chosen one." The guys had backed down immediately.

Now she flexed her toes downward, activating the sensors that controlled the suit's lower thrusters, and clenched her hands to engage the wrist thrusters. The suit hummed to life, launching her into the sky. She crowed with delight as the ground fell away beneath her.

Air rushed by her as she arched over the dry hills of Camp Pendleton. Ahead the smooth expanse of the Pacific Ocean called to her. She could smell the crisp salt air already.

Not wanting to stop flying too soon, she banked to the south and followed the coast line for several minutes before settling on an empty stretch of beach somewhere south of base. She hovered for a moment, a few feet above the sand, before hitting the deactivation button. Her suit telescoped into the belt pack. With a thump she dropped into the sand.

She shook her head to get her hair in place before breaking into a sprint. She went at full speed for a few minutes, but her velocity blurred the view. Wanting to enjoy the evening, she skidded to a halt, sending sand flying, then continued at a more leisurely pace.

Tanvi jogged along the shoreline. It was a beautiful night, with a cool breeze coming off the ocean, perfumed with the scent of salt water. The sun hovered right above the water, streaking the sky with oranges and lavenders.

A sudden longing to surf filled her. She needed to stop putting it off. Aiden wouldn't want her to give that up forever, no matter how much she missed him.

Grief for her lost friend pierced her soul, and she picked up her pace, pushing herself to run faster, harder, focusing only on the speed. She kicked up sand. The world blurred around her, whether from her tears or just the velocity she'd managed, she wasn't sure.

Several minutes later, she stopped, out of breath, heart pounding. Sweat pasted her dark hair to her forehead and neck. She inhaled, hand to her throat to check her pulse. How far had she gone? Where was she?

A series of beach houses over looked the water here, mission style stucco homes as well as rustic a-frames, all super nice and probably ridiculously expensive. Well lit picture windows revealed luxurious interiors with big screen TVs and fancy exercise machines facing the water.

"Nice digs." She laughed quietly to herself.

She wiped her hand across her forehead. Maybe she should turn back and run the other way.

Before she could decide, the lights in the houses all blinked out. She paused. That was odd. Had something taken down the power? As she watched, a figure rose from behind one of the homes and landed on the roof of the largest of the beach houses. Tanvi froze. Even from a distance, she could tell the figure was human. A flying human could only mean one thing.

Her throat tightened. Could DOSA be running some sort of operation in this area? They shouldn't be. While she'd run a good distance, she hadn't gone nearly far enough to be out of her own team's jurisdiction. DOSA sables didn't enter each other's turf without giving fair warning. Too easy for dangerous misunderstandings to happen with sables stepping on other sable's feet.

Still, flying types were rare. The chances of a flying type *villain* being in the area was less likely than DOSA having gotten some communications crossed. Thankfully DOSA had a set channel for contacting other on duty DOSA members. She could access it from her exo-armor.

Reaching down, she pushed the button to trigger her armor. It snapped into place, and her energy increased in response, ready for action. She tapped a button on the side of her visor to activate the comm-channel.

"All active DOSA agents in the Oceanside area, report in. This is Tanvi Anand, AKA Forte. Please apprise of any DOSA operations in my immediate vicinity."

The channel stayed silent except for the gentle buzz of static.

"I repeat, any DOSA approved operations—"

The unknown sable leaped from the roof then accelerated downwards. A distant crash echoed over the beach. Tanvi winced at what had to be a bone-cracking collision before the sable disappeared into the house.

"Hell with it." Tanvi clenched her hands to trigger her thrusters and rocketed off the beach. Whoever this sable was, he or she had interrupted the wrong hero's workout.

***

Alma landed with a crash in the middle of a large, empty room. Her feet went wrong and instead of the powerful crouch she'd envisioned for her touch down, she hit first her knees then her face. She got up, spitting plaster and sheetrock.

I need to work on that.

Still coughing from the dust and debris, she spun in a tight circle, only to find the room dark except for the twilight seeping through the hole she'd punched in the roof. Cursing, she fished a flashlight out of her hoodie pocket. Five minutes into her first solo heist and already she'd screwed up like three times.

Normally Shaina would use her electrical manipulation power to short out all alarm systems and security cameras. Alma had hoped cutting the power to the house would have the same results. She hadn't realized cutting the lines for this house would also result in the rest of the houses on the block going dark. That was likely to draw attention. Also, usually Jackson would use his scouting powers to plot the perfect entrance for the team. Alma had just had to guess, and now she didn't know where she was or how close she was to her goal. All that, plus she hadn't even looked cool on entrance.

Making sure her hoodie covered her face in case some of the security cameras operated on emergency batteries, she flipped on her flashlight. The beam swept across rows of chairs all facing in the same direction. As she turned it also illuminated a flat screen big enough to take up a full wall. She wrinkled her nose. Yeah, the mark she'd chosen wouldn't miss the money she'd take. If anything, she was just pulling a Robin Hood—the fact that her and her sister were the benefactors rather than some anonymous poor talking animals or whatever was just semantics.

She opened the door revealing a hallway and some stairs going down into the body of the house. Pulling a scrap of paper from her pocket, she wondered where the office was. She needed something of value she could easily carry out herself and could quickly convert into cash. Thankfully, Handler kept a list of potential heists for every area they visited. According to him, this particular mark was a numismatist, which according to Google meant coins which were practically just money.

Now if she were a rich old dude, where would she hide her coin collection? Assuming that he didn't have it under his pillow or something.

A faint buzzing caused her to pause. Was that a low flying plane? A drone? What if the pilot saw the huge hole she'd left in the roof? She needed to move fast—

The door behind her burst open. Alma whirled around, shining her flashlight directly in the face of a dark-skinned woman wearing white and hot-pink exo-armor.

Frick! DOSA sable! I recognize this one ... Forray? Form? Forte! That's it.

Alma chucked her flashlight straight at Forte. It bounced off the light armor on her chest.

Heat flushed through Alma's face. What had she thought that would accomplish?

The sable's eyes, clearly visible through the tinted visor, widened. "You new to this? Want to surrender now and save us both some time?"

Gritting her teeth, Alma kicked off the ground. No chance of finding the coins now. She needed to cut her losses and get out of there ... maybe she could rob a bank or something later.

Alma's powers flickered around her as a manipulable energy field that both pushed her off the ground and buffered her body when she crashed through things. She sent a burst through her feet but also pulled some of the energy around her hand. The foot burst propelled her forward. She slammed fist first into Forte. The energy around her hand cushioned her, making it feel as if she'd just punched a pillow. It offered no such cushion to her target.

Forte's mouth formed an "o" as she hurtled back through the doorway.

Alma chortled. "Who's new to this now?"

A theater chair shot through the air, straight at Alma's face. She squeaked and dropped to her hands and knees. Forte rushed Alma again, a blur of quickly thrown punches.

The first hit Alma in the gut before she had a chance to reposition her energy. Her air went out of her in a painful, "Oof!"

Forte's foot swept forward. Adrenaline kicking in, Alma pushed through her hands, springboarding herself towards the ceiling. Deactivating her power, she fell on top of Forte. Her arms surrounded the older woman's neck.

What am I thinking? Forte's a strength sable ... of course, even strength sables have to breathe. She tightened her hold with all her might. Forte clawed at her arm. Her breaths came in shallow gasps. Alma gave an elated laugh. Once Forte was unconscious she'd have plenty of time to find the coins and make her escape—

The thrusters in Forte's armor went off slamming them both backwards. Forte's body crushed Alma into the wall with a burst of pain. Alma's teeth jarred, and she tasted blood.

Losing her hold on Forte, she fell. The world swam. Gray closed in on her vision.

Forte crouched over her and ripped her hood back.

The sable's mouth dropped open. "A kid? You're a kid?"

Her voice seemed to come from miles away. Alma didn't care. She'd failed Lupita. She'd gotten caught, and now they'd never have a chance to be a family.

***

A cold wave of panic slapped Tanvi in the face as the

kid's eyes rolled back in her head and she went limp.

Oh, crap, did I kill her? Did I just kill a kid?

Tanvi dropped to her knees beside her. Should she try first aid?

Her brain scrambled for the crash course in emergency medicine Aiden—who had been a licensed EMT—had given her and the rest of the team. The memory of Aiden, though, immediately twisted her heart and confidence. He'd been so young, older than this kid by probably a decade, but still, barely an adult himself. If Tanvi had just killed a kid, did that make her as bad as the villain who had stolen Aiden from his loved ones?

No. I can't be that sort of a monster. This kid is going to live.

Vaguely remembering that it was a bad idea to move trauma victims, she carefully felt for a pulse. Still beating and she could see the girl's chest rising and falling.

"Hang in there." Tanvi's voice cracked. She forced herself to calm. "Oh, crap, I don't know what to do."

Keep her still.

Tanvi's heart thumped. The voice in her head sounded a lot like Aiden.

It continued, perhaps a forgotten memory of a conversation they'd once had.

Check for bleeding.

A trickle of blood ran from the girl's lip, but it didn't appear to be serious. Good there.

Watch for changes in breathing and alertness.

Breath steady, alertness—zilch.

Call for emergency assistance. This is one place you shouldn't try to be a hero. First responders are trained way better than you'll ever be for this sort of thing. If I'm not there, call 9-11 or a DOSA response team.

Tanvi flipped open a panel in the armor on her wrist. When her armor was on, her phone automatically synced with its communication systems. She hesitated. She really wanted medical response, but there was also a chance the teen wasn't working alone and other supervillains might be in the area. No need to draw innocent normie first responders into a potentially dangerous situation. DOSA could handle both securing the area and getting medical help for the kid.

"Phone, dial DOSA emergency response."

"DOSA Response Center. We have your location on satellite. Please confirm your identity," a woman on the other side said a half second later.

"Tanvi Anand AKA Forte."

"What is your situation?"

"Intercepted a burglary by a sable suspect. Suspect apprehended but injured. No sign of other sable agents. No civilians on site. Need medical help for the injured suspect. She's unconscious but breathing. Not sure how serious her injuries are but don't want to risk moving her."

"We can have a team dispatched to your location with a life flight in minus ten minutes. Please stay on the line."

Tanvi's shoulders slumped.

You did good, Aiden's voice whispered.

Thanks, she thought back, even though logically she knew she was talking to her own subconscious. Even dead, Aiden helped the team hold things together.

Not wanting the girl to come to and try to escape, Tanvi unhooked a metal coil from the utility belt part of her exo-armor. It unwound and activated with a faint buzz that prickled through her skin, weakening her powers. Pushing aside her discomfort with the power-numbing sensation, she snapped the coil around the girl's ankle.

Power dampening fields were an essential part of the DOSA tool kit. They were generally short range, needing direct contact with the subject to void their powers, but once they were on a sable, the sable immediately became a lot easier to deal with.

Prisoner secured, Tanvi leaned back against the wall and closed her eyes. Adrenaline fleeing, she felt cold, weak —of course, she was still far stronger than the average normie, but by her own standards, her muscles might as well have been jello. Her hands shook. If this kid didn't make it, she'd never forgive herself.

Okay, universe, you stole Aiden from me. I'm still ticked off at you for that, but if you let this kid live, I'll consider us ... not even, but close to it. Come on. Give me a break, just this once. Please.

"Please," she whispered to the silence.

In the distance sirens blared and helicopter engines buzzed. Help was on the way.

She put her hand on the teen's forehead. "Hold on, kid. You're going to be okay."

Chapter Five

Prism shivered against the wind coming off the Pacific Ocean, focusing on the warmth of Fade's hand in hers.

"Do you want to borrow my jacket?" he asked. "Or we could head to the restaurant early. Sit inside?"

"No. I'm fine." She didn't want to end their walk, not yet. "I just need to get my blood flowing." She bent down and unstrapped her sandals before beaming up at him. "Race you to the water?"

Holding her footwear by the straps, she bolted for the surf. Her feet sank into sand still warm from a day in the Californian sun. Fade quickly overtook her, fading through her then becoming solid to catch her as she ran into him. She yielded, melting into his chest, and allowing him to sweep her off her feet into a kiss. His lips moved against hers, further warming her. Breathless, she cupped his face in her hands and let the worry and tension that had built up over the last few days melt away.

He broke the kiss but continued to stare into her eyes. "You're beautiful, you know that?"

She blushed. "I think you've told me once or twice."

"Not enough." He brushed his lips across her forehead and into her hair before releasing her. "Since we're here—" He slipped off his sneakers and socks, sticking his socks into his shoes. "Want to sit and talk for a bit? Can't get a much better view." He nodded towards the waves lapping the shore only a few feet ahead of them.

She settled into the sand and rested her head against his shoulder. The sun dipped further beneath the surface of the water as his arm encircled her waist. Yes, the view was beautiful, but she didn't need it. She just needed Fade, his presence, his warmth. She closed her eyes.

After a few blissful moments, however, her thoughts began to churn again. The Adjudicator's threat to take Fade off their team—followed by Tanvi's comment that it might be better for the team in the long run if he were to go—her own doubts about the way their relationship was progressing … there were so many questions about how this was going to work.

And maybe Tanvi was right. Maybe she and Fade didn't have enough in common to make it last, but it didn't stop Prism from loving him more than she could ever remember loving anyone before. She wanted this to work. She needed this to work.

But what if I'm ignoring things that will bite us both in the future. Is Fade even interested in a long-term relationship? By his own admission, he's never really had that as a goal. Who am I to crash into his life and change that?

His hand waltzed up and down her spine. "What are you thinking about?"

"A little of everything." She smiled weakly. "Though, not to change the subject, but do I get to know what you, Tanvi, and Keeper were up to without me last night?"

"Just a few drinks between friends. Would've been more fun if you were there, but they wanted a chance to interrogate me about my intentions involving you." He chuckled. "I guess the team's noticed that we're going through some growing pains in our relationship."

Her insides filled with a disconcerting mix of hope and fear. "Is that what you call them? Growing pains?"

He stretched his long legs out in front of him and dug his toes into the sand. "Yeah. We're two individuals suddenly together both professionally and personally. It's natural to fumble a little, figuring how the pieces fit. I don't think we're doing that bad at it, all things considered." His hold on her tightened.

"I don't either, but when other people ..." She bit her bottom lip, trying to sort her thoughts into something expressible. "I tend to simply do what feels right to me, you know? What my instincts and my values say is what I should be doing, but when someone like Tanvi who knows us both so well points out all the reasons we shouldn't be together, I worry that my love for you is blinding me to problems that will hurt us later." She snuggled into him. "But I do love you, and it's hard for me to see past that fact to anything logical. It's not that I'm doubting us, but I'm doubting whether I should be doubting us or not, if that makes any sense."

"A little. I do love you, too. Differences aside, or maybe in some odd way because of our differences." He let out a long breath. "I've been losing some sleep over it lately too, and not just about you and me but about a lot of little details of reintegrating into DOSA. I'm trying to decide if this is what I want to do with the rest of my life. I know I don't want to be a villain again, but my record as a hero is less than impressive."

"I find you very impressive." She kissed his cheek.

He laughed. "Maybe that's all that matters." His fingers worked into her hair. "There is something I wanted to get your input on. I had planned to bring it up over dinner, but now's as good a time as any. Something Keeper pointed out stuck with me, and it really is an issue."

Her chest tightened. "What is it?"

"My name ... or lack thereof. It *is* kind of dumb signing only 'Fade' to everything."

"It's unique. I wouldn't call it dumb." She shrugged. Her anxiety eased. The name question she could deal with.

"Yeah, but it has little inconveniences. Too many forms require a first and last name, and 'Fade Fade' is the worst. Not crazy about F. Ade either."

"Well, you do have another name: Greg Curran," she pointed out. "Even though you left it behind, you could pick it up again, so to speak."

He grimaced. "Yeah, that's not me, though. I left it behind for a reason."

"It must've been you once," she pointed out. "When you were a kid, at least? I mean, it's the name your mother gave you, and while I know you don't really remember her, roots are important."

"The Curran part she gave me. She didn't name me Greg." His eyes grew far away as he stared out over the ocean.

She sat up a little straighter. "Who did then?"

"Doctor who delivered me, apparently. From what I could find out, my mom managed to get clean for most of her pregnancy, which considering who she was and how she ended up, is the closest I ever got to an act of love from her." He faded his fingers into the sand until his hand disappeared up to the wrist, then solidified and pulled his hand out, the grains sifting through his fingers. "However, according to the social worker who handled my case, as soon as I was born, she took off to shoot up again, skipped out of the maternity ward when they wouldn't give her painkillers. She left me behind without bothering to fill out my birth certificate. I don't know if he was supposed to, but the doctor penciled in his first name in the blank spot. Maybe out of hubris. Maybe because he didn't want to send me out into the world as 'baby boy Curran.'"

Prism searched Fade's face. He always spoke so matter-of-factly about his messed up childhood, but it had to hurt. She knew from experience that he wasn't the invulnerable cynic he made himself out to be, though she supposed it was possible he'd processed what he'd been through to the point that it no longer bothered him. If that were the case she'd just have to hurt for him.

"After that, it was easier to go with what was on the paperwork, even the few times that my mom resurfaced trying to get custody," he continued. "Still, the name never felt like me. It's weird, but when I took the handle 'Fade' for the first time, that immediately became my identity in a way that Greg Curran never was."

"I think Fade is an amazing name, and it suits you perfectly." She patted his knee.

"It does, but as I said, I wouldn't mind having an actual last name again. Not Curran. Definitely not Greg, but Fade *Something*. I'm ready for that."

"Fade Smith, Fade Jones, Fade Away." She winked at him, hoping to lighten the mood.

He smiled. "All good thoughts, but I was thinking, maybe, Powell."

She blinked. "Seriously?"

"It's the name of the man who plucked me out of villainy to join the first SVR, my mentor, if you will." His gaze wandered back to the water. "Your dad was more a father to me than the unknown sperm donor who knocked up my mom then disappeared from both our lives. Also ..." He put his hand in his pocket then withdrew it, now holding a small, dark blue box. "It's the name of the woman I want to spend the rest of my life with."

Prism couldn't speak. She stared stupidly at the box as he pried it open revealing a white gold band with a single blue solitaire.

Her hands quivered, wanting to reach for it, to claim it, but somehow uncertain this was real.

He cleared his throat. "It's a sapphire, partially because I know you like blue." His free hand caressed the colored tips of her blond hair. "Though, admittedly, also because diamonds are stupid expensive, and my DOSA paycheck hasn't let me save up what I'd need to get you something like that."

"It's beautiful," she whispered. "I do love blue. Do you really ... I mean, are you sure?"

"Do you want me?" he asked, his voice deep, his eyes intense.

"More than anything." She managed to nod.

He pulled the ring from the box and slipped it onto her finger. It felt cool against her skin, a little strange, but so right.

"Then yes, I'm sure. I'm a hundred percent sure. You're the woman I love, Lucia Powell, Luce, Prism, whatever your name is. Maybe I don't even have a name to offer you in return, but love and fidelity, to always have your back, to give you the best of myself, that I can offer."

She threw her arms around his neck.

"I'm guessing that's a yes, then?" He laughed.

"So much yes," she murmured. Their lips met for a long moment. He eased her into the sand, holding her close as they continued to kiss. Her whole being melted.

Prism tightened her hold on him, afraid she'd fall apart if she didn't, maybe dissolve into the sand in a puddle of happiness. His lips traced onto her neck. Her hands worked under his jacket to grip the back of his shirt.

Delight welled up within her. "Can we skip dinner and just get married tonight?"

He brushed his hand through her hair. "It's not that far to Vegas. Besides, I'm not sure if the restaurant will let us in when we're so sandy."

"We could always get it to go." She toyed with his ear. "I mean, the proposal was a nice surprise, but I was really looking forward to pasta."

He grinned. "That's one reason I love you. Your priorities are right where they should be."

He leaned in for another kiss.

Prism's phone went off, and he paused right before reaching her.

She flinched. "Sorry. I'll silence it."

He withdrew enough that she could get it out of her jacket.

Prism glanced at the display. "Huh. It's Tanvi." She paused with her finger over the "dismiss call" button. "Tanvi only ever texts. Why is she calling?"

Fade's brow furrowed. "That's weird. Do you think it's an emergency?"

"I better see." She hit the button. "Hey, Tanvi, are you —"

"Pris, it's awful! It's just awful." Tanvi's voice burst through the phone like a punch to the eardrum.

Fade's eyes widened, and Prism recoiled.

"What's awful?"

"I just ... I can't ... I'm at the hospital on base."

Prism's heart dropped to her stomach. "Are you all right? Are you hurt? Is Keeper—"

"No, it's not us ... it's ... it's hard to explain.

Prism's nerves settled—slightly. "Okay, calm down. If you're not hurt, then what—"

"I did something. I did something bad."

Prism blinked. Tears choked Tanvi's voice.

"What do you mean? What's going on?" Prism pressed.

"I can't ... I hurt someone."

Fade tensed. "Does she need us?"

"I think so," Prism whispered. She then raised her voice. "Hold on, Tanvi. We'll be there as soon as we can. Just hold on."

"Thanks. Sorry. Hurry," Tanvi sobbed. The line went dead.

Prism shoved her phone back into her pocket and refastened her sandals. Fade likewise turned his attention to his shoes. Prism's insides fluttered, but she tried to talk herself down from panic.

She's not hurt. Keeper's not hurt. Whatever it is, they're fine. If they're fine, I'm fine.

Fade slipped his arm around her and helped her stand. "It's going to be okay," he focused on her. "We'll get to her. We'll figure out what's going on, and whatever it is, we'll get through it."

She dusted the sand off her skirt then nodded. "Let's hurry, though."

Chapter Six

The drive back to base seemed to stretch on forever with every red light, stop sign, and slow driver adding to Prism's already heightened anxiety. Fade kept his hand on her knee the whole time, occasionally squeezing gently. It helped, but even with the comfort of his touch, by the time they pulled into the hospital parking lot, Prism was on her fifteenth worst case scenario. She needed to find out what was going on ASAP.

"Fade, could you text Tanvi and tell her we're about to park?" she asked.

"Sure."

Forcing her mind to clear, she focused on finding a parking spot while Fade took care of the communication. His phone buzzed almost immediately.

"She says she'll meet us at the emergency room entrance." Fade unbuckled as Prism put the car in park.

With one last deep breath and a quick prayer, she burst out of the car and ran through the parking lot, Fade right behind her.

Tanvi paced in the entrance. At Prism's approach, Tanvi rushed through the automatic doors and tackled her in a tight hug. Prism's ribs screamed for mercy. She sucked in a breath before using the fact that Tanvi appeared physically whole to calm herself.

"You okay?" Fade asked, looming over the two friends like a self-appointed bodyguard.

"Yes ... well, yes and no." Tanvi withdrew and sniffled. "I was on my jog, and I saw this burglary going down."

Prism stiffened. "A burglary? On base?"

"No, no, some rich dude's beach house." Tanvi's voice

cracked. "It was a sable. I know I should've called it in, waited for back up, but I saw her flying, and my instincts kicked in. You know?"

"You decided to pull a Leeroy Jenkins." Fade nodded.

Confusion momentarily pushed through Tanvi's obvious distress.

"He means you rushed in without a plan," Prism explained, mentally noting to question Fade on his knowledge of gamer memes later.

"Oh, yeah, then yeah, I ... Lee-whatever," Tanvi continued. "I thought it would be an easy takedown, and it was until—" She cringed. "I tackled her. Knocked her out, but when her hood came off—Pris, it was a *kid*. A literal kid, like maybe thirteen or fourteen—fifteen tops. Like she should be skipping school and gossiping with friends and flirting with boys, not robbing houses. Why was she robbing houses?"

Prism tensed. Teen involved crime certainly wasn't unheard of, but teen sables were generally registered and supervised. The most common methods of inheriting super powers being either laboratory manipulation—which was illegal on minors—or inheriting powers from parents—in which case the parents were likely DOSA registered sables who would keep their kids out of that sort of trouble. Because of this, supervillain teens weren't something she'd ever encountered.

"Is the kid going to be okay?" Fade asked, stepping closer.

"I'm not sure. The doctors took her in right before I called you. What if she's not? What if I just killed a kid, Pris?" Tears streamed from Tanvi's eyes.

Prism gripped her friend's shoulder. "If she's a sable, then she's likely resilient with a strong healing ability. That's just how we're made."

Tanvi drew a deep breath. "I guess you're right, but

when I saw her—" Her gaze fell on Prism's hand where the sapphire ring glinted in the overhead lights. Her eyes widened. She whirled away from Prism and punched Fade in the arm. "You punk! You proposed? And you didn't tell me you were going to? What the crap? Did you at least get pictures?"

Prism's heart lightened. In her worry over Tanvi, she'd almost forgotten her elation at her fresh engagement. Now she smiled.

"Ugh." Fade rubbed his upper arm. "Sorry, no. It was kind of a spur of the moment thing."

"Not spur of the moment enough that you didn't have time to go ring shopping." Tanvi scowled at him.

"Nah. I didn't buy it," Fade said. "I forged it myself in the fires of Mt. Doom. You know, the old fashioned way."

"Whatever. I'd better get the full story."

"On the beach, at sunset, and he's going to take my last name." Prism's smile broadened until her cheeks hurt.

Tanvi gave a theatrical gasp. "Oh gosh, does he have a brother? Can we clone him?"

Fade coughed. "Um, you do realize I can hear you, right?"

"Get over it." Tanvi cast him a disdainful glance that swiftly melted into a starry-eyed expression. "My girl and I gotta squee."

A black SUV pulled up to the curb. Prism's hand tightened around Fade's arm as the door opened and the Adjudicator emerged. He shot her a glare. She stood a little taller, hoping he'd have the decency not to bring up their previous conflict right now. A tall, gray-haired woman in a smart charcoal power suit followed him out of the car tailed by a pair of DOSA bodyguards in black suits.

"What are the Adjudicator and Shepherd doing here?" Tanvi whispered.

Prism shrugged. Shepherd, the woman in the suit, was

one of the older DOSA heads, a far-sight sable with a persuasion secondary ability. Though not as blustering and aggressive as the Adjudicator, she still wasn't someone Prism ever wanted to go up against.

To Prism's surprise, the Adjudicator stayed a step behind Shepherd as the woman approached the little band of heroes. She nodded first to Prism and Fade then focused on Tanvi.

"We were in the area for a conference and heard you'd apprehended an unregistered flying type sable." Shepherd arched a thin eyebrow. "We had received unconfirmed reports of a new flying sable sighted throughout the southwest regions over the last several months. It is good to have both confirmation and to have the villain in our control. You've done well, Forte."

Prism stepped forward. "Excuse me, but if DOSA was aware of an unregistered flying type in the area, why was my team not informed? Forte encountered this sable during her off hours. Fortunately, she wasn't harmed, but if I knew there was a threat of that nature in our immediate vicinity, I would have prepared my team members for the potential conflict."

"Simple answer, we didn't know she was in your jurisdiction." The Adjudicator stepped forward. "Our last sighting was in the San Diego area, and that was unconfirmed."

"There have also been sightings in Nevada and Arizona, but again, all unconfirmed," Shepherd added.

Displeasure rippled through Prism. She might not have jurisdiction in San Diego, but it was close enough that she should've been informed. Still, her relationship with the DOSA committee was strained enough, so she bit her tongue.

The door to the hospital slid open, and two uniformed Navy officers strode out to greet the DOSA heads.

"Master Chief, Captain." Shepherd nodded to each in turn. "You didn't need to hurry down here on our account."

"It's our pleasure, ma'am." The older offered first Shepherd then the Adjudicator his hand. "I just received an update on the patient you brought in. Apparently all scans are normal. There were some broken bones and other minor injuries, but she seems to have the near miraculous healing abilities we've observed in other super-abled patients. Her wounds have healed to a degree we'd expect to take a month in only a few hours. She's sedated for now, but we'd appreciate some help keeping her restrained when she comes to."

"Of course. As soon as she's well enough to move, we'll have her transferred to a DOSA holding facility so you won't have to worry about straining your resources to keep her in hand." Shepherd nodded.

Tanvi's jaw dropped. She grabbed Prism by the wrist in a painful, vise-like grip.

"Thank you for the update, Master Chief—" Shepherd continued.

Tanvi yanked Prism to the side. Fade arched his eyebrows before following.

"Easy." Prism pried Tanvi's fingers off and examined the spot she'd grabbed. "That's going to leave a bruise."

"Sorry, but we can't let that happen!" Tanvi whispered, glancing anxiously in the direction of the DOSA committee members. "Pris, she's a *kid*. We can't let her go to *jail*."

"DOSA holding cells aren't like civilian prisons, Tanvi. She's not going to be hurt or put in with dangerous people. I'm sure they simply want to keep her contained so she doesn't escape before they can figure out something to do with her. DOSA isn't going to treat a teenager like a hardened criminal."

Fade's mouth quirked down at the corners.

Prism frowned at him. "What?"

"I mean, this was nearly two decades ago, but based on my personal experience, I wouldn't count on that, Luce." He let out a breath.

"You were in your twenties when you were arrested," she pointed out. "Not a teen."

"I was in my twenties the first time they figured out how to keep me from escaping," he corrected. "I was sixteen the first time they brought me in. Not much older than this kid. At least at that time, they didn't have a system in place specifically for juvenile sable offenders. They were going to charge me as an adult, and would've if I hadn't been particularly hard to contain. I escaped, and it was another seven years before they got their claws on me again."

Prism swallowed. "Like you said, though, that was back in the early 2000s. Since then DOSA has had a lot more experience dealing with sable villains. The SVR's existence alone—"

Tanvi squealed and punched the air. Every head, including Shepherd and Adjudicator's, snapped to stare at her. "That's it! This solves everything! Pris, she has to be our next subject."

Prism choked. "You want the SVR to take on a teenager? Tanvi, that won't work. We do real crime fighting against dangerous sables." A shudder cut through her. "They could really hurt her. I don't want to be responsible for putting a literal kid in the line of fire."

"But what's her other option?" Tanvi scowled. "A holding cell until she's eighteen? Four years of being locked up like a failed experiment until DOSA knows what to do with her? That'll destroy the kid. She should be free, going to school, playing video games, making friends—"

"Just because she's under-aged doesn't make her any less of a criminal." The Adjudicator stomped over to glare at Tanvi. "Do you really want DOSA to release a suspect who nearly defeated one of our best sables in a one-on-one fight into the public school system with access to thousands of innocent, normie teens? Not to mention teachers who wouldn't have anything they could do if she went rogue?"

Tanvi returned his glare with her own fiery sneer. "First off, she didn't even sort of almost defeat me. I'm fine. For another, no, I don't think we should just turn her loose on the public at large. She's got superpowers. She needs to be treated like she has them, and that means she needs to be trained in how to use them."

"DOSA agents aren't babysitters." The Adjudicator grunted.

Prism's heart twisted. Most sable kids were born to sable parents who taught them how to use their powers. There were some exceptions—Tanvi had mostly gone to private schools back in India where she'd had tutors who were coached to deal with her still developing abilities—but homeschooling was often the accepted solution when a kid might randomly shoot lasers from their orifices or levitate household objects. "I'm sure she has parents who are worried sick about her. They really should be the ones who make that call."

"If she had parents who cared, she wouldn't be breaking into houses!" Tanvi's voice rose in pitch and desperation.

"Hey, deep breath." Fade held out his hand. "None of us want anything bad to happen to the kid, all right?"

Tanvi shut her mouth but kept an accusing gaze on the Adjudicator.

"Shepherd, if I may ask, do we know anything about the subject's identity?" Prism asked. "Are there any missing persons reports that match her description?"

Shepherd glanced at the captain who shook her head.

"No. We haven't had much time to look into it, obviously, but local law enforcement came up empty," the captain answered.

"Considering the reports you said you had, isn't it likely she came from out of state?" Prism said. "We need to do our due diligence."

"We will, but whoever her parents are, they obviously weren't equipped to deal with a sable child," Shepherd said. "We can't simply release her into their custody."

Prism's stomach twisted. *What am I about to get myself into?*

"Anyway, it's not something you need to worry about." The Adjudicator crossed his arms. "We're here. Thank you for bringing her in, Forte, but from now on, the girl's our problem."

Tanvi turned a pleading stare on Prism, and Prism's resistance broke.

"Adjudicator, you said you wanted the SVR to take on another subject. I would like to request this girl be released into our custody for rehabilitation." She let the words burst from her, not giving herself a chance to reconsider.

Tanvi bounced on her toes.

The Adjudicator's face hardened. "I gave you a *list*. This *child* was not on that list."

"Because you didn't know she existed yet," Prism retorted. "She's a perfect candidate. Flying sables are rare, and while this girl has apparently toyed with criminal activity, she's not too far gone into the life. She should be easy for us to bring around."

"But a child in the SVR?"

"Better than a child in a holding cell," Fade shot back.

The Adjudicator glared at him.

"Actually, Prism has a point." Shepherd glided forward, her calm gaze searching Prism's face.

Prism drew herself up taller.

"Underage supervillains are a rare enough occurrence that we don't have a program in place for them yet,"

Shepherd continued. "We will, of course, need to attempt to find the girl's legal guardians. However, if none come forward, she will be considered a ward of the state, and I feel confident in entrusting her care to Prism and the SVR."

The Adjudicator coughed. "Really, Shepherd, this should be discussed with the full committee—"

"For goodness sake, Frank," Shepherd's tone reminded Prism of an exasperated grandmother whose grandchild had asked for yet another cookie. "You're the one who has been pressuring Prism and her team to take on a new charge. Well, here we have one handed to us, and a flying type at that! Whoever this girl is, she'll be of far more use to DOSA training with the SVR than she will in a holding cell."

The Adjudicator's jaw—the whole exposed half of his face, really—tensed. "I hope you know what you're doing, Shepherd. I want it on the official record that this was not my idea."

"Yes, yes, you get that written down in blood and stone." Shepherd rolled her eyes. "Cover your butt, all you want. Thankfully some of us at DOSA are still willing to risk our political standing in order to do what needs to be done."

Prism blinked, and Fade snorted. The Adjudicator's face turned crimson before he spun about and stomped back to their SUV.

"If you will excuse me, Prism, Fade, Forte." Shepherd nodded to each of them in turn. "I would like to speak with the girl's doctors before I retire for the evening."

The Navy personnel led her into the building, the automatic doors swishing closed behind her.

Tanvi squeaked and pulled Prism into another rib-crushing hug. "Thank you, thank you, thank you, thank you!"

"No problem." Prism withdrew and examined her friend. Beneath the happiness, red still rimmed Tanvi's eyes. "You should get home and rest, though."

"Rest? I need to tell Keeper what happened!" Tanvi pulled up her shirt just enough to reveal her exo-armor belt. Hitting a button, she activated it. The armor snapped in place, expanding to cover her exposed skin, before she engaged the thrusters and hovered a few feet above the ground. "See you at HQ!"

As Tanvi zoomed off into the darkening sky, Prism's muscles gave out, her posture slumping.

"Dang it, what have I done?"

"The right thing." Fade came up behind her and worked his hands into her shoulders, easing the tension from her body. "Like you always do."

"I hope you're right," she breathed. If this went wrong, it could cost her a lot more than political capital.

Chapter Seven

Alma sat on her hospital bed, knees against her chest. The power dampening device on her ankle chaffed but not in the normal way something rubbing against her would. No, she'd checked over and over again, certain she'd find the skin beneath the DOSA restraining device red and blistered only to find no physical damage. Even so, she could feel it, seeping into her, weakening her.

She hadn't been strong enough to break through the window and escape. When she'd tried to manipulate her energy to push off the ground she'd gotten about an inch up before the field gave out and she dropped to the floor. She hated it. She wanted her powers back.

Did normies always feel like this? How did they survive?

At least the device didn't interfere with her healing factor. The normie nurses and physicians had gone on and on about how impressive it was that she'd healed from her injuries in less than two days. Alma barely remembered half of it. There'd been painkillers involved, probably to keep her sedated as well as pain free.

Even with the power-dampener, the doctors watched her as if she could snap and take their heads off at any moment. Not a big surprise. The first time her powers had manifested, the foster family she'd been placed with acted as if they'd had a bear loose in their house. No reason to think that would ever change, that she'd ever have a place among normal people.

She pressed her nose up against the window, staring across the parking lot towards the main road. Handler had to have noticed she was gone by now. He'd be furious, but what could he do? As scary as he was, Handler was no match for the combined forces of DOSA. At least in their custody she was safe from him. Of course, she was safe in the way a bird in a cage was safe. Chances were she'd never see Lupita again.

Someone rapped on the door.

Alma cringed and tightened her robe around her body. "Go away!" she snapped.

The door opened anyway.

A tall woman with a thin face and gray hair done up in a severe bun strolled in.

Alma glared at her. "What do you want?"

The woman pulled up a chair and sat beside the bed. "First off, introductions. My name is Susan Harper, but I'm more commonly known as Shepherd."

Alma shrank back. Shepherd wasn't as public as the other DOSA heads, but everyone in the US still knew the name.

"Okay," Alma said slowly.

"And now it is traditional for you to introduce yourself in turn." A faint smile crossed Shepherd's lips.

Alma's mouth clamped shut.

"No matter. Nurse!" Shepherd called out.

A nurse entered the room carrying a bundle of clothing which she passed to Alma before darting back out. Alma unfolded the first thing in the bundle: a gray sweatshirt with "DOSA" written across the chest in bold, black letters.

She wrinkled her nose. "I'm not wearing this."

"Your shirt and coat were damaged during your treatment," the woman said. "We'll provide more appropriate clothing for you later, but we can't release you half-naked."

Alma froze. "I'm being released?"

"Conditionally." Shepherd drummed carefully manicured nails on the arm of her chair. "You're a hard girl to keep in one place, Alma Ramos."

Alma forced her face to remain blank. "Who's that?"

"Don't play games." The older woman reached under her suit jacket and pulled out a tablet. She tapped a few times on the screen before turning it around to show Alma a picture of herself, slightly younger. "It took a little research to put together, but there are only so many runaways whose handlers claim they literally flew away. That was nearly four years ago. Where have you been in the meantime?"

"Around." Alma shrugged. If they knew who she was, did they know about Lupita?

"I see." Shepherd scrolled down the document on the tablet. "Unfortunately the reports of your superpowers didn't go far enough up the chain to catch DOSA's attention at the time. From what I can tell from the limited records, there appears to have been some suspicion that those involved were making up the story to save face about allowing an eleven-year-old to disappear from their care so easily. Also there was no record that you had any relatives who had demonstrated sable tendencies. Parents both deceased. One younger sister on record ... also listed as missing?" Shepherd narrowed her eyes at Alma. "I don't suppose you know anything about that?"

"We were separated when I was eight." Alma shrugged. "I barely remember her."

I won't let you get your claws on Lupita. You might be Shepherd, but we aren't sheep.

"What are the conditions of my release?" She pushed the conversation back in a more relevant direction.

"Have you heard of the Supervillain Rehabilitation Project?" Shepherd slipped the tablet back into her jacket pocket.

Alma blinked. "Kinda. It was in the news a bit ago, I think."

"It's a program where sables with a history of criminal activity can be retrained to function as DOSA agents."

Alma shrank in on herself. "No thanks."

"Your options are that or a holding cell until you hit eighteen. The foster system can't handle sable children. They're too great a risk, too expensive to supervise. DOSA has many branches, but none of them deal with babysitting."

"I can take care of myself." Alma's lips curled in defiance.

"If by taking care of yourself you mean robbing houses and living on the streets, that is simply not an option." Shepherd stood. "If you would prefer the holding cell, that was our original plan for dealing with you, and we're ready to enact it. You got lucky, though. The sable who brought you in, Tanvi Anand, or as she's known professionally, Forte, is a key member of the team overseeing the current SVR. They've only taken on one subject previous to you and were looking to recruit another."

"Yeah, lucky," Alma sulked.

"More than you realize," Shepherd said. "You had a small number of personal effects on your person when you were detained. The security team has them at the front desk, but we'll claim them on the way out. There might be a change of clothes in there you'll like more than the sweatshirt, but you need to wear what I gave you until we can check you out of here and hand off your custody to the SVR."

Custody.

Alma had always found it ironic that people used the same word when referring to the guardianship of a minor and the arresting of criminals. At least with her, it was doubly accurate. She was both a minor and a criminal.

Shepherd scrutinized Alma. "One last thing. You may not want to tell us where you've been for the last few years, but that doesn't mean we don't have an idea. There have been sable-involved heists throughout the southwest recently, and while we can't prove you were involved with all or even most of them, we are aware of the likelihood." She took a step closer.

Alma cringed back for a moment then drew herself up again.

"Most of those heists you could not have pulled off on your own," Shepherd continued. "If you were running with a gang, you'd be wise to tell us about them now."

Alma narrowed her eyes right back at Shepherd. "I have no idea what you're talking about."

Sure, she had no love for Handler, but Shaina and Jackson didn't deserve to be arrested. Hopefully they'd find a better way out of their situation than Alma had stumbled into.

"All right, if that's your choice." Shepherd opened the door to the room. "Get dressed. There are a pair of flip flops under the bed. The SVR team should be downstairs ready to collect you in five minutes."

Pushing aside her distaste over the DOSA sweatshirt, Alma quickly dressed, tossing aside her all too flimsy hospital gown and robe. She exited the room. Shepherd stood in the hall, still as a statue. The moment Alma emerged, she beckoned for her to follow.

The nurse at the reception desk handed Alma a paper bag claiming it contained all of Alma's belongings—minus the clothing items that the emergency workers had destroyed. Alma's heart rocketed to her throat. Had they found her picture of Lupita sewn into the lining? What if something had happened to the picture? Even if she never got a chance to see her sister again, she wanted to have that picture. If she lost it—her throat closed in on itself, and she dropped her gaze to the floor.

Not crying. Not crying. Not crying.

Shepherd continued marching her through the Naval hospital as if nothing were wrong. Soon they arrived in the lobby of the building. Two women in their twenties—one of whom Alma immediately recognized as Forte—stood waiting for them.

The woman who was not Forte—a blonde with blue streaked hair who wore a pale blue bomber jacket—approached first.

"Thank you for agreeing to this, Shepherd." She offered the older woman her hand. "It means a lot to our team to pick who we get to work with."

"The girl has potential. Good power base, young enough to convert to the hero path." Shepherd shook the woman's hand then reached into her pocket. She took out a small object that resembled a car key fob. "Here's the remote for her anklet. Considering her flying abilities, I'd suggest only releasing her from it when you're absolutely certain she won't be able to escape … or that she no longer wants to."

Every muscle in Alma's body tightened, waiting to spring. She needed to get that remote.

"Of course." The woman in blue pocketed the remote before turning to Alma. "My name is Lucia Powell, but professionally I'm known as Prism. You've already met Tanvi." She waved at her companion.

Alma shrugged.

"I'll leave you to your new charge. Thank you, Prism, and good luck." Shepherd walked away.

Forte hurried towards Alma as soon as Shepherd left, grinning ear to ear. Prism took a few steps back, also smiling, but more tentatively.

Irritated at the feigned excitement for her arrival, Alma clutched the paper bag filled with her few belongings closer to her chest and scowled at the two sables.

"Glad you're finally getting released!" Tanvi put out her hand as if expecting a high five.

Alma considered it but didn't say anything.

After an awkward moment, Tanvi dropped her hand and cleared her throat. "It's almost noon. You want to get something to eat?"

Alma shook her head. "*No hablo inglés.*"

Tanvi's lower lip fell. "Oh, dang it … Pris! An assist?"

Prism stepped forward. "*Tienes hambre? Quieres comer?*"

"I don't speak Spanish either." The bag crinkled as Alma's hold tightened.

Tanvi blinked at her, but Prism shrugged it off. "She's just being a teenager, Tanvi. Shepherd would've mentioned if there were a language barrier." She motioned towards the waiting car. "Even if she's not hungry, I am … and now I want tacos."

Tanvi pulled out her phone. "It's only eleven. Do you think that food truck that parks near the carwash would be open yet?"

"Maybe, but there's always a line." Prism's mouth quirked down at the corners.

"They accept pick up orders by text." Tanvi exhibited her phone. "I have their number."

"Of course you do." Prism chuckled wryly. "I'll take the fish taco platter. Alma, do you want anything?"

Alma's mouth watered. As much as she wanted to maintain stony silence, she also wanted to eat.

"Who's paying?" she asked as they started towards the parking lot.

"It's on DOSA's tab this time." Prism put her hand in her pocket, the opposite one from where the remote had gone, and took out a set of car keys. "Taking care of you is a business expense, after all. I just need to keep the receipts."

I can at least get a few good meals out of this before I run.

"Carne asada," Alma said.

74

They stopped beside a blue sedan, and Prism took out her phone. "Let's pick something up for the guys too. We'll introduce Alma during group lunch. I'm texting Fade to see what he and Keeper want."

"You want shotgun?" Tanvi waved to the passenger seat.

Alma shook her head and slipped into the back seat.

"Suit yourself." Tanvi took the seat beside the driver.

Prism finished texting and got behind the wheel. She handed Tanvi her phone. "If they text back before you've got the order in, get whatever they want. If not, get a variety. Just be sure said variety includes my fish tacos."

"I wouldn't dare deprive you of your fish tacos." Tanvi buckled up.

With the DOSA people distracted, Alma risked getting into her paper bag of possessions. The ripping noise as she pulled off the tape jarred her, but neither Tanvi or Prism reacted to it. She eased open the top of the bag. There was her backpack, her personal belongings still inside. She could tell at a glance they'd been searched. Her clothes were folded neatly rather than jammed in place like she'd left them. Her shoes were on top of the pile.

She ran her fingers over the lining and found the spot where she'd sewn in Lupita's picture. She could feel the stiff paper of the photograph beneath the softer cloth of the lining. Cool relief washed through her. At least she still had that.

Not daring to take it out, she instead closed her eyes and remembered what the photograph looked like. How Lupita was missing her two top front teeth at the time they'd taken it. How there had been a smudge of ketchup on her sister's chin that looked a little like blood, but how they'd both been so happy in that moment, together, if only for a short while.

The car stopped, and she opened her eyes to watch

Prism walk up to a colorfully decorated food truck only to return a minute later holding a collection of brown paper bags in a cardboard box. Prism placed this on the passenger seat next to Alma and lovingly buckled it in. The smells of meat, spices, and salsa permeated the car. Alma's stomach rumbled.

The car started up again, and they were off, driving deeper onto base.

"So, Alma, we haven't really had formal introductions yet." Tanvi leaned over the seat to smile at Alma. "I mean, we've sort of, kind of met—"

"We ran into each other, you could say." Alma rubbed the back of her neck which was no longer sore, but she wanted to drive the point home.

Tanvi's face fell. "Oh, yeah, sorry about that. My name is Tanvi, though."

"Not Forte?" Alma arched an eyebrow.

"Nah, that's way too formal for me. Prism, though, she mostly goes by her hero-handle."

"I picked out my hero-handle when I was nine and insisted all my friends call me that." Prism laughed. "It became a habit."

"Now that you've met me and my girl, Pris, that just leaves the boys," Tanvi continued. "Keeper, or Bob, is older but a great guy, chill, loves animals. Seriously, if you like any sort of animal, he can probably introduce you."

Alma slumped in her seat. That actually sounded a little cool, but she didn't want to let on.

"And then there's Fade, the team's quiet badass. Doesn't have a second name. He's smokin' hot, but he's also taken by Pris here, so don't get any ideas." She punched Prism in the arm causing the car to swerve, thankfully still staying within its lane. Alma clutched the seat beneath her.

"He's old enough to be her father." Prism frowned, keeping her eyes on the road. "Also, Tanvi, what have I told you about doing that while I'm driving?"

"No way. He can't be that old." Tanvi's brow furrowed.

"He's thirty-four. That makes him twenty years older than her, well within paternal range."

Tanvi whistled. "The guy keeps himself up. I always forget he's got that many years on you."

Prism shrugged. "I'm not exactly a kid anymore either."

"Speaking of—" Tanvi's attention and enthusiasm switched its focus to Prism. Alma let out a relieved sigh. "You guys set a date yet?"

"Haven't really had time. We'd literally been engaged for five minutes when we got your call about Alma." Prism tapped her fingers on the steering wheel. "It's a little awkward. Neither of us have any living family left—not close anyway. I guess I have a few second cousins or something like that on my dad's side, but most of my mom's extended family is in Italy. They aren't going to fly all that way for someone they haven't seen in twenty years. Fade's even worse. No real family to speak of."

Alma's ears perked up. For some reason she had always assumed DOSA sables had TV families, with grandparents and cousins and siblings all over the place. Prism sounded even more alone than Alma was. At least Alma had Lupita.

"We do have some good friends, obviously, but it's a small circle." Prism continued. "I wish I could be excited about a wedding, but who would walk me down the aisle? Who would be Fade's best man? Having a wedding would shine a huge light on empty places in my life where people who aren't here anymore should be." Prism's voice cracked. She rubbed at her eyes with the sleeve of her jacket.

Tanvi's expression softened. "Oh, Pris, I'm sorry. I didn't mean to—I mean, I just assumed you'd be all excited about a dress and flowers and a really big party."

Prism laughed half-heartedly. "Yeah, all that sounds nice. I'm sorry to be a downer. I think it's going to be a really small wedding, though, maybe just you and Keeper as witnesses and the two of us for the ceremony. A nice dinner and some champagne afterwards. I'll wear something white, but not a big puffy dress, and I don't care if he wants to wear jeans. He looks great in jeans." The lines around her eyes eased, and a real smile overtook her face. "Yeah, that'll be perfect."

"It will." Tanvi patted her shoulder.

Alma's gaze shifted to the rolling hills outside the car window. Apparently even DOSA sables had their problems.

I need a plan. I need to get this freaking anklet off me, find a way to get some money, and escape.

It would be nearly impossible to pull off a score under DOSA's very nose, but that was exactly what she had to do. She glanced at Prism and Tanvi. The sun glinted on a ring on Prism's left hand. Engagement ring probably. Those were usually pretty expensive—and perhaps the other sables would have equally valuable possessions. It wasn't as straightforward as cash or gold coins, but it could work.

Stay quiet. Keep my eyes open. Be patient. Man, I hate being patient.

The car stopped in the parking lot of a large, blocky building.

"This is it!" Tanvi jumped out of the car and opened the door for Alma.

Alma glared at her. "Unless we're on a date, you don't need to get doors for me."

Tanvi gave an awkward laugh. "But you were injured —"

"I feel fine." Alma pushed past, still cradling her bag of belongings. She wrinkled her nose at the building. "It looks like a hospital. You know I just got out of one of those, right?"

"It used to be a hospital," Prism explained. "The Navy abandoned it when they got the funds to build the bigger, better one near the front gate. We took this over a few years ago and repurposed it as our headquarters."

"What was wrong with this one that the Navy didn't want it anymore?" Alma frowned.

"Haunted." Prism replied. "The ghost of a moody teen who sulked herself to death on the premises stalks the halls, angsting and making sarcastic comments towards people who are just trying to get to know her."

Alma started then scowled at the woman. "Whatever."

"Let's get inside." Tanvi hurried ahead. "I want you to meet the boys, and I also want to eat my tacos."

Prism pulled out her phone. "I'm telling them to meet us in the first floor break room."

"After we're done eating, I'll show you your room." Tanvi keyed in a code, and the sliding doors opened onto a lobby filled with houseplants. "It's kind of boring right now, but if you want help decorating, I have free two-day shipping accounts with pretty much every online retailer."

Alma paused. She hadn't considered that this arrangement would mean she got her own room. She didn't think she'd ever had her own room. Before she could process how nice that could be, she pushed the thought away. No, she wasn't staying here long enough to get comfortable, let alone decorate.

Now, how do I get out of here?

Alma scanned the area. A couple of visible security cameras, and probably more she couldn't see, but no other obvious obstacles. She wondered if they had a guard watching the live feeds or if they were just for recording.

Prism led them into a small kitchen with a table, chairs, and a TV on the wall. Two men, one black and maybe thirty, the other older, white with a gray-streaked brown beard, waited there for them. Prism set the takeout on the table as the guys stood to greet them.

"Fade, Keeper," she motioned to each man in turn. "This

is Alma Ramos, our newest team member."

"Welcome aboard, kid." Fade offered Alma his hand.

She shied back. He loomed over her. While logically she knew Tanvi, who she'd already encountered, was far stronger than most men, something about a towering, broad shouldered dude made her anxious. After all, for all she knew, Fade could be a strength sable as well.

Don't let them know I'm afraid.

She hardened herself. Tucking her belongings under one arm, she grasped his hand as firmly as she could. She tightened her hold, maintaining eye contact and waiting for him to pull away.

A slight smile twitched at the corners of his mouth before his hand literally moved through hers. She gasped and jumped back. An odd humming power radiated through where his hand had penetrated her skin.

"What the—?"

He smirked then passed his hand directly through the table. "It's my power. Tanvi said you're a flying type? Any other abilities."

Alma shrugged. "Not really." Truthfully, she was stronger and faster than other kids, but no need to give away everything about herself. They already knew too much.

"I'm an animal charmer." The older man stepped forward. Alma tried not to reveal her surprise at his weird, Harry-Potter-character accent. He stooped down and picked up a black cat from under the table. "I go equally by Keeper or Bob, whichever you like, and this is my wee lass, Yui." He nodded towards the cat. "Do you have a hero-handle yet?"

Alma scoffed. "I'm not a hero."

Keeper's eyes twinkled. "But isn't that why you're here? To change that?"

Alma shuddered. No, she was here because she had no

choice. Because she'd always had the worst luck. Because Tanvi had knocked her into a wall and nearly broken her neck. She spun to face Prism who was sorting through the takeout bags, probably looking for her precious fish tacos.

"Can I go to my room? I'm tired."

Disappointment creased Tanvi's face. "Are you sure? I mean, you've barely had a chance to meet the guys. I was hoping we could show you Keeper's—"

"I really want to be alone, all right?" The smell of the tacos made it hard to keep up her resolve, but she couldn't hang out here, pretending this was normal, pretending she could ever fit in with these shining DOSA heroes.

"You can take your food to your room." Prism picked up a paper clamshell container marked with grease and sauce stains. She passed this to Alma.

The warmth of the food inside seeped through the thick white paper into the girl's hands, and it took all her willpower not to pop it open and dig in.

"I guess," she said.

"I'll show you to your room," Tanvi volunteered.

"Take some napkins." Prism opened another clamshell. Her face brightened when this revealed morsels of fried fish sitting on top of shredded cabbage and fresh corn tortillas. "Looks like this batch is especially saucy." She placed a handful of napkins on top of Alma's to-go container.

"Okay." Alma pressed her chin against the napkins so she could hold them in place without releasing her belongings or the food. She then followed Tanvi out the door.

In the short term, they could force her to stay, but they definitely could not make her like it.

Chapter Eight

Prism rested her elbows on the table between the now empty takeout containers. She sank her face in her hands. "Well, that went great."

Fade ran one of the few remaining tortilla chips through some taco sauce. "What did you expect?"

Tanvi and Keeper had already left, Tanvi saying something about the gym while Keeper wanted to feed his animals. Prism hadn't felt like going anywhere.

"I don't know, but not that." Prism thought back over her interactions with Alma. "I mean, I didn't expect her to be over the moon happy to be here, but with her other option being jail, I guess I thought we'd be a better enough alternative that she'd at least be a little relieved. She seems so angry and suspicious—"

"She's a runaway foster kid, Luce." Fade gave her a smile that on any face she didn't love so much would've seemed a little condescending. "She's been programmed to be angry and suspicious. It's going to take more than tacos to break through that."

"I guess." Prism massaged her forehead. "I hate how DOSA failed that kid."

"Hate it, sure, but are you really surprised?"

"Sort of." Prism tried to sort through her thoughts on the matter. "It bothers me that any kid can fall through the cracks in the system like that, but it seems like we should be able to keep track of a sable kid especially, you know? Not that we deserve special treatment, but we have a whole community in place. It should be able to protect kids like Alma. If only so we don't have more supervillains popping up for us to deal with."

Fade shrugged and pushed aside his now empty to-go container. "Being a sable doesn't protect you from the world sucking. I wasn't much older than Alma when I got into the villain life."

"Yeah, but you were in and out of foster homes and never met your biological dad. I always thought sable kids in the system were the exception because most sable kids have sable parents who should be registered with DOSA so they wouldn't be allowed to drop off the radar like that. At least that's how it's supposed to work."

The familiar energy of Fade's powers flickered around her as he toyed with a plastic fork, fading it first into then out of the tabletop. "According to something Talon told me once, it might be more common than you think. He said that while most sables either inherit their abilities from parents or receive them from laboratory manipulation, there are anomalies where certain sables appear out of nowhere. He thought that natural stressors might trigger the genes to activate."

Prism brow furrowed. "Did he think you were one of those?" She'd always assumed Fade got his powers from his unknown father.

"He wasn't sure. It's still possible my abilities are hereditary since no one knows who my dad was. However, my powers did emerge when I was thirteen and in a rotten foster home. I used them to run away. Faded my way into the public library after hours and lived there for almost four months before someone caught on and brought me back into the system."

Prism arched an eyebrow. "Let me get this straight. You were a thirteen-year-old boy who suddenly manifested superpowers, and your first decision was to run away to a *library*?" The idea tickled her, and it was hard not to giggle at him.

"It was a well-considered decision," his tone grew

defensive. "A library is a public space with access to entertainment and information where most people don't question a kid hanging out for hours."

Gears turned in Prism's head. "I'm starting to put a few things together about you. Like the fact that in less than a year with the team, you've set high scores on almost all the video games in the entertainment room, read through every book in the building, and referenced Harry Potter, Lord of the Rings, and World of Warcraft in casual conversation." The giggle escaped. "Is the badass supervillain secretly a nerd?"

"I didn't think I was being secretive." He let a smile slip. "But people who decorate their rooms with *Princess Bride* and *Labyrinth* posters and clock hours farming virtual cows can't really throw stones over nerdiness."

She leaned across the table and whispered conspiratorially, "I have a level 89 Elven Loremaster in *Lord of the Rings Online*."

He eased closer to her. "Really? That's sexy. How'd you keep that hidden from me?"

"I haven't had time to play much since you joined the team, so it never came up." She looked him over. "I'm thinking you'd enjoy the burglar class."

He shook his head. "Too obvious. What do they have that carries a big ass sword?"

She laughed, her tension easing.

He wrapped his fingers around her wrist, rubbing his thumb in circles into her palm. "I know you want this to be perfect, but it's going to take time. Alma needs to see that we can be trusted, that we're not going to turn on her or abandon her like people have in her past. There's a barrier there, one I didn't get through until I was in my twenties and started working with your dad. Before that, I just assumed nobody cared and everything was out to get me."

A thought crossed Prism's mind. "Do you think you

could talk to her? Let her know you understand what she's going through?"

Fade coughed and pulled away. "First off, I'm not a mentor type. Second, the last thing that kid needs is some thirty-four-year-old dude pretending he knows the first thing about being a fourteen-year-old girl."

"Yeah, you were born in your thirties. You were never a vulnerable teen in the exact same state as Alma." Prism clicked her tongue.

"Of course." He kissed her cheek. "Though if you think about it, the person who really wanted the girl on the team was Tanvi. I know the SVR is kind of your baby, but you have a team for a reason. If Tanvi cares the most, she might be the best one to oversee the girl's rehabilitation."

Prism tapped her fingers on the tabletop. "I'll ask her if she would be willing to take it on. Even if Tanvi doesn't want to take the lead here, the team thing goes both ways. Alma needs to incorporate with all of us. Maybe some training exercises would be a good place to start."

"I'm always up for a good workout." Fade stood and stretched. "Speaking of which, I think I'll go on a run. Want to come?"

"Sure." She smiled. "Let me go change."

"Meet you in the lobby." He brushed his hand through her hair one last time before striding out the door.

Prism stood and tossed the last few empty containers into the trash. Some exercise might ease her tension temporarily, but she wouldn't feel right until Alma was settled.

I have to make this work. We can't fail the poor kid.

Chapter Nine

Alma sat on her bed watching the numbers change on the bedside digital clock.

2:24.

She willed her heart to beat silently. An air-conditioning unit hummed in the distance but other than that silence. No voices or footsteps. The DOSA HQ lay quiet, asleep.

Rising from the bed, she double checked all her belongings, verifying nothing had fallen out of her backpack. That only took a moment. She didn't have much.

She glanced around the room, trying to see if there was anything worth taking. The room she'd been given was bare bones. Just a few pieces of cookie cutter furniture. Still, it was a bed of her own, a space she could be alone in. She wished she'd had more time to enjoy that. As she searched through the drawers of the room's dresser, looking for anything of value or utility, she remembered Tanvi's promise that they could decorate the space any way Alma wanted. What would that even look like? She wouldn't know where to start with that kind of thing.

After opening several drawers, she found only some spare bedding. She snatched a pillow case to use if she found some valuables she could fence for starter money. As she unfolded it, a faint memory crossed her brain, of walking door to door in a quiet neighborhood, dressed as a princess in a ridiculous, flimsy purple dress that constantly threatened to rip to reveal her jeans and T-shirt beneath it.

"Remember, say 'trick or treat,' mi Pajarita!" a nearly forgotten voice echoed through her heart and soul. "They'll give you candy! Don't be shy."

Alma dropped the pillow case.

Sitting down to put on her shoes, her fingers brushed against the cool metal of her disruptor anklet. Her lips pursed. She wouldn't get far with that on. When she slipped her finger beneath the cold metal band, a prickling sensation crept up her hand into her arm. She searched for a latch, but from what she could see, the disruptor was a single, solid piece of metal. It couldn't be, though. It had to open to be able to come on and off.

If something opened, she could get it open. She simply needed the right tools.

Her hoodie had been shredded by the hospital personnel, and she had no other coat. She glanced out the window. Clouds crossed in front of a pale crescent moon. Could she make it without a jacket? The DOSA labeled sweatshirt sat, balled up, at the end of her bed. It would have to do. She pulled it over her head, took up her backpack, and walked to the door.

They hadn't locked her in. At first the act of trust had surprised her, but then she'd realized that with the anklet serving to both track her and keep her from accessing her full powers, they probably didn't think they needed to do more than that. They were wrong. Alma couldn't be held down by a stupid piece of metal. She was going to get out of here and make a life for herself. This DOSA crap was only a detour.

Fluorescent lights flickered along the dim hallway. She eyed the various doors leading off of it. A couple doors down a *Princess Bride* poster had been taped to a door. Across from that another door sported a picture of a woman playing a violin in a birdcage. Good guess that those were probably inhabited. A shadow moved near her feet, and she inhaled sharply to keep from screaming. A soft, light creature brushed against her ankles, and a pair of glowing eyes gazed up at her.

Keeper's stupid cat.

The cat meowed.

"Go away." Alma nudged at the cat with her toe. "You'll wake them up."

The cat flicked her tail and slank away from Alma.

Alma started in the opposite direction, towards the stairwell. Her shoes squeaked on the floor beneath her. Her anxiety increased at every step but she kept going, slow and steady.

When she made the stairwell, however, all resolve evaporated, and she burst down the stairs at a sprint. Alma hit the first floor landing and collapsed against the door. She panted and sweat beaded on her forehead.

What the frick? She'd never gotten winded on a short run like that before? Why—

Her gaze fell on the anklet. Stupid thing. It had to be suppressing some aspect of her powers she hadn't even realized she was using—super stamina? Something like that.

Got to get this thing off me or I'll never get away.

She dabbed at her forehead with the sleeve of her sweatshirt. Everything could be removed with the right tools. Handler had taught all his charges lock picking as well as other skills. Where could she find tools? The break room had a full kitchen. Kitchens had tools. She'd start there.

She flipped on the lights for the break room. Everything was quiet and clean though the ghosts of the tacos consumed there lingered in the form of a faint odor of cumin and chipotle. She considered the fridge. Maybe she should take some food to go. Of course, she wouldn't be going anywhere if she couldn't get the anklet off.

Alma pulled open a drawer and found it full of silverware. She considered a butter knife but swiftly rejected that idea. The next drawer slid open with a loud clank. She froze. For a moment, she paused to listen. The fridge hummed. The lights flickered overhead. Alma exhaled.

Various kitchen gadgets cluttered the drawer. At a glance she identified whisks, a corkscrew, some knives, and a dozen other objects she had no reference for. She picked up a long bladed knife. It seemed the most likely candidate, but it also had the most potential to do physical damage to herself. She put it back and chose the corkscrew instead. Sitting in a chair, she rested her ankle on the knee of the opposite leg and examined the anklet for any visible weak points like cracks, screws, or joints. Nothing.

Alma grunted in frustration. She knew these things were one-size-fits-all, yet it fit her perfectly. The only way she could figure for that to work would be if it were made of small, interlocking pieces that could telescope in and out of each other to change size and shape. If that were the case, there had to be space between the pieces, right?

Running the pointy end of the corkscrew along the smooth metal, she tried to feel out the cracks she knew had to be there. Again nothing. She returned to the drawer. Maybe sawing through it would work. Taking up a long bread knife with a serrated blade, she sat in her chair.

The blade scraped across the anklet. A fierce smell of friction-heated metal rose from where she was working and flakes of metal appeared along the blade. She laughed. This was it. It was working. She pulled away the blade and blew away the flakes. The metal beneath shone smooth and unmarred. Her hopes sank. She rubbed her eyes with the back of her hand before examining the knife. The teeth along the blade had worn down to dull nubs. The metal flakes had come from the anklet destroying the knife, not the other way around.

She choked on her frustration. "Ugh!"

She slammed her palm into the anklet. With a sharp

whirring noise, it loosened then fell to the floor, leaving her leg free. She breathed easier as her powers rushed through her, enlivening her muscles. How had that worked?

Crowing with delight, she leaped to her feet and spun around. Her heart jumped into her throat.

Tanvi stood in the doorway, conspicuously holding the remote to the anklet. "You would've been sawing at that for hours if the cat hadn't woken me up."

Alma swallowed, glancing from the remote to the deactivated disruptor. What had just happened?

"I thought Prism had that." As soon as the words escaped her lips, her face heated. Of all the stupid things to say. She needed to run. Did it really matter why Tanvi had taken off the anklet? No, what mattered was that Alma could escape. Somehow, though, her feet didn't move.

"She gave it to me. Said if I wanted to, I could be in charge of acclimating you to the team and deciding when you were ready to be trusted without the anklet." Tanvi stepped into the room but left the door open behind her. She didn't even try to block it. Maybe she felt she didn't have to. Tanvi had already taken on Alma and won once. Alma wasn't eager to get crushed against a wall again.

"You think I can be trusted?" She glanced down at the ruined knife.

"No, but I don't like the idea that I'm keeping a teenager prisoner." Tanvi's shoulders slumped. "Before you take off, can I have a minute to convince you not to leave?"

A cold splash of realization hit Alma in the face. "You won't stop me?"

"If you hear me out and still want to go, no, I won't stop you." Tanvi pulled a chair out from under the table and settled into it. "Could you put down the knife, though? I'm hard to kill, but I don't like getting stabbed. It stings."

Alma dropped the knife onto the tabletop. "I pretty much ruined it anyway." She crossed her arms over her chest. "Nothing you say is going to change my mind. I don't want anything to do with DOSA or hero crap. That's how people get killed."

"Do you want to be a villain?" Tanvi arched an eyebrow. "Because that's as dangerous as hero work—maybe more so because there's always someone after you."

"I just want to be left alone!" Alma snapped. "I am tired of people using me. I want to make choices with my life."

"Choices that include robbing houses?" Tanvi leaned closer.

"I needed the money, okay?" Alma averted her eyes. She *still* needed the money. Even if she got away, even if she found Lupita again and somewhere safe for them to hide, she'd need money for food and clothes and Lupita needed to go to school which meant they might need to fake having parents, and an illusion like that would be expensive to maintain. She wanted to be with her sister, but not on the streets, not in a way that doomed Lupita to a life as cruddy as hers was.

"We all do, but getting it that way is going to lead to a lot of pain for you down the road," Tanvi said.

"It already led to some significant pain, remember?" Alma gave an exaggerated wince and rubbed the back of her neck.

Tanvi cringed. "Sorry about that, but that's exactly why you can't keep doing this. I'm not the only DOSA sable out there, and I'm not even the most powerful of them. If you'd gone up against Glint or Fireball or any of a dozen top tier DOSA sables, you might've been hurt a lot worse. You could've been killed. You're a flying type sable, which usually hints at a lot of power. Breaking gravity isn't exactly a weaksauce ability, but you have no idea what you're doing. You need training, if only to protect yourself. Yeah, DOSA isn't perfect, but the villain world sucks people in and won't let them out. It's not something you can dabble in."

"I don't want—" Anger stole Alma's words. What if Tanvi was right? Handler was small time, a single man with compulsion powers traveling around the country in a trailer, and she'd still barely escaped him. It wasn't a safe world to bring Lupita into. "I don't want to be in the villain world or the hero world or any world but my world, all right?" She kicked at the nearest chair. "This is stupid. I'm a kid. I should be going to school and having friends over and …"

And a family. I want my family back. Not some stupid fake DOSA family. My real family.

Sympathy deepened the lines around Tanvi's eyes. Alma wished she could punch her.

Don't pity me. Don't pretend to care. You just want to use me, just want me to join your perfect little DOSA team. Well, I won't.

"I wish I could give you that. If you want, I can talk to someone at DOSA about looking for extended family for you, someone might be out there who can take you in. An aunt or a grandma? There aren't really foster homes set up for sables—"

"I don't want to go to a foster home."

"What about something more permanent? Like adoption?"

"It wouldn't be real. They'd only want me because of my powers." And they might not want Lupita at all. After all, Lupita was a normie. DOSA wouldn't want anything to do with Lupita.

"You don't know that." Tanvi stood. "Look, Prism is planning to run the team through a few training exercises this week—with you. You'll learn how to protect yourself. Please, at least stay for that."

Alma narrowed her eyes at Tanvi. "And if I take that training and use it to become a real villain? Use it to learn how to fight you and win?"

"That's a risk I'm willing to take because I don't think you're a bad kid, Alma."

"You don't know me." Alma snorted.

Tanvi sighed. "No, you're right. I don't, but I'd like to. When I realized I'd hurt a kid, it made me … remember some things that happened that I didn't want to remember." Pain etched lines across her otherwise youthful face.

Alma tilted her head to one side. What was that about?

Clearing her throat, Tanvi continued. "Whatever happens, I want you to be able to protect yourself. I also hope you don't choose the villain path because if you do, and we end up fighting against each other—I'd hate that. I don't mind slamming down some piece of trash villain who is old enough to make his own choices about being an a-hole, but you're a kid. From what I can tell, you haven't had a choice in what path you've taken, and that's not fair."

"I've always been told that life's not fair."

"No, it's not, but people can be if they try hard enough."

Alma mulled over this. Tanvi seemed sincere. Maybe she wasn't malicious, just naive.

Remembering how quickly Alma had lost their fight still stung. If she could learn to defend herself, she'd have a better chance. Also, if Tanvi were serious about keeping her out of the anklet, she'd be able to leave whenever she wanted.

"All right, I'll stay for a little longer."

Tanvi's face immediately brightened.

Alma's insides twisted. Why did people have to pretend to care about her? It never lasted. No, she would use Tanvi and her DOSA pals to improve her chances, but then she'd get away. To be with Lupita, her real family, the only one who would always care.

Chapter Ten

Rap. Rap. Rap.

Alma groaned and hid her face deeper in her pillow. She cracked an eye open. Light streamed through the window blinds, casting striped shadows over the room. Her backpack lay on the bed next to her and she still wore her clothes from the evening before—even her shoes.

The person on the other side of the door knocked again.

"Alma? It's almost eleven. You still in there?" Tanvi called.

"No!" Alma yawned. "I ran away. You'll never see me again. Now let me sleep."

"Come on! Keeper fried up a whole pan of sausage and eggs for you."

Alma sat up. Her stomach grumbled.

Her sweatshirt had hitched up during the night, so she pulled it back into place and hurried to open the door.

Tanvi grinned. "Thought you'd open up for that." She passed Alma a plate piled high with breakfast items. "You'll need to eat fast. Prism's already got a training exercise planned."

Alma's heart did a backflip. "What sort of training exercise?"

"No idea, but I'm sure it will be fun." Tanvi shrugged.

Alma sat on the edge of her bed, balancing her plate on her knee, as she shoveled scrambled eggs into her mouth. Her appetite had fled, but she didn't want Tanvi to see that. Sure, the whole reason she'd agreed to stay was to get training, but Prism and her team were serious, full-time superheroes. Chances were Alma would look like a fool to them. Well, at least she wouldn't face it on an empty stomach.

After a few bites of eggs, she sampled one of the sausages. Smokey, savory juice burst onto her tongue, and her appetite returned full force. It only took her a couple of minutes to clean her plate.

Tanvi whistled. "If you always eat like that, we're going to have a hard time keeping you fed."

"Been living on hospital food for the last few days," Alma pointed out. She wiped her mouth with the back of her sleeve. "Ready to go."

Tanvi pulled a phone from a pocket of her yoga pants and tapped on the screen. A moment later the device beeped. "Prism and the boys are going to meet us in the gym. That probably means Prism's going to start you out easy with some one-on-one training. Let's go."

They descended a couple of floors and entered a wide open gym space complete with basketball hoops, weights, and other equipment lining the walls. The center, however, had large mats spread out. Prism and Fade stood next to one of these.

"Where's Keeper?" Tanvi asked.

"He drew the short straw on dishes." Fade chuckled. "I don't think he minds. He and Yui were chatting over the leftovers."

Tanvi laughed. "He's so odd with that cat. Sometimes they remind me of an old married couple."

Fade guffawed. "More than you know."

Alma swept her eyes up and down Fade. Of all the team members, she knew the least about him. She'd gotten a good idea of who Tanvi and Prism were on the ride to HQ the day before, and Keeper seemed pretty easy to understand, a little crazy but in a pleasant sort of way. Fade, however, was quiet, and her one encounter with his powers—his hand cutting right through her as if she wasn't even there—made her curious. How could she defeat him if her fists would go right through him? Would she be fighting him today?

"So, what's the plan?" she asked.

Prism shrugged off her bomber jacket revealing a close fitting T-shirt beneath. She also wore yoga pants and a pair of running shoes. "Until we've gotten used to each other's abilities and fighting style, I'd like to have you go up against the team one at a time. Starting with me."

Alma tilted her head to one side. She didn't know a lot about Prism's abilities—something light related she thought—but of the team members she was definitely the least physically imposing. "Why you?"

"For one thing, Keeper's not here. Fade's a little old fashioned about hitting girls, and you've already fought Tanvi. Based on my experience, you'll learn more about your powers facing a new challenge than repeating an old." Prism tossed her jacket onto a bench along the wall. "For another, as team leader, it's my prerogative to break in new team members."

Fade's lips curled into a mischievous smile. "I remember when you broke me in."

"Hush you." She playfully slapped him on the arm.

Alma rolled her eyes. "Are you two going to make out? Because I forgot my barf bag."

Tanvi crowed with laughter and put up her hand for a high five. Without thinking, Alma clapped her palm against Tanvi's. She then flushed. She didn't want to start liking these people.

Prism pulled off her engagement ring and offered it to Fade. "Would you hold onto this for me? I don't want to risk damaging it."

"Just so long as you put it back on when you're done." He bent down to kiss her before taking the ring and tucking it into the pocket of his leather jacket.

Tanvi and Fade retreated to sit on the same bench

Prism had thrown her jacket onto.

Prism bent down and picked two small white objects off the mat where they'd escaped Alma's immediate notice.

"I want to show you how these work before we start—so you know what you're getting into." Prism strapped one of the white things on each of her wrists before extending her right hand and pushing a button on the part of the wristlet that overlapped with her palm. With a hum and a crackle of energy, a beam of fierce yellow light shot from the wristlet. It impacted into the wall, bursting into sparks.

Alma leaped back a step.

"Don't worry," Prism soothed. She hit another button, and this time instead of a blast a sustained beam rose from her hand. "These are my lasers. I have natural abilities too, but I've found that supplementing them with a little tech goes a long way."

Alma swallowed, eyeing the sword-like rod of light. "Do they cut through things?"

"They can." Prism turned a small knob on one of the wristlets. The blade hummed at a slightly different frequency before she rammed it into the mat beneath her. It penetrated the floor covering with the putrid scent of burnt rubber. When Prism flipped off the beam, a blackened hole remained. "For training bouts, though, I almost never use them at full power." She adjusted the knob again. "I like to call the settings kill, stun, and 'man, that stings.'" She flashed Alma a bright smile. "I can't punch nearly as hard as Tanvi—or I'm guessing you—so this evens the game a little."

Alma nodded slowly. "Man, that stings" didn't sound like much more fun than getting punched into a wall by Tanvi did.

"I'm a kid, so you're going to take it easy on me, right?" Alma asked.

"Would you return the favor?" Prism winked.

In spite of herself, Alma laughed. "Probably not."

"I have no interest in actually hurting you, but you also won't learn anything if I treat you like you're breakable, which I'm pretty sure you aren't." Prism stretched her arms over her head before circling her torso around her hips in a long stretch. "So, with it being one-on-one, the point to this exercise is to try and restrain the other party. DOSA prefers capture/incarcerate to outright killing villains, plus it's easier to simulate in a training scenario."

"Have you had to kill a villain, though?" Alma frowned. Tanvi had come pretty dang close to killing her.

Prism's face grew grave. "A couple times. It's never pleasant, and I hope you'll be able to avoid the same. If it comes to a choice between letting yourself or an innocent person die or taking the life of a villain, though, you have to be ready to make the call."

Alma fell quiet. She wasn't sure how she felt about that. Before she'd fallen in with Handler, the line between good guys and bad guys seemed much starker. If she'd been asked when she was younger, she would've said killing villains wasn't a big deal. After all, they were villains. Now, though, having gotten herded into that life, she had to wonder if most villains were truly evil or more like her and simply desperate.

"Ready to start?" Prism asked.

Alma shook herself out of it. "Sure."

"Good. Catch me if you can." Prism's body shimmered and appeared a foot or two away from where she'd been standing.

"What the—" Alma's powers flared in response. Her energy catapulted her off the floor.

Teleportation? Is that her power? That's not so bad.

Balling her hands into fists, Alma swooped at Prism's face. She dove right through her. Alma gasped. She flailed, trying to stop her own momentum, crashed onto her knees, then her face.

The slap of the mat against her skin sent her adrenaline rushing. Okay, so not teleportation. She hopped up and pushed herself to hover next to the ceiling.

Prism walked towards her, but there was something off about the way she moved. Alma scanned her, trying to place what it was.

"I thought Fade was the one who could be unsolid." She glanced at the observing sables. Fade leaned forward, watching intently but with a bemused smile that irritated Alma to no end.

"Oh, she's solid." Tanvi giggled. "She's just—"

"Shush, Tanvi." Alma's gaze shot back to Prism. The voice was off, as if it was coming from somewhere other than her location. "Let her figure it out."

Yeah, that was it. A slight delay between when Prism's lips moved and when Alma actually heard the words.

A projection? That's it! Alma's eyes lit up, and she scanned the room. There, a few feet from where Prism stood, the mat had two indents as if someone's feet were weighing it down even though no one stood there. No one visible, at least.

Alma dove towards the spot, feet first, channeling all her power into her legs for a massive kick.

Prism's projection blinked out and a burst of light exploded from the area Alma targeted. The brightness hit Alma like a slap to the face, tangible in its ferocity. Blinded, she slammed into the mat, landing hard on her butt. Pain jolted from her tailbone up her spine.

Ouch. That's gonna be a bruise.

Her vision cleared of the dancing dots just in time to see Prism's laser-blades swooping towards her face.

Alma squeaked and rolled out of the way. The blades hit the mat where she'd been a second before, a now visible Prism right behind. A blast of light shot from Prism's outstretched wrist. It impacted against Alma's side like a shock from an electric fence. Alma whimpered and toppled head over heels. Ears ringing, she lay on her back, eyes closed, for several breaths. When she dared to open her eyes, Prism hovered over her, laser-swords going full blast.

"You okay, Alma?" Tanvi shouted from across the room.

"Yes," Alma answered through gritted teeth. So much for Prism being easier than Tanvi.

"You actually have a lot of promise." Prism powered down her blades and brushed a stray lock of blue-tipped blond hair out of her eyes. "You caught onto my projection ability way faster than I expected. Nice work."

Alma glared at her. Undeserved praise was far more annoying than deserved criticism.

She's making a mistake, not taking me seriously.

Prism offered Alma her hand. Jaw clenching, Alma took it then with all her strength yanked Prism off her feet and over Alma's head. Muffled sounds of surprise rose from the spectators.

Alma got to her feet and spun to find Prism already bouncing out of her tumble.

The team leader's eyes flashed. "Oh, so you want to play dirty, huh?" Her lasers buzzed to life. "Bring it on, kiddo."

Prism threw her hands forward and another flash of radiant light shot from her. Dazzled, Alma staggered backward, throwing her hands over her eyes. Knowing she'd be safer on the ceiling, she pushed off the floor. Too late. Prism darted forward, blades spinning. Pain shot through Alma as one impacted against her calf. She screamed and dipped. She cartwheeled into the far wall. Prism bounded towards her in a whirl of light.

Alma charged only to go right through her. Dang it. Another projection.

Prism's invisible foot hit Alma between the shoulder blades. The girl crashed down again. Every muscle in her body ached.

Alma whimpered. Desperation spiked within her. Her heart was in her throat. Her powers screamed for her to fight back. Energy surged through her and without thinking she thrust her hands forward in the direction the kick had come from.

A blast of silver light rushed like an outbreath from her fingertips. A wave of sparkling energy swept across the gym. It slammed into Prism who flashed back to visibility a second before she hit the wall.

"Luce!"

"Pris!"

Fade and Tanvi sprang from the bench.

Alma trembled as she stared at her own fingers.

Prism hopped up and raised her hands as Fade rushed to her.

"I'm all right!" she said, still sounding out of breath. She stepped past Alma, her brows melting together. "How did you do that?"

"I ... I don't know," Alma stammered. "That's never happened before."

"The girl has energy pulses!" Tanvi punched the air. Concern for Prism faded from her face to be replaced with a beaming smile. "Awesome!"

"Energy pulses?" Alma turned her hands this way and that. Her fingers tingled as if coming alive again after falling asleep.

"It's actually a pretty common secondary power for flying type sables." Prism stepped closer moving gingerly. "Oof. I wouldn't mind an aspirin after that."

Fade slipped behind her and rubbed her shoulders. "I've got you."

"Super strength, flying, and energy pulses." Alma's nose wrinkled. That combination seemed familiar. "Weren't those the powers of that one sable who went rogue last year?"

Prism's face fell, and Fade and Tanvi both tensed.

"What?" Alma frowned.

"Her name was Cosmic, and she didn't just go rogue," Prism's words came out tight. "She went full on monster."

Alma's stomach twisted. Was Prism suggesting Alma could also be a monster? After all, she was a villain with the same powers as Cosmic. "She couldn't have been that bad."

Tanvi's hand clamped down on Alma's shoulder. "Trust us. She was."

Prism turned away. "Look, it was a good bout. You … why don't you …I'll see you all later." She rushed out the door. Fade hurried after her.

"What's her problem?" Not wanting to show her discomfort, Alma forced an air of unconcern.

"Cosmic killed her brother," Tanvi murmured.

Alma's heart dropped to her feet. "What?"

"When Cosmic went rogue, as you put it, she hurt a lot of people, including Aiden Powell, Prism's little brother." Tanvi swallowed. "He was also my friend. The why is a long story, though it was partially because Cosmic was certifiably nuts. The important points are, Aiden was important to Prism. Cosmic killed Aiden, and Prism straight up destroyed her for it."

Alma gaped. "Prism killed Cosmic?" While Alma didn't exactly follow DOSA sables, everyone knew Cosmic had been one of the most powerful in their arsenal. Prism—she just didn't seem that scary.

"Don't underestimate her, especially not after you've hurt someone she cares about." Pain creased Tanvi's face. "She cared about Aiden a lot."

Guilt flooded through Alma. She hadn't meant to make light of Prism's grief. If Alma could understand anything it was loving a little sibling. Alma didn't know what she'd do if something happened to Lupita.

Prism must think I'm a jerk.

"I didn't know," Alma whispered.

"Prism isn't mad at you," Tanvi assured her. "It's just an open wound, one you didn't know you were poking." She patted the girl's back. "You did great today. I know fitting into a new team is hard, but you'll get there. Just give it time." Tanvi glanced over Alma.

Alma looked down and found her sweatshirt stained with perspiration. Now that the fight was over, her skin cooled. Goosebumps prickled on her arms.

"We need to order you some more clothes. How about I loan you some tank tops so you can get a shower, then we can do a little online shopping? We can have a whole new wardrobe delivered by tomorrow, I bet."

"Sure," Alma mumbled.

Alma shuffled her feet as they left the gym. How could she be part of the team when she kept screwing up so monumentally? Prism had to hate her now. It was only a matter of time until the rest of the team followed suit.

***

Prism drifted in and out of consciousness, vaguely aware of her blankets around her, the pillow beneath her head, and the light from her moon-lamp as it gently faded from blue to green to yellow to orange. She smiled and let out a deep breath. Comfortable. Safe. Warm. Tired. So soft.

Her eyes fell shut, and the darkness flowed around her like warm water. She started to float, awareness slipping from her as her muscles relaxed and the cares of the day fled her body.

Lucia!

A jolt of anxiety rocketed through her, but not her own. No, there was a foreignness to the emotions, as if she were observing them, not experiencing them. Even so, they were real, and they were in her brain. She could feel them like an electric current zapping through her blood. She whimpered. Her hands tightened into her sheets.

Luce! Help me! Please, you have to hear me.

Aiden?

A tremor cut through her. It couldn't be. He was gone, but the energy around the emotions was achingly familiar. It was his power, his presence.

Aiden, where are you?

He reached for her. She could almost see him, leaning across the quiet of the night, hand outstretched, searching for her, flailing for her like a drowning man fighting for the surface. Then as swiftly as his presence had appeared it disappeared. Snapped. Snapped like his neck had snapped in that horrible moment, his energy fading even as she remembered the light escaping his beloved eyes.

Prism sat up in bed, screaming.

Her gaze flitted about the room. It was empty, quiet.

"Aiden?" she whispered.

No answer. Only the silence of the night.

She jumped out of bed. Closing her eyes, she tried to focus her mind, tried to reconnect, tried to find him again, but nothing responded to her attempts.

"Dang it!" What had she expected? She didn't have the power to reach out. Aiden was the one with mind powers. Hers were just stupid, useless light abilities. Her heart pounded. She needed to find him. Needed to get to him.

She rushed towards the door at full speed only to collide against Fade as he ghosted through the wall.

She collapsed into him, and he grabbed her by the arms to steady her.

"Luce, are you okay? I heard you scream?" The faint, color-shifting light illuminated his worried dark eyes.

Her whole body shook. "Aiden! Fade, I felt him calling for me. He needs me. He needs help."

Pity softened his expression. "Lucia, Aiden's gone. You were dreaming."

She made a feeble effort to pull away, not enough to break his firm but gentle hold on her arms. "No! I felt him! It was real. He ... he ..." Energy fled from her as she realized how silly she sounded. Aiden had died. She'd watched him perish in this very building. He couldn't call to her. He was gone.

Her knees gave out, and she slumped against Fade. "It felt so real."

His arms surrounded her as she began to cry.

"I'm sorry, but it was just a nightmare." He kissed her forehead. "Where Aiden is now, he doesn't need your help. He's at peace. I promise."

She tried to hold onto that, but her chest still felt empty, sucked dry.

Fade rocked her from side to side, his hand massaging her between her shoulder blades. "You should go back to bed. It's after one, and we have a training session tomorrow."

She gripped his T-shirt. Aiden's cry for help still echoed in her brain. "I'm not sure I can sleep."

He kissed her forehead. "I don't want to leave you alone. Would it be all right if I stay with you? I promise, I won't try anything."

A shiver cut through her, and she managed to nod.

Together, they settled onto her bed, and he pulled her blankets around her once more.

Prism nestled into his chest. "Thank you for being here, Fade."

"I plan to always be here." A faint smile flitted across his beloved face. His hand brushed over the back of hers, momentarily pausing to caress her engagement ring. "Do you want to tell me about what happened?"

She tried to put her thoughts together. "You're probably right. It was just a dream, but I swear I could hear him calling to me, as if he were reaching out to me with his powers, you know?"

"Yeah, I do. I've been on the receiving end of Aiden's abilities." He stroked her short blond hair. "It's not something I'll forget."

"It's silly." She squeezed her eyes shut, hoping to block out the memory. "Even when he was alive, Aiden's abilities only had a short range. For him to call to me like that, he'd not only have to be alive but in the building. I don't know how I let myself believe it was real."

"The brain is funny, especially when half asleep." He kissed her forehead. "Still, Luce, I love you, and I don't want to sound like I'm calling you crazy, but you went through a lot when you lost Aiden. You've never really ... Do you think you should see someone about it? You might actually have some PTSD, and while I love you, I don't know how to help you with that."

She bit her bottom lip. "It was just a dream, Fade. I'm fine."

"No, you're not." He cupped her face in his hands. "There's no shame in getting help, real help. DOSA probably has people on call for that sort of thing. They certainly put their agents through enough crap that I'm sure you aren't the only one who needs therapy."

Prism snuggled closer to him. He felt warm, solid, real, more real than the nightmare that had seemed so undeniable only moments before. She breathed in his scent, a spicy perfume that probably had a lot to do with the bodywash he used but which she would allow herself to pretend was just his natural odor.

"I promise, if it gets worse, if I have more nightmares, I'll talk to someone, but right now, I really just need you, all right?"

"All right, but please, remember that you need to look out for yourself as well as the rest of us." His lips caressed her cheek. "You've given everything to this team. There's no shame in taking a little back for yourself."

"I took you for myself." She smiled, the tension melting from her body as she continued to cuddle with him. "That's all I need."

She settled in, her eyelids growing heavy again. Maybe he was right. When everything calmed down with Alma as a new team member, she'd see someone. Now, though, she was going to sleep.

Chapter Eleven

Air rushed by Alma's face as she pushed herself faster and faster through the warm afternoon air. Below, the muddy blue of Lake O'Neill sparkled in the sunlight. She cast a glance behind her. The pink and white streak that was Tanvi chased after her, but she was still far enough behind that she wouldn't be able to stop Alma now.

Kicking herself into a downward dive, Alma plummeted towards the lake.

"Easy!" Tanvi's warning echoed through her earpiece.

Alma spun to face the older sable just long enough to wave before flipping around and skating across the surface of the water. Water rose in a huge wave. A group of black and white waterfowl flapped desperately for the sky, quacking their displeasure at Alma's intrusion.

Pushing upward again, Alma stopped to hover just as Tanvi reached her.

Tanvi crossed her arms over her chest. "Don't do that. It's hard to come out of a dive. You're lucky you didn't go headfirst into the water."

"Lucky?" Alma tossed her head so that her ponytail flipped from one shoulder to the other. "That was all skill."

"Luck or skill, you can't always count on it." Tanvi motioned for Alma to follow before engaging her thrusters and zooming over the beds of reeds to the shore beyond.

Alma alighted next to her on the grassy bank.

Tanvi slipped off her visor and wiped sweat from her brow. "If I get you killed on a routine training flight, Prism will never let me hear the end of it."

Alma deflated at the mention of Prism. She still hadn't figured out a way to apologize or explain herself for bringing up Aiden's killer so flippantly. It was probably too late now to do so gracefully. Prism had been business as usual in the weeks that had passed since then, but that didn't necessarily mean she'd forgiven Alma.

Tanvi flipped open a panel on her wrist armor and skimmed the readout beneath it. "It's almost lunch. We should probably head back."

Alma's shoulders slumped. "Can't we take another lap around base? Maybe head to the beach?"

A smile tickled Tanvi's lips. "You really like flying, don't you?"

"Well, yeah." Alma hesitated. "I guess I didn't realize how much I did." Handler had kept a tight watch on Alma's powers, not wanting her to attract DOSA's attention. "I didn't exactly get a lot of chances to do it where I was before," she mumbled.

"You ever going to tell me where that was?" Tanvi kept her eyes on the panel, pushing buttons to rotate through the various displays.

"No." Alma launched herself into the air. She'd already said too much. "How about we race? If you win, we'll be lame and go home. When I win, we'll go to the beach."

Tanvi chuckled. "You mean 'if,' don't you, short stuff?"

"No, I mean when."

"How about to HQ, then? That way we'll be able to go inside immediately after you lose."

"Sure." Alma smirked. "It's on the way to the beach."

Tanvi fired up her thrusters, and the two sables burst into the air. At first they traveled so close together Alma could feel the air from Tanvi's wake. Then Tanvi swerved to one side. Alma squeaked as Tanvi collided into her, knocking her off her flight path. Alma somersaulted in mid-air, pushing her energy in all different directions trying to regain control. By the time she righted herself, Tanvi was a dot in the distance.

"Cheater!" she snapped through their comm line.

"Sorry, you mispronounced that. It's actually said *winner*," Tanvi all but cackled.

"I'll get you back for this." Alma pasted a scowl to her face as she shot after Tanvi again. Inside, however, something tickled in her chest, a laugh threatening to escape.

"Meet me on the roof. We'll debrief before we go in—both of us need to get our story together so Prism doesn't gripe about us goofing off during training hours."

"Yeah, we don't want the mother hen to be disappointed in us." Alma scoffed.

By the time she landed on the roof of HQ, Tanvi had removed her armor and now sat cross legged next to the door to the stairs wearing just her yoga pants and tank top. "Good run, Alma." She hopped to her feet. "So we have things straight, we did timed laps around HQ. No diving into water. No racing with stakes on the line. Just safe and practical timed laps."

Alma forced a sober expression. "Yes, exactly that."

"Great to be on the same page." Tanvi clapped Alma on the back. "Hey, while you were catching up after I smoked you in our race—"

"After you cheated," Alma interrupted.

"Same difference. Anyway, I started thinking, it's about time you took on a hero-handle, you know? I mean, secret identities are almost impossible these days, but it's still easier to see your professional name in the news rather than your personal one. Besides, it's just cool." Tanvi picked up a jacket that lay on the roof beside her. "Here, you might want to wear this. You're sweaty and the breeze up here will cool you down fast now that we're not moving."

Already feeling goosebumps break out on her arms, Alma accepted the garment. "I don't know. Do I really need one?"

"Need, no, but it's expected and other sables—both villain and hero—" Tanvi gazed pointedly at Alma. "They won't take you seriously unless you have a cool name."

"How'd you pick yours?" Alma asked as she pulled on the jacket.

"It took me a while to come up with it, but I like music, and I'm strong, which is what Forte means, basically. It also means loud, but I can be that too." Tanvi laughed. "I wanted something that could double as a stage name if I ever decided to ditch heroing and go back into music."

Alma rubbed at her arms. "I don't have any ideas for a name, though."

"It could have something to do with your powerbase, like Burst for your energy bursts or something plus flyer. Burstflyer. Powerflyer. Flyergirl."

"Nuh-uh. Nothing with 'girl' in it." Alma shook her head.

"Fair enough, though I did know a forty-something sable with psychic abilities who called himself 'Brain-Boy' completely unironically." Tanvi grimaced. "Between the two of us, Butt-Head would've been a better name for him."

"I bet." Alma snorted.

The team had converted the roof of HQ to their purposes. Keeper kept a collection of beehives, a small vegetable garden, and even a dovecote there, and one area had a series of deck chairs. Alma and Tanvi now settled into these, watching Keeper's birds flutter around.

"You can use something personal to you, though. It doesn't always have to be about your powers," Tanvi continued. "Keeper's handle is sort of related, but he told me it was a jokey nickname he had as a kid even before his powers developed because he always had animals around him, so the locals in his small town started calling him their little zookeeper."

"That's cute." Alma considered her options. "Something to do with my heritage could be nice. Like maybe in

Spanish?"

"You'd have to talk to Prism about that. My Spanish is limited to counting to ten and anything that might be on the menu at *Tacos 2 Go*, but yeah, the Spanish word for flying or bird or something might work."

A thought struck Alma, "My ... my mother used to call me Parajita. It was kind of a made-up name that meant her little bird."

Tanvi's eyes softened. "That's really sweet. That could be it."

Alma hardened herself. "No. It's silly." Still something in her longed for that, to be someone's little bird again, and the memory was nice. Of course, a sable name should make her feel tough and invincible, not soft and nice. "What about Something-Bird?"

"Burst-Bird? Powerbird? Bird-girl?" Tanvi winked.

"No." Alma tapped her fingers against the arm of her folding chair. "What about Soulbird? Alma means soul."

"Oh, that's slick. I like that." Tanvi gave Alma a thumbs up. "Soulbird it is."

A strange warm feeling crept through Alma.

Soulbird. Yeah, that could be me.

The sound of a car pulling into HQ's parking lot caused Alma to get up and walk to the edge of the roof. All of the team members were home so it couldn't be them. Maybe one of them had ordered pizza for lunch.

A wash of cold fear swept over Alma as she gazed out on the parking lot and saw the ominously official black SUV.

"Tanvi, were we expecting anyone?"

"No." Tanvi sidled up to stand beside Alma. Her face darkened. "Ugh, those are DOSA vehicles." Her mouth crinkled. "I hate it when they show up unannounced. It's almost never a good thing. Let's go inside and see if Prism needs backup."

Alma considered the figures emerging from the distant SUV. They'd be inside well before she and Tanvi could navigate several flights of stairs down to the lobby. "Let's take a shortcut."

She jumped off the roof.

"Alma, slow down!" Tanvi yelped.

Alma's breath hitched as gravity snatched her. Before she could fall far, her powers snapped on, and she glided gracefully to the stairs leading up to the door. She came to a stop, hands on her hips, hovering a few inches above the ground, and flashed the arrivals a haughty smile.

A man in a dark hood and mask glared at her. Her smile faded. She knew that mask. She'd seen it in more than enough online articles.

The Adjudicator?

Tanvi's thrusters hummed as she lowered herself next to Alma, her arms crossed.

"To what do we owe this unexpected honor?" she asked.

The Adjudicator pointed at Alma. "What is she doing out without her disruptor anklet?"

The door behind them slid open, but the Adjudicator kept lecturing without so much looking up to see who it was. Prism stepped out and positioned herself directly behind Tanvi's hovering form.

Alma glanced at Tanvi. For some reason she'd assumed DOSA would be aware that the team was letting her go without the anklet.

"It's a training session." Tanvi landed and hit the button so that her exo-armor telescoped back into her belt. "She can't very well train if she's got her abilities muted."

"Don't be smart with me, Miss Anand." The Adjudicator's finger whipped towards Tanvi as if it were a gun he was eager to fire at someone. "I pulled the reports on her anklet before I came here. It's been inactive for some time now."

"Well, if you knew that, why did you ask?" Prism smiled sweetly. "The restraining of SVR subjects has always been the purview of the SVR. I decided when Fade's anklet came off. Before me, in the original SVR, it was my dad's call. Alma is a low flight risk—well, she's high risk for actually flying, but low for fleeing." Prism laughed at her own joke.

"The girl is literally a runaway." The Adjudicator's face showed no amusement. "I wouldn't consider that low flight risk."

Alma let her powers flag so that she dropped to the ground. Prism and Tanvi immediately flanked her. A strange tightness overtook Alma's throat, and she averted her eyes.

The sliding doors swooshed open again. Keeper and Fade strode out, Keeper with his black cat draped over one shoulder. The cat tilted her head, gazing directly at Alma. Alma shifted uncomfortably and turned away, finding it easier to focus on the Adjudicator for some reason.

"Is that why you're here? Because of the anklet reports?" Prism asked. "If that was a concern, you could've just emailed, and I would've given you the same explanation." She glanced at the SUV. Alma followed her gaze.

Though the tinted windows made it hard to see who was in the back, the front passenger window was rolled down, revealing a single uniformed driver behind the wheel. Still, no one else emerged from the vehicle which suggested the Adjudicator hadn't brought backup.

"I know an important committee member, such as yourself, must have more important things to do than travel across the country to check in on us." Prism's tone softened to a diplomatic hum.

The Adjudicator stood a little straighter. "I actually came because I had some good news that I wanted to deliver in person." He reached under his coat and pulled out a tablet. "While we were loath to sentence a minor to a holding cell—"

Fade coughed, loudly.

The Adjudicator glared at him before continuing. "Myself and the other committee members have debated the wisdom of inserting a teenager into an active DOSA team. I took it upon myself to seek out alternatives, and I've found one that should suit all parties."

He handed Prism the tablet. She took it gingerly, as if it might self-destruct in her hand, and glanced it over. Alma tried to crane her neck to see, but between the distance and the angle, she couldn't make out anything.

Prism swallowed. "What does this file have to do with Alma?" She passed the tablet to Tanvi.

"I think it should be obvious," the Adjudicator answered. "A married sable team currently on inactive status in a childless home? Tapman and Melodica are the perfect candidates to be the girl's guardians." He dropped his voice, though since there was no one outside of the team nearby to listen, Alma assumed he was only doing it for dramatic effect. "Don't tell her I said this, but Melodica has been struggling with infertility for the last year or so. She and her husband took time off from DOSA specifically to deal with the issue, but sometimes these things aren't meant to be—"

"I'm sure the lass appreciates you sharing such things with strangers on the other side of the continent." Keeper stroked Yui who gave a peevish meow.

All emotion drained from Alma to be replaced with a hollow ache. She knew where this was going.

"But it seems to be a win-win. The girl gets a new home and family with a couple who both desperately want a child and have the capability of handling her super abilities. Of course, I would suggest they keep her in the disruptor anklet for longer than you have seen fit to." A smile curled across his face. "Once the SVR is through with their stint at babysitting, you and your team will be free to take on a new villain. I imagine you still have my list of recommendations?"

Alma's stomach tightened. It was happening again. She was going to be relocated, sent away, disposed of. How had she been stupid enough to hope this time would be different?

"Clumsy me. I misplaced that somehow." Prism scowled. "Shepherd legally granted guardianship of Alma to the SVR, not DOSA as a whole. We'll consider this, but whether or not Alma leaves is up to Alma, not the SVR, and definitely not the committee."

The other team members nodded. Hope flickered back to life within Alma.

The Adjudicator's expression hardened. "Don't be a fool, Powell. DOSA, and the SVR in particular, are no place for children. It's dangerous. Are you really going to pit a fourteen-year-old girl against supervillains? You, of all people, should know how deadly this game can get. Remember what happened to your brother?"

Alma gaped.

Prism's shoulders hitched towards her ears.

Fade stepped between her and the Adjudicator. "You should leave."

The Adjudicator drew himself up, though Fade still towered over him. "You have no authority to—"

"I don't need authority to tell you that you're an entitled —"

"Fade!" Prism put her hand on her fiancé's arm. "Thank you, but it's okay. I'm okay."

Fade glanced at her, considered for a moment, and nodded before shooting one last challenging glare at the Adjudicator and taking a step back.

Alma deflated. It would've been very nice to see Fade punch the Adjudicator's smug face.

Prism let out a long breath. "I take Alma's safety very seriously. However, she's not a piece of equipment that can be requisitioned by any DOSA team that wants her. She's a person, and she needs to have a say in this. I'll talk it over with her, but it's between her and my team." As she spoke she placed her hand on Alma's shoulder. Alma's tension eased. "Is there anything else you came here to tell us? If not, my team would like to go over the information you presented amongst ourselves."

The Adjudicator grunted. "Remember, if the girl can't hold it together as a hero, her only other current option is a holding cell. This offer from Melodica might be her last chance at a normal life. Don't deprive her of that because you're too stubborn to admit you were wrong."

"Oh, I'm often wrong, but considering the Cosmic incident, that's a trait the committee seems to share with me." Prism's blue eyes chilled to points of glaring ice. The corners of Fade's mouth quirked into a smile and even Yui meowed her approval.

The Adjudicator spun on his heels and stomped back to his SUV. As soon as the door shut behind him, Prism's posture softened like a popped balloon.

"Second floor conference room, now," she said.

The team scurried to obey, and a few minutes later they were all situated around a table.

Prism sat at the head of the table with Fade, who had scooted his chair in order to be closer to her, at her side. Keeper and Tanvi each took places across the table from each other while Alma, feeling like she was about to be grounded, positioned herself at the foot.

Prism glanced at Tanvi, who still carried the Adjudicator's tablet. "Could you let Alma see the file?"

Tanvi dropped her gaze to the tabletop but slid the

tablet towards Alma.

Alma took it. A photo of a couple gazed back at her. They were dressed in jumpsuits—a fairly common uniform amongst DOSA sables—and looked to be in their thirties. She scanned their file. Lifetime DOSA sables, second generation—meaning they'd each also had parents who were sables—with *music* based powers. She furrowed her brow. What was that like?

She skimmed through information about their qualifications and accolades to get to the important part.

Location: North Carolina.

Her throat tightened. "They're on the east coast?"

"Yes, I believe so." Prism nodded. "They used to work out of Langley, if I remember correctly, but accepted a less demanding assignment a few years ago."

Alma set the tablet down on the table. "So if they were to take me, I'd have to move to where they are?"

"Probably. I can't imagine they'd relocate." Prism's gaze penetrated Alma who focused on the table rather than meet the team leader's eyes. "Alma, I won't lie, the Adjudicator is probably right that this would be a better option for you than the SVR."

Alma slumped in her chair. If she accepted this move, she'd be across the continent from Lupita. She'd never be able to see her again. Maybe she could ask this family if they'd take Lupita too, but to do so she'd have to tell them she knew where Lupita was hidden, and then the government would put Lupita back in the system if the couple didn't want her. And why would they want her? They wanted Alma because Alma was a sable, to make up for the sable kid they couldn't make themselves. Lupita wasn't a sable. Taking on one orphan was a lot of work. Taking on two?

No. I can't risk it. I won't go to any family unless I'm sure they'll take Lupita as well as me.

"I won't." Alma shoved the tablet. It slid across the table and crashed to the floor. With an irritated meow, Yui hopped up from where the tablet had landed. She settled on the tabletop, glared at Alma, and started to wash her paws. A slight smile crossed Keeper's face before he turned to face Alma.

"I wouldn't write this couple off so quickly, lass. They're looking to start a family, which isn't a bad thing."

"And honestly, Alma, as much as I hate to admit it, the Adjudicator is right." Prism flinched as if the words brought her physical pain. "The SVR is dangerous, and the missions we go on aren't something I would ever feel safe for you to participate in."

"But I'm a sable!" Alma burst out of her chair. "I'm strong. I'm fast. I'm practically indestructible."

"Being a sable doesn't make you invincible, let alone immortal." Prism scowled. "Also, don't you want some sort of a normal life? To go to school? To have friends your age? A family?"

"Family is overrated," Alma lied.

My family isn't. Lupita isn't. Everything else that pretends to be my family but isn't is overrated to the max.

Tanvi swallowed. "I hate to see you leave, kiddo, but Pris is right. This is dangerous work. While I am willing to train you, I don't think I'd be comfortable putting you in the field until you're at least eighteen. That's a ways away."

Alma's jaw dropped. She'd thought if anyone would have her back it would be Tanvi. If Tanvi wanted to get rid of her, what hope was there?

Tanvi's shoulders slumped. "I don't want you to leave, but a real family might be better for you than … this." She waved her hand towards the rest of the team.

"A girl needs a mum," Keeper added.

"I don't!" Alma pushed her chair back. It slammed to the floor. Tanvi winced, and Yui's fur stood on end. "I've taken care of myself for the last three years without any help from a 'mum' or a dad or any of you. I don't need a family. I don't need DOSA either! I'm only here because you made me be here, and if you try to make me go to that freaking family in freaking North Carolina, I will leave! I'll leave, and you won't be able to stop me."

"Alma—" Prism stood.

"No!" Alma slammed her fist into the table. Rage boiled within her. This wasn't happening again. She wasn't going to be packed up like unwanted luggage and shipped across the country to live with strangers. She wasn't going to leave her sister behind. "You said this was my choice, Prism. Were you lying? Were you just saying that to save face in front of the Adjudicator? I'm not a pawn in your game. I'm a person, and I want to make my own choices."

"Easy!" Prism held up her hands. "I didn't mean it like that. You do have a choice. I promise. However, I think you should consider—"

"No!" Heat rushed through Alma.

She couldn't listen to this. It had all been a lie. It was always a lie. How had she been stupid enough to hope this time wouldn't be a lie?

"I'm not going! I'm not going to listen! You think you know what's best for me. You don't know anything! You don't know what it's like to be me. You can't know because you're all spoiled, shiny heroes. You don't know how hard I had to fight to stay out of the system, and now you want to put me back? Give me away to another fake family?"

"Alma—" Tanvi rose from her chair and took a step towards her.

"No!" Alma thrust her hands forward without thinking. A burst of energy knocked Tanvi backwards over her chair. Alma gasped as Tanvi somersaulted into the wall.

"Tanvi!" Prism rushed to her friend.

"I'm all right!" Tanvi leaped up and brushed herself off.

Cracks spread in the plaster of the wall.

Alma cringed. Oh, they'd never let her stay now. She needed to run. She needed to run far away before they made her go someplace where she'd never see Lupita again.

Prism faced her. "Alma, you need to settle down or I'll have to put the disruptor back on you."

"I won't let you!"

"Lass, we're not trying to hurt you." Keeper stood, his face softening. "We all care about you."

"No, you don't!" Alma's pitch rose to a shriek. "You're just pretending to care because it makes you feel good to help the poor little orphan girl. You don't know the first thing about what it's like. You're all spoiled, privileged, DOSA puppets. You won't understand. You'll never understand."

Tanvi's mouth opened, perhaps to protest, but Alma shoved the table at her and turned to storm out.

Fade stepped between her and the door.

"Out of my way!" Alma shouted.

Fade grabbed her arm. A strange energy sparked through Alma, and before she could pull away from him, she fell through the floor, him landing next to her. She glanced around. They were in one of the many office rooms on the first floor. There was a desk to one side and a few chairs and file cabinets, but a layer of dust spoke to the room being mostly abandoned.

His powers released her, and she jerked away. "What the frick, dude?"

"Shut up and listen!" he barked. "You aren't the only kid in the world who has taken their share of hits, all right. Maybe you've convinced yourself that you were dealt a bad hand in life, and so you have the right to do and say whatever you want, but that's not how the real world works."

"What does a DOSA sidekick know about the real world?" She sneered. "You're just as—"

He thrust his phone in her face. "Google me." He frowned, his dark eyes dead serious.

She arched her eyebrows. "You're kidding."

"Not even a little."

Torn between defiance and curiosity, she took the device. "Just 'Fade' is going to get me a lot of hair cuts and garbage. Do you have a last name?"

His glare faded. "For the time period you're interested in, it was Curran. I haven't let anyone call me that in a long time, though." He spelled the last name for her.

Several news articles and a hero-wiki page came up. Wanting the condensed version, Alma chose the wiki. *Former villain and master thief Fade, AKA Greg Curran, first caught the attention of law enforcement and DOSA investigators in the early 2000s—"*

Alma's cheeks warmed, but she shrugged off her embarrassment. "So you pretended to be bad for a while. That doesn't mean you know—"

"My mom abandoned me to the system when I was only a few days old. She played with the idea of regaining custody enough to keep me from getting adopted, but she could never stay clean long enough to make it happen. When I was six, she OD'd, and that ended any delusions I had that we'd ever be a family." His words came out clipped, as if they physically hurt him to say.

"You were in the system?" She swallowed. She glanced at the wiki's oldest photos of Fade—or at least a boy she assumed was Fade. He looked to be close to her age, and it was already a mug shot.

"Until I got my powers." He strode across the room and pulled two of the chairs away from the wall. He offered her one. Hesitant, but needing to know where he was going with this, she took it. "It was a rush. Thirteen-years-old, never had a say in my fate, suddenly with the power I needed to take control. You know what I mean?"

Her throat tightened. She'd been eleven when she'd figured out there was something weird about herself, but her thought process had been similar to what Fade was describing. "What did you do?"

"The obvious. I ran away, decided I was going to use my powers to make a life for myself." He sat in the other chair, facing her. "At first I told myself I was just going to take enough to keep myself alive and fed, but it never ends that way. I got addicted to it. It seemed like I always needed more. Food and shelter wasn't enough. I wanted money to be comfortable, to keep myself entertained, to buy friendship because I sure as hell didn't know how to make friends, not when I was used to everyone in my life abandoning me or me having to leave them when my time in whatever home was up." His shoulders slumped. "The thing is, no matter how many times I told myself I wasn't hurting anyone, I was. Maybe they were people who didn't feel the loss of what I took as much, maybe I didn't physically hurt anyone, but there was damage done."

Alma's nose wrinkled. She liked to think she would only ever target rich people who didn't care if they lost a few hundred dollars or a flat screen TV, but it didn't always end up like that. Sometimes only poor people were convenient.

"It also wasn't the life I wanted," Fade continued. "DOSA got me on their radar the moment I used my powers to escape from a detention center, and after that, life was one long chase. I might've bought a few weeks or even months at a time if I found a particularly good place to lie low or a group of criminals looking for someone to join them in a heist who could offer me protection, but it never lasted. Every time I started to build a life for myself, the authorities would get closer, and I'd be on the run again." He leaned forward. "Trust me, kid, it's not the life you want, and I get it. I didn't think I was DOSA hero material either. I still doubt that I am some days, but I stick it out because I know it's a lot better than the alternative."

"So do you only stay because they'd arrest you if you left?" She hadn't considered that Fade could be as much a prisoner as she was.

"No. I mean, I won't lie, there was a short time after I was finally apprehended and before I settled into the life where that might've been true." He scratched at the back of his neck. "But what really happened was joining DOSA helped me find a family."

Her lips curled in contempt. "Oh, so true love changed the big bad villain's ways? Come on, dude. Don't try to sell me that fairy tale."

"Falling for Prism was a part of it, but it's more than that. You need something to fight for. A purpose. For a lot of DOSA heroes that's the idea of doing the right thing, helping others. For some it's the fame and the public adoration. For me? It's the people I've come to care about within DOSA. Prism, yes, but also Keeper and Tanvi." His eyes burned into her. "What you said back there about the team only helping you to feel good about themselves? Maybe you'd have a point if we were trying to train you to shove you off on another DOSA team or back in the system, but that's not what we're trying to do. We're trying to bring you into our family, and if you knew these people as well as I have come to, you'd know that's a big deal. This little group of mismatched misfits is everything to them—and to me too." He stood. "I'm not going to force you to apologize to them, but I'm going to encourage it. I know the path you're walking better than most. You might think it's a track you're stuck on, but every little choice you make along the way is a chance to get off it. The longer you're in the villain life, the harder it gets. I wasn't able to escape it until my twenties. You've got an opportunity to get out ahead of that, and if you don't appreciate it, you're an idiot."

Alma crossed her arms and slouched in her chair.

How can he say they're trying to bring me into their family when at the first suggestion, they want to kick me out to be with some strangers? Maybe Fade's bought into this, but I haven't.

Fade narrowed his eyes at her. "Well? You ready to go back up and talk this over like a big girl?"

Alma's face heated. "There's nothing to talk about."

"For now." Fade opened the door. "Look, I know Prism. She doesn't lie. If she says you don't have to go to that family unless you want to, she means it."

"Everybody lies," Alma scoffed. "If you think she doesn't, that just means she's extra good at it."

He laughed. "You know, you remind me a lot of me, kid. I wish that were a good thing."

Fade exited, leaving the door open. Alma didn't follow. Even if Prism were telling the truth, the Adjudicator obviously wanted Alma gone. It would only be a matter of time before he got his way.

Chapter Twelve

Prism blinked as Fade and Alma sank through the floor. Tanvi hurried to the spot, but the pair was already gone.

Brow furrowed, Tanvi turned towards Prism. "What's he up to?"

"I don't know, but I trust him," Prism answered.

Yui hopped onto the table and stretched before walking up to Keeper and allowing him to pick her up. Stroking his cat, Keeper walked around the table. "Do you want me to go look for them?"

Prism considered Tanvi's face. Her friend was obviously fighting to remain calm, the corners of her mouth quavering.

"No, let them be. I'm sure Fade knows what he's doing. If you wouldn't mind, though, I'd like to talk to Tanvi alone."

"Of course." Keeper nodded and left the room.

Tanvi fiddled with her ponytail.

Prism approached her and put one hand on her shoulder. "You all right?"

"Oh, yeah." Tanvi shrugged. "It wasn't that hard of a hit. Wouldn't have knocked me down if I hadn't been caught off guard. I'll be fine."

"That's not what I meant." Prism gave her what she hoped was a comforting smile. "I know how invested you are in Alma's rehabilitation. This was a major step back. If you need to talk, let me know."

Tanvi's shoulders rose and fell in a great breath. "I guess I was an idiot thinking this would be easier. I mean, what kid wouldn't want to be a superhero? I know I did."

"Alma didn't exactly have a choice in the matter, and

this is probably overwhelming." Prism shook her head. "The Adjudicator's right, though. We can't have the girl fighting with us when it comes to real villain attacks. It wouldn't be right."

"I know, and I feel stupid for not realizing that sooner." Tanvi eyed Prism. "When did you figure it out?"

"Almost immediately." In spite of her best efforts, Prism smiled wryly. "I agreed that the girl would be better with us than in a holding cell—and that she needed to be trained to use her powers, but on active missions? No, that was never my plan. I had kind of hoped we could just draw out her training—" Guilt twisted at her insides. "Also, I thought having a long term trainee who couldn't graduate into active hero work until she was eighteen might keep the committee off our backs about replacing Aiden."

Tanvi's mouth quirked into a scowl. "Of course the Adjudicator couldn't make it that easy."

"No, and it does put us in an awkward position." Prism sat on the edge of the table. "My thinking was Alma would train with us while attending the school here on base once the summer was over, then once she graduated high school, she could pick her next step, whether that be college or full time hero work. Now, though—"

"Maybe the Adjudicator is right that what she needs is a real family," Tanvi whispered.

"I don't think she's going to see it that way." Prism cringed.

"But what if it were *her* real family?" Tanvi's face brightened.

Prism's eyebrows melted together. "Her parents are dead, and the social workers couldn't find a next of kin."

"There has to be somebody. Her parents had to have had families. Grandparents, aunts and uncles, cousins—" Tanvi punched her fist into the palm of the opposite hand. "I'm going to find them. If they exist, they'll be her legal guardians, and DOSA will have nothing they can do about it."

Doubt chewed at Prism. "But if they don't exist, it'll just disappoint her. I know you're good at this kind of research project, but this isn't some criminal we're trying to trace back to their origin point or stolen artwork we need to find the provenance of. This is a person who has been through her own personal version of hell over the last few years."

Tanvi tugged at her ponytail. "I won't tell her until I find something for sure, then, but I need to look. I can't help feeling that the kid wouldn't be in this mess if I hadn't interfered."

"Yeah, she'd just be robbing houses and living God only knows where." Prism rolled her eyes. "You didn't do anything wrong, Tanvi. It's not you who screwed up. It's the system."

The women sat in silence for a moment before the door opened and Fade strode in. Prism hopped off the table to greet him.

"Where's Alma?" Tanvi asked.

"Downstairs taking a minute to cool off." Fade shrugged. He came to stand behind Prism. His strong hands settled on her shoulders and started to rub. Every muscle in Prism's body went melty as a chocolate bar left in the sun. She hummed appreciatively.

"You gonna tell us why you ghosted her away like that?" Tanvi narrowed her eyes at him.

"She needed some perspective I was in a unique position to give," Fade answered. "I'm not sure if it made a difference, but it calmed her down a little."

Prism's heart lightened. "I thought you said you weren't the mentor type?"

"I'm not, but I can on occasion be the 'give someone a dose of reality' type," he said. "Whether or not that gets through her thick coat of teen angst or not is up to her."

"Do you think I should talk to her?" Tanvi asked.

"I'd give her some time," Fade said.

"You're probably right." Tanvi's shoulders slumped then she perked up again, bouncing on her toes. "But I have a project to get to. See you later, Pris, Fade-o." She ran out of the room.

Prism arched her eyebrows. "Fade-o?"

"You're not allowed to call me that!" Fade shouted after Tanvi.

"Try to stop me!" her response echoed down the hall.

"It's slightly better than the things Aiden used to call you. Madonna, for instance?" Prism laughed at the memory only to immediately have a pang of grief cut through her, reopening the wound in her heart. Her gaze dropped to her feet.

"Hey there." Fade gently turned her around and pulled her against his chest. "You all right?"

"Yeah, I'll be okay." Letting her guard down, she didn't try to stop the tears from seeping from her eyes onto his T-shirt. She slipped her arms around his waist and savored as he rocked her back and forth. "It comes and goes. It's not a bad thing. It just means I haven't forgotten him."

He massaged her between the shoulder blades. "Luce, you know I respect you as the team leader and I know you can take care of yourself, but if that jackass brings up Aiden's death in an attempt to manipulate you one more time, I swear, he's losing teeth."

She shook her head. "I don't want you to get in a fight because of me."

"Oh, it won't be because of you." Fade's expression darkened. "The Adjudicator knows what he's doing. If he hasn't realized there are consequences for that sort of crap yet, he needs to be taught a lesson."

Her fingers tightened into his shirt. A part of her would take great pleasure in watching Fade kick the Adjudicator's butt. However, him doing so might have repercussions that would endanger the little family she'd built. Remembering the Adjudicator's threats to reassign Fade, she shuddered and pressed him closer.

"Be careful. You tend to think you can get away with things, but you're in the hero world now." She pulled away enough to look him in the eyes. "You have to play by the rules, remember?"

He grinned. "I'd like to see you make me." He leaned in for a kiss.

Their lips met for a long moment. She brushed her hand up his arm onto his neck and toyed with his ear until they parted.

His dark eyes studied her. "So what are you going to do about Alma?"

She sighed. "Tanvi has a plan to try and find her actual family, which I guess would be the closest thing this mess could get to a fairy tale ending. In the meantime, though, we keep training her. No matter what path she chooses, she'll need to know how to manage her powers if she wants to stay safe and avoid hurting those around her."

"Those are good long term goals, but in the short term, the now?" He tilted his head to one side. "Do you think she should be back in her anklet?"

Prism balked. "I really don't want to do that. Especially when she hasn't really done anything to lose our trust."

"But has she really done anything to gain it? Alma's been with us for less than a month." He pulled a chair out from under the table and sat before her. "When I was in the first generation of the SVR with your father, I spent nearly two years in a disruptor anklet. Even when you rebooted the program, you had me wearing one for the first three months."

"And I hated that." Prism shook her head. "I felt guilty every time I snapped the anklet on you—"

"But you weren't wrong to make me wear it. I wasn't trustworthy yet. After what happened today, I'm not sure Alma isn't going to try and make a break for it."

Prism rubbed her forehead. Tanvi had told Prism about her promise to let the girl leave if she really wanted. The fact that the girl had chosen to stay even with that freedom had been a point of pride for Prism, but it also put them in a precarious situation. If the girl did run, Prism had no way of guaranteeing that the rest of DOSA wouldn't go after her. It could discredit the SVR and ruin Alma's chances at further rehabilitation all in one go.

Fade was probably right. The logical thing to do was to put Alma back in her anklet. Still, something deeper than logic, a deep-seated hope, made Prism hold tight to the idea that she could make this work without going back on their promises to Alma. She didn't want to argue with Fade, though.

"I'll think about it," she whispered.

Oh, please, let me not be making a horrible mistake.

Chapter Thirteen

Alma stuck her head out the door and paused to listen for any sign that the older sables were still awake. Once again, the halls were quiet and empty—except for a small, black shadow.

Alma scrunched her nose at Yui. "You again? What's up with you, cat? If I didn't know any better, I'd think you were spying on me."

Yui leaned forward in an impressive stretch, her tail curling and uncurling gracefully as her mouth opened to reveal needle sharp teeth.

"Yeah, play it casual. Sure." Alma pointed at Yui. "I'm watching you."

Yui sat up and flicked her whiskers, her glowing eyes never leaving Alma.

Alma pulled her hood over her braided hair before starting down the hall. The cat padded after her.

"Cut it out!" Alma hissed. "We're not friends."

Yui slipped in front of her to stand before the entrance to the stairwell. She gave a meow that was either judgmental or just especially catty.

"Don't worry," Alma said, more to assure herself than anything else. "I'm not going to be gone for long. I just have an errand I need to run, all right?" She pushed the door open. The cat darted into the stairwell after her.

As much as Alma wanted to run away, she didn't have the resources yet. While the DOSA team provided everything she materially needed, they didn't give her access to cash she could squirrel away or valuables she could easily sell. If she wanted to start off on her own, she needed money.

Whether she ran away or not, though, she couldn't go another night without seeing Lupita.

Tightening the strings of her hoodie so that only her eyes and nose were exposed, she jogged up the stairs. The cat pranced along with her.

Finding out the code to the roof door had been stupid easy. Neither Tanvi nor Prism bothered to cover the keypad when they punched it in.

Emerging into the darkness, she paused to draw a deep breath through her nose. Cool air with a faint scent of sun-baked grass filled her lungs. The cat brushed against her ankles again. Alma groaned and bent down to push Yui away. She blinked. Instead of the black cat, a small gray bird —some sort of sparrow—sat beside her feet.

"You better get out of here before the cat sees you and decides to have a snack." She nudged at the bird. It puffed out its feathers and fluttered into the air, circling her once before disappearing in the direction of Keeper's dove cages.

Alma pushed herself into the air. Her powers rushed through her veins, propelling her into the sky above the HQ building.

Convincing Handler to move their operations from Nevada to southern California had been one of Alma's greatest triumphs. The months before that, when they were too far from Lupita's hideaway for Alma to sneak away for a visit, had been torture. She'd managed some minor contact with her sister, chatting in various online games that allowed for anonymity, but always with the fear of Handler catching on or seeing something suspicious over her shoulder.

Being under constant surveillance with the SVR hadn't increased her chances much, but now, with Tanvi and even Prism seeming to trust her, she felt she could risk slipping away.

Alma glided over the rolling hills of Camp Pendleton, into the built up sections along the coast. She followed the flickering lights of cars zooming down the 5 as close as she dared. Hopefully the dark skies, as well as the typical SoCal resident's already distracted state, would mask her.

Within a few minutes, she hovered above Encinitas. She swooped over the Botanical Gardens, some of which was lit up with fairy lights. Settling in one of the great trees, she stopped to listen to the strum of a string quartet, performing a concert at the nearby gazebo. A memory of walking alongside the turtle pond in the garden's bamboo grove softened her and made her long to stroll the winding paths once more. Shaking herself out of it, she launched again, flying over the trees, businesses, and cookie-cutter McMansions until she found it: a retirement community on a dimly lit street, an older area with smaller homes but close enough to the nicer neighborhoods with the good schools.

Perfect if we were anything the state would recognize as a family.

Bitterness gripped her. She landed on a back patio beside a torn and faded deck umbrella and sun bleached plastic lawn furniture. Beside these, however, a series of potted plants thrived, including a tomato plant, a small orange tree, and a collection of herbs. Alma plucked a sprig of cilantro from the last pot and crushed it between her fingers. The fresh fragrance elicited a faint smile. Moths buzzed over the flower beds filled with a mixture of pale blue salvia, bright yellow poppies, and bold red penstemons. Everything was homey and perfect, just like she remembered it.

Pressing her face against the sliding glass doors, she gazed in. A tiny, wizen old woman sat before an ancient tube TV, a black and white rerun of some old show playing before her. Alma's chest tightened. Sometimes the woman would react with confusion and panic when Alma returned, not recognizing her or understanding where she'd come from. If tonight were one of those nights, and the woman's fuss was loud enough to draw the attention of her neighbors—Alma cringed.

Cautiously, she tried the door. It slid open. Alma's nose wrinkled. While it made this easier, she didn't like the fact that gaining entry was so simple. She closed the door behind her, intentionally flipping the latch in place.

Tia Maria didn't look up from her shows. A half eaten TV dinner sat on the coffee table between her and the TV. Beside it, however, was a plate with a few untouched dinosaur nuggets and a smear of Tapatío sauce. Alma chuckled. Still with the baby food.

"Alma!" a voice cried.

Alma whirled around to see Lupita emerge from the kitchen, a can of soda in one hand and a napkin in the other.

Alma's gaze flicked up and down her eleven-year-old sister. Not too thin. Looked as if she'd recently bathed. Her clothes fit and appeared to be laundered. All good.

Lupita cast a worried glance towards the direction of the living room then motioned for Alma to follow her down the short hall to the apartment's only bedroom. A walk-in closet had been emptied to make way for a small blow up mattress and a plastic dresser stuffed to the brim with clothing and a few toys. Lupita flipped on the bare bulb light and settled onto the mattress, pulling a blue mermaid scale pillow against her chest.

"I was worried about you. You said you'd be back—"

"I know!" Alma interrupted. She didn't want to go over everything that had happened since they'd last parted. "It's hard to get away sometimes. I'm sorry."

Lupita's chin dropped, and guilt flooded through Alma.

"How's Tia?" Alma quickly changed the subject.

Lupita shrugged. "She has her good days and bad days. Mostly she knows who I am. Sometimes she calls me Mama's name or just seems out of it."

Alma's stomach twisted. Tia was their great-great aunt, and as far as Alma knew, their only living relative. After their parents had died, the court had decided the woman's dementia made her an unfit guardian, a decision that broke Tia's heart every time the haze cleared enough for her to remember it. When Alma had gotten Lupita away from her last foster home, Tia's had been the obvious place to hide.

"Do you think anyone suspects you're here? Has anyone seen you?" Alma pressed.

Lupita shook her head. "No. I don't think so. Sometimes when the nurses do their check in, Tia talks about me, but I think they don't believe her. I always make sure to stay out of the way. Under the bed, mostly."

The idea of her sister hiding under the bed like a child afraid of a monster while Tia's caretakers did the bare minimum to ensure the woman was all right irked Alma. At least Lupita's presence made sure that the wellness checks found Tia capable of living on her own for a little longer. Lupita cleaned, brought in deliveries, and even cooked for the older woman. It provided Lupita a home, food and shelter, but it wasn't the life Alma wanted for her little sister. Still, she was safe and she was fed—which was more than Alma could say for herself for a lot of the last few years.

Alma stood and examined the bedroom. Tia's bed had been made with excess precision, not so much as a pin-width wrinkle on the quilted coverlet. A serene Santa Maria watched over the tiny room. Everything seemed in order.

"Alma," Lupita's quavering voice returned Alma's attention to the closet sleeping area. "When are you going to come live with us?"

Alma's mouth hardened into a frown. "You know I can't.

Not yet. Maybe someday—"

"You say that every time! When is someday? I can't—" Lupita choked.

Alma settled next to her. "Hey, Lupita! Don't cry. I'm working on something. Something new, and it'll help us. I promise." Alma prayed that wasn't a lie. "Trust me a little longer."

"I want to." Lupita curled her knees up towards her chest. "I just get worried if I don't see you for very long."

"Niña, I promise, everything's gonna be fine." Alma placed her arm around her sister. "As long as you haven't messed with the accounts, Tia's benefits should go in and the bills will go out. You can even switch up the grocery delivery if you want a change of pace, just keep it under the budget, all right?" She squeezed Lupita's arm. "Both you and Tia will have everything you need." She settled more comfortably beside her sister. "So, anything new happened since last time I was here?"

"I found a snake on the back porch. Tia screamed so loud when she saw it, so I got the broom and pushed it into the bushes."

"Brave girl." Alma clicked her tongue. "What about school? Did you finish the workbook I bought you?" While Alma couldn't risk Lupita attending a local school or even signing up for an online one with her current address, she always made sure to buy her workbooks and show her the educational games that she could get on Tia's computer.

Lupita shrugged. "Most of it. I don't really see the point to fractions."

"I like to think about them in terms of pizza slices." Alma laughed. The sister's chatted for a little while before Lupita fell quiet again.

"Hey, hermana." Alma poked her. "What's wrong?"

"Alma—is it true you're a thief?" Lupita's lower lip quivered.

A jolt cut through Alma. "Why?"

"It's just ... I logged into one of our games the other night, and your account was online, but it wasn't you. When I tried to talk to you, whoever it was said they needed to find you because you stole something from them and if I didn't tell them where you were, they'd find me and take it from me instead."

Alma's breath left her.

Handler.

It had to be. It would've been easy enough for him to hack his way into her accounts. He knew all the logins, and she suspected he used key-loggers to track her and the other kids' online interactions.

"Did you tell him who you are? Or where you live?"

"I'm not stupid." Lupita pouted. "As soon as I realized it wasn't you, I logged off. I've been afraid to log back in since then."

"We'll have to set up new IDs." Alma's shoulders hunched. That was something she hadn't counted on. Hopefully Handler assumed Lupita was just some anonymous online contact.

"But is it true?" Lupita pressed. "Are you a thief?"

"No ... not anymore anyway." Alma hesitated. "I was for a while, but I didn't want to be. A bad man made me do things I didn't like, though, and that's why we have to be careful. I can't risk him finding out about you. Don't talk to anyone online until we've both had a chance to make fresh accounts. Okay?"

"Okay. What are you doing, though?" Lupita tilted her head to one side. "How'd you get away from the bad guy? Are you sure he won't find you again?"

"Even if he could, he couldn't get to me," Alma assured her. "I'm with DOSA."

Lupita gasped. "The superheroes? Alma, are you going to be a superhero?"

Pride filled Alma only for her to immediately feel silly. She wasn't, at least she wasn't going to be for long. She wanted to run away, after all, get out on her own again.

"They're trying to train me to be one, but I'm not sure if I want to stick it out—"

"You have to!" Lupita's eyes widened. "You would be an awesome superhero. Oh, Alma, I'd give anything to be a superhero. Fighting bad guys, wearing a flapping cape—"

"Most of them don't wear capes," Alma corrected her.

"But some do, and it looks so sweet!" Lupita clasped her hands in front of her. "Oh, Alma, you should wear a cape. You'd look so cool in a cape."

Alma laughed. "I guess I would."

"Oh, I wish I could tell someone that my sister is a superhero!" Lupita leaned against the wall, beaming.

Alma fiddled with her hoodie strings. She hadn't expected Lupita to care about that sort of thing. She'd never had a reason for anyone to be proud of her before. It felt strange. Good, but strange.

"Are you going to have a cool costume? A superhero name?" The light in Lupita's eyes kindled a strange warmth in Alma's chest.

Alma sat taller. "I don't know about the costume—they call them uniforms, just FYI—but I've got a name. It's Soulbird."

"Awesome!" her little sister breathed. "Do you think I can have a name too?" Her smile faded, and she dropped her gaze to her lap. "I mean, it would be fun. I guess it's silly."

"It's not silly. You can have a name," Alma reassured her. "If you want I'll help you pick it out."

"Could I be your sidekick? I know I don't have powers, but some heroes don't, right?" Lupita's dark eyes looked hopefully at her sister.

Alma's throat tightened, but she managed to rasp out,

"Yeah, sure."

Lupita beamed.

Dios mio, what am I doing?

Alma cleared her throat. "When you're bigger though. For now, just lie low for me, okay? It'll be easier to convince my team that you can join when you're my age."

"Okay, I can wait." Lupita nodded. She bounced a little as she sat, though, as if already imagining herself springing into action to fight crime and save the day.

The old cuckoo clock on Tia's wall chimed out. Alma swallowed. She'd already lingered too long. If the rest of the team realized she had sneaked out, there would be questions.

"What about your costume, though?" Lupita continued. "That's important—"

"I'm sorry, hermana, but I have to go." Alma stood. "I wish I could stay—"

"Wait!" Lupita leaped up and ran to her dresser. After rummaging through it for a few seconds, she pulled out a gauzy length of pale blue fabric.

Alma furrowed her brow. "Isn't that from that princess dress you wore when you were eight?"

Lupita waved the cloth at her sister. "It's the only cape I have. At least try it on."

Alma made a face but tied the thin ribbons around her neck anyway. The cape only came to her knees. "It's a little small for me."

"I want to see how it looks when you fly. Can I watch you leave?"

"Sure." Alma tried very hard to sound nonchalant, but her throat was tightening again.

Maybe being a hero isn't such a bad thing after all.

When they emerged into the living room, Tia Maria snored in front of the TV, a dated re-run of a game show still playing on the screen in front of her. Lupita hurried to turn off the TV and the living room lights before opening the sliding glass door for Alma.

"Remember to lock it after I leave, all right?" Alma reminded her.

"Okay, but not until I've seen you fly with the cape." Lupita crossed her arms as if to prove she couldn't be budged.

Alma huffed out an exasperated breath. "All right, all right." She turned to face the yard and froze. A small gray sparrow sat on the top of the privacy fence, dark eyes glinting in the light from the streetlamps. Alma swallowed. It couldn't be the same bird. That would just be weird. Shaking herself off, she gave Lupita a quick, one armed hug. "Stay safe, hermana. I'll see you soon."

Then she pushed off into the sky, cape flapping behind her. Lupita's laughter chased her into the night, and Alma's face hurt from smiling.

Chapter Fourteen

Not wanting to think about her sudden doubt over her long term plans, Alma focused on flying and made the trip to base in about half the time the trip to Tia Maria's had taken. She landed on the roof and walked to the edge to look out over the rolling hills. She wanted to think for a little longer before she went in for the night.

A light rustling stirred the air behind her. The hair on the back of Alma's neck stood on end. Was it that creepy bird? No, that would be too much. She spun around, hoping to catch the little sneak, and nearly shrieked as her gaze met a pair of glowing eyes. She clamped her jaw shut. Her heart pounded painfully.

"What the frick, Yui?" she snarled.

The black cat licked her paws.

Alma grunted. "At least you're not that stupid bird."

The cat's body hitched in a way that almost made it look like she were laughing. Already confused enough without starting to wonder if she were going crazy, Alma pretended she didn't notice.

A strange whirring sound echoed from the other side of HQ. Alma paused. Was that a helicopter coming in? No, it was too quiet and too close. Maybe a drone? She tiptoed past the deck furniture and Keeper's birdcages before peering over the edge of the roof. Her heart leaped into her throat.

A man hovered about halfway down the outer wall. The slight glow of an exterior security light showed that he wore some sort of blocky jet pack but a brimmed hat shadowed his face. Alma's throat tightened. What was he doing?

The man zoomed forward and latched onto the side of HQ like a spider. He reached for the nearest window, something silver glinting in his hand. Alma's mouth hardened into a scowl. She knew a break in when she saw it. She pushed off the roof, but before she could zoom in to confront him, she hesitated.

What am I doing? I want no part of this. This is stupid—

A slight breeze rippled around her, and Lupita's cape fluttered. Resolve crept through Alma. She dove from the roof straight at the figure.

The man glanced up. "What the—"

She slammed into him. With a muffled shout, he lost hold of the wall and hurtled into the air. Weirdly, his hat stayed firmly in place.

With a roar from his jetpack, the man rocketed upward right before he would've hit the ground. He spun about and glared at her. A bandana covered the lower half of his face, but his exposed eyes were dark and angry. He extended a hand. Metal spikes shot from his palm, forming a four pronged weapon.

Alma's heart jumped. He zoomed towards her. Alma pushed her hands forward, and a power burst exploded down her arms. He flew backwards but only for about ten feet—unfortunately not crashing into anything. He landed on the grassy area between the building and the surrounding brush.

"Get out of my way, kid," he snarled. "Last warning."

"Get away from my home," she snapped back.

"Suit yourself." He pointed towards her with his spike-enhanced hand. Something clicked, and the barbs shot forward like grappling hooks.

Fear raced through Alma. Her powers surged, pulling into her chest and arms. The spikes hit against her—but not her. They crashed into an invisible field a few inches from her body. The impact shuddered through her but as a weak hit rather than stabbing pain. She gaped. She hadn't known she could do that.

The man cursed under his breath as the cords attached to the spikes retracted, zipping them back into his hands.

Alma gritted her teeth. She slammed forward with another blast of energy. He skidded across the ground, collapsing into a bush with the cracking of branches.

"Alma!"

She spun around.

Two figures rushed around the corner. A roar from the bushes alerted her to the villain's escape. He shot into the sky and flew away as Prism and Fade reached Alma's side. Prism wore a tank top and what appeared to be polka dotted pajama bottoms while Fade was in a T-shirt and loose athletic shorts—probably what they'd both been sleeping in.

Prism gripped Alma's arm. "Are you all right?"

Alma gave a breathless nod then pointed towards the retreating villain, already a small dot in the night sky. "He's getting away."

Prism and Fade exchanged a glance.

"Do you think Tanvi could catch him?" Fade asked.

Prism shook her head. "By the time she gets out here suited up—"

"I can." Alma pushed off the ground, but both Prism and Fade clamped down on her shoulders.

"No, you're not going anywhere," Prism said. "Alma, what were you thinking? Who was that, and why were you fighting him?"

Alma hesitated. She didn't want to tell them about her visit with Lupita. She'd just have to leave that part out. "I don't know. I was on the roof getting some fresh air when I heard him trying to get in through the side of the building." With the attack over, her adrenaline faded leaving her muscles tired from a long night of flying topped off by an unexpected supervillain attack. "He looked like he was trying to break in, so I stopped him."

"You shouldn't have risked that." Prism's brow furrowed. "If Fade hadn't—" She paused and faced her fiancé. "While we're on the subject, though, how did you *know* she needed help? Whoever the attacker was, he didn't set off any alarms. I didn't hear anything, and I was in the room right down the hall from yours."

"Yui got me." Fade shrugged. "She was probably looking for Keeper but ran into me in the hallway first. I was headed to the kitchen for a late night snack."

"Yui?" Prism blinked.

"Long explanation. Not my story to tell." Fade then faced Alma. "Prism's right. You shouldn't have taken him on your own. All of us were right inside, and we're a team for a reason."

Alma folded her arms. "I got him, didn't I? I would've had him beat if you two hadn't distracted me."

"Even so, it was dangerous." Worry crinkled Prism's face. Real worry, not the "if you'd have gotten hurt, I would've had to fill out paperwork" variety that Alma was used to. Something within her chilled. Other than Lupita, she couldn't remember the last time anyone had really, truly worried about her.

Shame overwhelmed the feeling of strangeness. She'd made Prism worry.

"I'm sorry," the words surprised even her.

Prism's expression softened. "I'm just glad you weren't hurt." She nodded towards HQ. "Let's get inside. We need to put out an alert for a villain attacking DOSA facilities. Speaking of which, can you tell us what he looked liked and what his powers were?"

Alma nodded. "Sort of. He wore a bandana over his face and a hat, but he had a jetpack and could shoot metal out of his hands."

"Jabz," Prism and Fade said together.

"Seriously?" Alma scoffed. "What kind of a name is that?"

"With a 'z' on the end, too." Fade snorted. "In his defense, he picked that name out when he was maybe seventeen. We were on the villain scene together for a few years before I got caught and ended up in the SVR. Apparently DOSA never apprehended him?" He eyed Prism.

She shook her head. "A few close shaves, but in spite of the awful name, the guy is a topnotch master thief." She glanced at the looming shadow of HQ. "Which makes me wonder, why was he trying to break in here? We don't have anything valuable enough to tempt someone like him, and especially not anything worth poking a nest of DOSA sables." She hummed thoughtfully. "This worries me. Let's get inside and file that report. I don't like how exposed we are here."

As they started to walk, Fade glanced at Alma. A smirk crept over his face. "Are you wearing a cape?"

Alma flushed. She yanked hard on the garment, snapping the ribbons. "Was just goofing off is all. Didn't expect to actually have to fight in it."

"I like it." His smile softened. "It's a bold choice, but you pull it off."

Again that weird warmth crept through Alma. "Thanks." She rolled the cape up and tucked it under her arm as they approached a side door to HQ. Prism keyed in a security code, and they entered a dimly lit stairwell. Somewhere above them a door slammed followed swiftly by pounding footsteps.

Tanvi rounded the corner a moment later. Her glance darted from Prism to Fade before resting on Alma. "I heard shouting and banging and saw someone darting away from here on a jetpack. What's going on?"

"Supervillain trying to break into headquarters." Prism

frowned, her shoulders slumping wearily.

"A supervillain? Who? Why?" Tanvi swallowed.

"Jabz, and we don't know." Prism rubbed her arms as if cold.

"I don't like this. The last time someone attacked headquarters—" Tanvi choked on her own words. Fade's face grew grave, and Prism's gaze dropped to her feet. Fade placed his arm around her and drew her closer.

"What happened last time?" Alma murmured.

"I don't want to get into that right now," Prism said quickly. "It doesn't matter. He's gone, thanks in part to you, Alma, though I don't want you to ever challenge a supervillain on your own again—"

"You did what?" Tanvi's pitch rose to a shriek.

Alma recoiled. "I chased him off. Beat him. That's what you've been training me to do, isn't it?"

Anger contorted Tanvi's face. "I've been training you to protect yourself, to keep yourself from getting hurt, not attack full-grown supervillains like Jabz. That man kills people! He could've killed you!"

"I'm fine. Don't have a cow, all right." Alma drew back, scowling. She didn't need another lecture on how stupid she'd been. After all, she'd won the fight.

"I'll have a cow if I damn well want to!" Tanvi shouted.

"Tanvi." Prism stepped closer, reaching towards her friend. "It's all right. No one got hurt—"

"But she could've! She could've got hurt, and it would've been my fault for bringing her here!" Tanvi wrenched away from Prism's offered embrace. "What was she thinking? Why wasn't someone watching her?"

"I can make my own decisions," Alma growled. "I don't need a babysitter."

"Yes, you do! You don't know how dangerous it is. What could happen to you, how you could get hurt. I won't let you get hurt, Aiden!" Tanvi snarled.

"Aiden?" Alma blinked.

Tanvi's lower lip went slack, as if just realizing what she'd said. Prism and Fade stared at her. It felt as if the air had suddenly been sucked from the space around them.

"I mean ... I ... just don't ... don't get hurt." Tears welled from Tanvi's eyes, and she spun around and ran up the stairs.

"I need to go after her." Prism pried herself away from Fade. "Fade, can you make sure Alma gets settled?"

"Yeah, if you need me, text, okay." He kissed her forehead. Prism gave him a weak smile and sprinted after Tanvi.

"What just happened?" Alma swallowed.

"Let's just say you broke open a wound that hasn't quite healed for any of us," Fade explained.

"Aiden was Prism's brother, right?" she said. "The one who Cosmic killed?"

"He was Prism's brother, but he was a lot of other things to a lot of other people, too. Tanvi—she cared about him." Fade nodded towards the stairs. "Come on. It's late, and while I don't know what Jabz was up to, I have a bad feeling we'll need our full strength for whatever is to come."

***

Tanvi collapsed onto her bed and hid her face in her pillow. Waves of grief passed over her as tears streamed down her face.

Stupid, stupid, stupid. Calling Alma that in front of Pris. What must she think? Then not even having the courage to stay and face my mistake. I'm such an idiot. Stupid, stupid, stupid—

A light rapping rose from the door. "Tanvi, it's me. Are you all right? Can I come in?"

Tanvi flinched. Well, she couldn't avoid Prism forever. That was one of the advantages and disadvantages of working with her best friend. Wiping her eyes with the edge of her T-shirt, she walked over and opened the door.

Prism peered in at her. "You want to talk about it?"

Tanvi hung her head. "Not really anything to say except I'm sorry. I didn't mean to bring up painful memories for everyone. I don't even know why I called her that. It just slipped out."

Prism put her hand on Tanvi's shoulder. "First off, as much as missing Aiden hurts, pretending he never existed at all would be so much worse. Second—Tanvi, I think all of us know why you called her that. Especially you, if you take a moment to think about it."

Tanvi let out a breath that caught on the edges of her throat. "I guess you're right. I just—having HQ attacked—I don't want to have someone else I care about hurt."

"None of us do." Prism entered the room and eased the door shut behind her.

The women sat together on the edge of Tanvi's bed. Prism draped her arm around Tanvi.

"It's stupid, but when I caught Alma in the middle of that burglary and saw I'd knocked out a kid—it made me think of Aiden, how we'd lost him so soon, how I didn't protect him." A sob shook Tanvi's chest. "I know I shouldn't have, it was stupid, but I watched the security feed from the night he—" She choked.

Prism stiffened. "Oh, Tanvi, why?"

"I don't know. I needed to see it to believe it was real, I guess—it was right after he'd died but before we knew who had done it. I convinced myself there might be something on the video that could offer some clue about Mymic's identity so we could stop her." Even in the grainy black and white of a security camera feed, it had been a horrible thing to see. Tanvi had tried to push the images out of her mind, but they'd stayed with her. "He looked so frightened and so young. I know he was only a year younger than me, but his eyes … I kept going over and over in my head what I could've done to stop it, to save him."

"I think we all have done that." Prism's voice grew raspy. "Any one of us would give everything to go back and change what happened, but we can't, and you can't make it better by clinging to Alma like this. It's not the same thing. For one thing, Alma's a kid. Even though he was my baby brother, even I have to remember, Aiden was a grown man who chose this life, this work, fully knowing it was dangerous. He knew the risks. He accepted them because he believed in what we were doing. He believed in our team, and he wanted to work with us because he was my brother and Keeper's friend. Also, he was more than a little in love with you." A faint smile crossed Prism's lips.

Tanvi's cheeks warmed. "I wish we'd had a chance to figure out if we could've worked." She sniffed back her tears. "It doesn't make it any easier with Alma, though." She closed her eyes. "The kid shouldn't be here. I was stupid to think this could work."

"That's not true." Prism drew Tanvi closer. "At the time, it was the best solution to a bad situation, but you're right. This isn't sustainable. There's a reason my father didn't want Aiden and me joining DOSA until after college. Adults can understand the choice to put themselves in danger for the greater good. A fourteen-year-old girl shouldn't be having to make a decision like that." Prism cleared her throat. "What about your magic research skills? Any closer to finding her family?"

"No. Just one elderly aunt with health problems that rule her out. I might try and talk with her, see if she remembers anyone the courts might've missed." Tanvi shook her head. "As much as I hate to admit it, maybe the Adjudicator is right. Maybe that family who wants her is the best thing for her, two parents, a safe home, a chance to be raised by superheroes but not as a superhero?"

"You're not wrong, but you saw how Alma reacted to the idea." Prism pushed a stray lock of hair from her forehead. "Maybe we can get her to at least consider meeting them. If she understands that she still has the final say in whether she goes with them or not, she might consider it."

"Maybe, but let me figure out a way to ask her." Tanvi frowned. "She's had enough choices made for her. I need to tell her in a way that makes it absolutely clear that it's her choice."

As much as saying good-bye to the kid would hurt, it was the best thing.

Now to figure out how to make Alma see it that way.

Chapter Fifteen

Handler glowered into the foam on top of his beer. The laughter of patrons watching the game on the bar's big screens and chatting over drinks only worsened his foul mood.

Years of scheming come to nothing in less than a month. Down their strongest member, his team couldn't complete any of the heists he'd planned for this leg of the journey, and his original goal of heading up coast for even bigger scores looked even more dubious. Sure, runaways were a dime a dozen, but sable kids? Especially ones as powerful as Ramos had been? It could take years to find and groom another like her.

No, he needed to find her again, force her back ... but based on Jackson's tracking powers, DOSA had her in their clutches. Handler didn't have the resources to break into one of their holding facilities. His hand tightened around his glass.

Irritating giggles drew his attention to a flirting couple a few barstools away. The woman, an attractive blonde in a crop top, playfully patted at a tanned, tank top wearing guy's arm, cooing over his muscles. The bartender wiped up a spill nearby, doing his best not to look.

A sly smile spread over Handler's face. He focused on the bartender, imagining his hand making the same motion as the man now made, swiping the towel in wide circles. After a few seconds, Handler could feel the cool of the damp towel in his own fingertips, the slick surface of the polished bar top. His awareness spread up the man's arm into his chest.

Gotcha.

Handler ran his own hand over the bar in front of him. The bartender mirrored his movements, his eyes widening in horror and confusion as his body moved without his permission. The bartender's hand slid onto the hand of the blonde and up her arm to caress her shoulder.

The woman yanked away with a cry of consternation.

"Hey! Watch it, dude!" tank top guy snarled.

Intent realized, Handler released the bartender to splutter incoherently.

"I didn't mean to. I mean ... I'm sorry ... I ..."

"You've got a lot of nerve touching me in front of my date!"

"No, I didn't!"

"You liar!"

Chaos erupted as the dude took a swing at the bartender. Snickering, Handler took a long swig of his beer, draining it, grabbed a bottle left behind by a patron too engrossed in the fight to notice, and ambled towards the exit.

He stepped out into the cool night air and drew a deep breath.

A large figure slammed against him. Handler hit the door jamb. The beer crashed to the pavement, shattering and spraying his pant legs.

Cursing he threw up his arms in front of his face. A tall man in a leather fedora with a red bandanna wrapped around the lower half of his face glared down at him with glinting eyes.

"Dammit, Jabz, what did you do that for?" Handler grumbled.

"You know damn well what I did that for!" the man growled. "What are you up to, having your brats interfere with my scores?"

Handler blinked. "My brats?"

"Don't BS me, Handler." Jabz spat but didn't stop

Handler from getting back to his feet.

Handler rubbed his side where he'd collided against the jamb. That'd be a nasty bruise. "My brats are back at my trailer. If they got out tonight, it's none of my doing, and I'll be happy to teach them a lesson on your behalf. First, though, tell me why you're so sure it was my brats?"

"Who else could it be?" Jabz asked. "It's not like there's an unending supply of teenage flying types darting around the country."

Handler's ears perked. "Flying type? You saw Alma Ramos."

"You really gonna play dumb? As if you didn't send her?" Jabz crossed his arms. "Lay off, Handler. We both know you've got your kids on too short a leash for that."

"I swear. She isn't with me right now." Handler considered what this meant then motioned for Jabz to follow him to the other side of the parking lot, well outside of the reach of any security cameras. They paused under a street light next to Handler's beat up truck. "Ramos got herself nabbed by DOSA agents a while back. I assumed they had her in some holding cell, but if she's free to roam —Where did you see her?"

"On Camp Pendleton, outside the HQ for the local DOSA unit." Jabz pulled down his bandana, revealing a weathered, stubbled face and a chin pointy enough to be used as a weapon in its own right.

Out of habit, Handler tried to calculate how to best take him down with a single use of Handler's ability. The length of time he could control any given person was limited and differed greatly from individual to individual based on their strength of will. Teens were far easier to manage than any adult, especially a hardened villain such as Jabz—which was the main reason Handler used them even though they were hard to find. Jabz's ability might be strong enough to take himself out in one hit if Handler wrested control at the right moment. Hopefully it wouldn't come to that.

"The Pendleton unit, huh?" Handler chewed his bottom lip.

Why was that familiar? Something he'd read in the news—

Realization crept over him. "They put the girl in the SVR."

Jabz's eyes widened. "I'd forgotten DOSA had resurrected that dinosaur. I had a former partner who flunked out of the original program back in the day. They're taking on kids now?"

"Apparently." Handler wiped at his pant legs, dislodging a few remaining drops of beer. This was both good and bad news for him. On one hand, if Ramos had some freedom of movement, it would be easier to bring her back into his control. On the other, if DOSA had decided to make a hero of the girl, he'd have limited time before she would be too indoctrinated to work with.

"However she got there, the kid foiled my heist and now DOSA will be hyper vigilant. My client is going to want answers as to why I wasn't able to pull a basic smash and grab on an understaffed facility."

"Your mistake." Handler grunted. "Understaffed or not, it's still a DOSA facility with multiple sables housed there. I would've talked up the difficulty to get a high payday."

"Sables are there, but the security is low. If the girl hadn't been lurking around outside, I could've gotten in and out before they could react. It's not like minor DOSA units are high value targets." Jabz leaned against Handler's truck.

"If that's the case, what did you want with breaking into one?" Handler narrowed his eyes at Jabz.

Jabz raised his hands in a shrug. "Client request. Wanted a personal laptop belonging to someone who lived there. Nothing I could see any value in, but the pay was good."

Handler mulled over this. He personally wouldn't take a job unless he understood exactly what he was getting into, but with DOSA agents crawling all over the country, a good payday was sometimes hard to come by. He couldn't begrudge other villains being less choosy than he was.

"So what are you going to do to get me my money?" Jabz's finger stabbed into Handler's chest. Thankfully he kept his metal bits inside.

"Easy!" Handler waved him off. He let out a huffing breath. "Look, Jabz, I doubt I have the money to pay you whatever your client owes, but I might be able to help you in other ways. Maybe we can work together to get you your score ... and for me to reclaim something stolen from me." His jaw tensed.

That brat was going to return to his team. No one ran away from Handler and lived to talk about it.

Chapter Sixteen

Prism cupped her hands around her warm coffee mug and breathed in the nutty fragrance. The supervillain attempt on HQ the night before had left her uneasy, mostly because she couldn't see a reason for it. Sure, supervillains often had it out for DOSA sables, but as far as she knew, Jabz had no particular vendetta with anyone on her team. Also, attacking a DOSA HQ with four fully trained sables in residence—in the middle of a military base no less—was worse than stupid. It was suicidal. What could Jabz have been after, and did she need to protect whatever it was?

The door to the break room opened, and Fade strode in. When he saw her, an easy smile illuminated his face. Prism's tension quieted.

"Good morning." He leaned across the table to kiss her forehead.

"Good morning to you, too." She nodded to the coffee maker. "Pour a cup and join me?"

"Don't mind if I do." He opened a cabinet. "Any word from the higher ups about Jabz?"

"He was sighted by a couple of civilians zipping through Oceanside, but the path went cold. My guess is he'll lie low until he's certain we're not actively looking for him, but just in case, I've put in a request to both the LA and San Diego DOSA teams to see if they'll send us some back up, maybe keep an eye open for Jabz in case he retreats into their jurisdiction."

Fade put a coffee mug on the counter and filled it. "Did anyone have any insight into why he might have been trying to break in here?"

"None at all. In fact, what DC said only makes me more

confused."

Fade settled across from her, his mug steaming.

She let out a sigh. "According to every source we have on him, Jabz is considered semi-retired. He has emerged a few times over the last couple of years, but only for high profile, high paying heists, usually with a team. That he'd go after us—I don't know. It just doesn't make sense." She eyed Fade. "You two were both considered master thieves before your rehabilitation. Did you ever clash in a way that might mean he still has a beef with you? Competing for a job or something?"

"Not really. Yeah, we were both thieves, probably the two best in the business during our early twenties, but our MOs were different enough that we rarely went after the same contracts. He was a smash and grab guy who wasn't afraid to do collateral damage. My selling points were stealth and the promise that the mark wouldn't even know they'd been robbed until after the goods were secure with my client." He chuckled. "If anything, there was a little begrudging respect between us but no ill-will to my knowledge."

"That was my understanding as well, but I kind of hoped you'd have some personal insight that might explain what he was trying to do." She sipped her coffee. "I don't like not knowing what we're up against."

"That's something we have in common." He reached across the table to stroke her hand.

She entwined her fingers with his. As she did, she considered her engagement ring. "We haven't set a date yet."

"Yeah, I've been meaning to talk to you about that." He squeezed her hand. "I don't know about you, but I'm a fan of short engagements."

"I don't want to wait too long either, but there's a bit of a favor I'd like first. The pastor at my church does premarital counseling." She glanced up at him, searching his face for a reaction.

His brow furrowed. "Do you think we need that? I thought we were getting along pretty well."

"Oh, we are, but a marriage is a big deal, and there are a lot of things we should talk about before we jump in head first," her words quickened as she slipped into her prepared speech. "How we feel about kids, about our careers, about ... well, just a lot of things."

"Makes sense." He nodded slowly.

"It's not because we have problems, but because if there are potential problems, I want to get ahead of them. Pastor Mark is great about facilitating that kind of discussion, or so I've been told. No matter how much we love each other, eventually we're going to have disagreements, and this is just prep so they don't completely blindside us, you know?"

He faded his free hand into his coffee mug then out of it again. "Makes sense. I'm not crazy about baring my soul in front of some strange dude, but personal cringe factor aside, you're probably right." He grimaced. "Okay, we can do that."

"There's an opening this afternoon." She gave him her best smile.

He laughed. "Why do I think you've already made the appointment?"

"I emailed him yesterday asking about availability, is all." She took another sip of coffee. "You're the most important thing in my life right now, and I want to make sure we're giving ourselves the best possible start."

"I'm all for that." His hold on her hand tightened before he raised it to his lips. Pleasure danced through her as he repeatedly kissed her fingers. She closed her eyes, humming quietly like a purring cat.

The door to the break room opened again, and her eyes

snapped open.

Alma strode in. She opened a cabinet, pulled out a cereal box, and groaned. "Who put an empty Sugar-Os box back in the cabinet?" She tossed it to the side. "Ugh, all we got is boring old Bran Squares."

"Sorry. I set up an online delivery for groceries, but they got delayed. Supposed to be here last night." Prism pulled out her phone and checked an app. "Yeah, it says they are out for delivery, but I guess that doesn't help you much right now. There's some orange juice and everything you need for eggs or toast, at least."

"I guess that'll work," Alma said. She popped a couple of slices of bread into the toaster, poured a glass of orange juice, and sat across the table from Prism and Fade.

Fade eyed Alma. "Where's the cape?"

Her mouth wrinkled. "Can we just forget you saw me wearing that?"

"Never." He grinned.

"Give her a break, Fade." Prism patted his wrist. "For what it's worth, Alma, capes are a totally legitimate uniform choice for DOSA sables, especially flying types. I know at least three high profile heroes who choose to wear them. If you're serious about creating your own uniform, I can help you put it together."

"Yeah, I guess that would be okay." Alma gave an uncertain nod.

Prism took another drink and finding her coffee had started to cool followed it up with a great gulp. She dabbed at her mouth with the back of her hand. "Write up a list of your ideas and get it to me. I have some sources I can order from and get you pieces to try on before the end of the week."

"Thanks," Alma murmured, her eyes focused on her orange juice until her toast popped.

A few minutes later Keeper joined them followed by a

bleary-eyed Tanvi. The group casually discussed their plans for the week—a training session the day after tomorrow, some paperwork that needed to be filed, basic chores that had to be done—while sipping coffee and eating boring Bran Squares. Through it all, Prism watched Alma out of the corner of her eye. The girl was quiet, but not in the sulky way she had been when she originally joined the team. No, she seemed begrudgingly content, if that was even a thing. Every so often a slight smile would creep across her face only for her to return to a mopier expression, as if she'd just remembered that she wasn't supposed to like it there.

I guess we could call that progress. Prism's heart lightened before she immediately tensed again. As much as she wanted this to work, Tanvi was right: the best thing for the girl was life with a real family where she wouldn't be in danger every day.

A buzzing noise echoed through the building's intercom system.

Tanvi looked up. "Were we expecting anyone?"

Prism stood. "It's probably my grocery delivery. Looks like you might get your Sugar-Os after all, Alma."

"Score!" The girl popped up and jogged out of the break room.

Prism laughed. "Hey, wait! You don't know the door code."

"She probably does." Fade shrugged. "You're the worst at keeping secrets. You never remember to hold your hand over the keypad when you punch it in. I knew the code to every door in the building the first week of my parole."

Prism wrinkled her nose at him. "Not everyone is as sneaky as you."

He raised his coffee mug to his lips. "Alma is."

Prism hurried after the girl, trying not to think about what Fade had said. No, she had to show Alma that she trusted her. Alma needed to know that the team had her back, not feel like she was under constant surveillance and suspicion.

Alma was halfway to the front door when Prism caught up. They reached the lobby together. Outside the glass doors, a woman in a blue delivery driver uniform stood, holding not their groceries but a bouquet of flowers.

She smiled and held it up when the women approached. "Flower delivery."

Prism's brow furrowed. "We weren't expecting one."

"I guess someone wanted to send you a nice surprise." The delivery woman shrugged.

Prism's caution spiked. She approached the door and gazed out. The woman had a delivery van from a company she recognized as doing business on base and there didn't appear to be anything potentially harmful about the flowers. Still, between Jabz's attack the night before and the unexpected nature of the delivery, she needed to be cautious.

"Do you mind if I see your delivery credentials?"

"Oh, sure." The woman set the flowers down and held up a card that dangled from her neck by a lanyard. There was a scan code on the card. Prism stepped outside and let her phone read the code. A document popped up with security clearances to make deliveries to DOSA owned, low-risk facilities for both the driver and the company she represented.

"Thank you." Prism returned her phone to her pocket before taking the flowers. The vase was see-through, no sign of anything but flowers stems and water inside. A small pink envelope was pinned to the side of the vase. "Hopefully this will clear things up."

She opened it and read, *Happy late Mother's Day. See you tonight! Remember, family comes first.*

Her brow furrowed. "No signature."

"I guess whoever it's from thought you'd know who

they were," the driver said. "Unusual bouquet. Poppies, salvia, and penstemons. We don't offer a mix like that on our website, so it had to be custom ordered."

"Yeah, I guess, but they aren't for us." Prism passed them back to the delivery driver. "None of us are mothers."

"You sure?" The driver checked her handheld. "This is definitely the address."

"Sorry, I don't know what to tell you." Prism shrugged. "Whoever ordered them made a mistake." She turned and found Alma staring at the flowers, lower lip quivering. Something tightened in Prism's chest. There was more than surprise or confusion in the girl's expression.

Is she frightened?

"Are you all right?" Prism pressed.

"Yeah," Alma answered quickly. "Just disappointed that they weren't my Sugar-Os." She cleared her throat. "I forgot something in my room. Let me know if the groceries get here." With that she darted down the hall.

Prism swallowed. Something was up. Maybe Fade was right. Maybe Alma was still hiding something.

***

Alma crouched on the edge of the roof, her hands jammed in the pockets of her hoodie.

It has to be a coincidence. It can't be real. He can't know about Lupita and Tia Maria. He can't. He can't.

Even as she tried to reassure herself, though, panic swelled within her. The adult sables had dismissed the mystery of the mistaken delivery far too easily. Alma had done her best to appear unbothered for the rest of the day, even though her insides still quivered every time she thought of the flowers in Tia Maria's flower bed and the message, "Family comes first."

The ominous "see you tonight" part of the message hadn't included any instructions, but Alma knew Handler couldn't get into a DOSA HQ. He might manage to get on base—she knew from experience that sneaking on and off base wasn't that hard—but into HQ itself? No.

Still, he had to have a plan. A plan that probably depended on her watching based on the message he'd sent. The roof provided the best viewpoint allowed to her, so there she sat. Waiting.

She didn't have to wait long.

A light flashed in the brush behind the former hospital, a beam of gold snuffed out almost immediately, then followed up ten seconds later by another pulse.

With a deep breath, Alma pushed off the building and slowly glided down to the source of the light.

Thick brush and long grass, a fire hazard in this dry section of the state, rose to greet her. Her powers fizzed within her like the buzz from shotgunning an energy drink. Maybe she'd imagined it. Maybe it was one of the inhabitants of the nearby base housing out looking for a lost pet. Maybe it was anything but who she feared, and knew, it to be.

Twigs cracked.

Alma flinched. "Who's there?"

Cold washed through Alma's veins as Handler stepped out of the shadows, the pale light of a shuttered camp lantern barely revealing his hated features.

"How did you find me?" she snapped. She was more worried about how he'd found Lupita, but on the faint hope that somehow, someway, the flowers had been just a coincidence, she didn't want to jump right to that. There was still a slight chance he didn't know who Lupita was or what she meant to Alma ... and if Alma could pretend that she didn't care about Lupita, maybe he'd forget about her.

"If you want to keep your location a secret, you shouldn't go around fighting supervillains." He simpered. "Jabz came at me, assuming you were still under my control. I'm glad to finally get a chance to talk to you when your babysitters aren't around." He leaned up against a tree. "I'm a little disappointed. I thought you were smarter than this."

"Smarter than what?" The initial spike of fear at his appearance calmed to a general wariness.

"To let yourself get caught and used by these DOSA creeps." Handler waved at the looming shadow of the team's headquarters.

"Yeah, sure, I should've stayed and gotten used by you instead." Alma narrowed her eyes at him.

"At least with me you could've eventually earned your freedom. Now that DOSA has you registered, they'll never let you go, not without a lot of effort to disappear, anyway." He drew closer, his eyes glinting in the lantern light. "Effort I can help you with."

Alma stood a little taller. "Thanks, but no thanks."

"Do you really think your little team will accept you once they learn about all the terrible things you did while working for me?" His lips curled in contempt. "All the things you stole, the people you hurt? If they find out—"

"They already know about me being a criminal," she interrupted. "They caught me in the act, and they don't care. That's the whole point to the Supervillain Rehabilitation thing. If I weren't a villain, they wouldn't *need* to rehabilitate me."

"Sure, that's what they're doing." He clicked his tongue. "Be smart, Ramos. You know they're just using you. A flying type is a valuable resource. DOSA will milk you dry then cast you aside. That's who they are. They don't care about you."

Defiance flared within Alma. *Prism cares. Tanvi cares. Even Fade and Keeper care in their own ways. Besides, what does Handler know about caring?*

"Do they know about your sister?"

A spike of fear drove through Alma's heart. Her powers

burst, sending her a few feet into the air before she calmed and hovered, staring at him. "What sister?"

"You're a bad liar." He placed the lantern at his feet. "Did you think I was an idiot? I knew you were pressuring the group to move into this area for a reason. You sneaking off only heightened my suspicions. It was easy enough to force Jackson to use his powers to trace out your most recent paths. I don't keep the kid around just for casing buildings."

Pulse pounding, she considered him. He didn't know how much her control over her powers had grown. One energy blast and she could send him flying, maybe kill him if it hit just right. Her fingers twitched.

"Don't think about trying anything," he said. "I can see it in your eyes, wondering if you can take me on—and maybe you could, but your sister'd die with me. Jabz is watching her location, and he knows I'm meeting with you. If I don't check in within the next ten minutes, he'll take out your sister and the old crone watching her." Handler winked. "You're fast, but you're not that fast. You'll never be able to get to her in time to stop it."

"What do you want?" Alma hissed through clenched teeth.

"A few things." Handler pulled a piece of folded paper from his jacket pocket. "For one thing, my pal, Jabz, wants you to make it up to him for foiling his heist. He provided me with the details of the item he wanted from your DOSA team, and I took advantage of the opportunity and added my own requests to the shopping list. If you don't want your sister to disappear on you, you'll bring them to me tomorrow."

Alma snatched the paper but didn't open it to read the contents. "So that's it? I just bring you some stuff, and we're both free?"

She didn't believe it. Handler wouldn't release his claws

from her life so easily. She wanted to hear it though, to have the lie plainly stated.

"Sure." He shrugged. "Unless you've come to your senses and want to join my team again. I offer protection, a chance to earn your own way."

"Thanks, but I've had enough of your protection." She sniffed. "Where do you want me to bring the stuff?"

"There's an address with the list. Abandoned warehouse not far from here. Come alone, or I say the word and the friend I have watching your sister from a distance gets a lot closer." He sneered. "Good to be working together again, Ramos."

"No, it's really not." She kicked off the ground and zoomed back up to the roof. When she glanced back, the area appeared empty, no light, no movement, no Handler.

She let out a long breath as she landed next to the birdcages. The birds cooed gently, the silent rustle of feathers and wings soothing the edges of her tension but not doing anything for the knot of stress in her gut.

How had she been so stupid? She'd seen Handler use Jackson's mapping powers to trace the routes of night guards and police cruisers. Of course the ability could be extended to tracking her as well. She'd led Handler right to Lupita.

The list crinkled in her fist. Moving into the light over the door to the stairwell, she unfolded the paper, and her brow immediately furrowed. Some of the items, she understood why Handler might want them: DOSA issued disruptors would give him more ability to control his charges—including her. "As much cash as you can grab," needed no explanation, though Alma didn't think the team kept much on hand. "The laptop kept in room 510," however, seemed oddly specific. Headquarters contained a lot of different laptops. Also 500 rooms were on the level with the team's private quarters. Her own bedroom was there. So this was someone's private laptop? Why would that be of more value than a DOSA issued one?

She shoved the list into her pocket and started down the stairs into the building. What were her options? If she went along with it, Handler would have her under his control. It would be just like before, but now with the added horror of him being able to threaten Lupita whenever he wanted her to do something particularly odious.

I could try and run away with her. Even if we don't have enough money yet, anything would be better than this—but if Jabz sees me coming, he might hurt Lupita before I can get her away. Also, what's to stop Handler from tracking us down and coming after us?

No, for them to be truly free, Handler needed to go down, but Alma couldn't be in two places at once. She couldn't take down Handler and protect Lupita at the same time. She needed help.

She paused on the landing to the floor with her and the other sables' rooms. She had a team. Would they back her up here? Even if it meant telling them about Lupita?

But once they knew, they probably wouldn't let Lupita stay with Tia Maria anymore. Even Alma knew that wasn't the best place for her sister. She didn't get to go to school there. She didn't have friends. Heck, she barely got to go outside. Maybe Prism could help, though. If Alma could stay at HQ, maybe Lupita could too. Maybe they could go to the base school with the kids from the nearby family housing. It might work. At least it was a better chance at life than anything Handler offered.

Throwing her shoulders back to strengthen her resolve, Alma marched down the hall and knocked on Prism's door.

No answer.

Alma hesitated. It had to be almost two in the morning. Prism usually was in bed by midnight. She knocked again.

Still no answer.

Resolve weakening, she turned to the door across the hallway, Tanvi's, and knocked. After an aching forever with no one opening the door, she wandered downstairs to the first level. Light eased under the break room door a little down the hall. At least someone was up. She padded down the hall, wanting to be sure who it was before she entered. She'd had enough nasty surprises for one week.

"I can't believe you," Tanvi's accented voice echoed towards her. "How did Fade take you sobbing like that?"

"Oh, like a prince as always, though I could tell he was a little worried." Prism laughed uncomfortably. "I don't blame him. It was our first counselling session, and I cried at, well, pretty much everything. When the pastor asked Fade to list off the things he loved about me, I cried. When Fade said he also wanted to have kids and said he agreed we should name the first Aiden—I sobbed. Not upset crying or overwhelmed crying, but water works every time we had to bare our souls."

Alma eased up to the door and gazed through the crack. Prism and Tanvi sat at the table, a bottle of red wine and two glasses between them.

"Honestly, it was kind of embarrassing, but I couldn't stop myself."

"Not surprised. You cry at the end of like half the movies we watch." Tanvi rolled her eyes. "If Fade can't handle that, he can't handle you."

"Oh, he handles me very well." Prism giggled.

"I bet." Tanvi gave an amused hum.

"We have another session tomorrow. I'm hoping I can hold it together better now that I've gotten accustomed to the format."

Alma hesitated. They weren't talking about anything super important, but it was personal, and she didn't want to walk in on them.

Prism sipped her wine. "So, did you make the call like we talked about?"

"Yeah." Tanvi rubbed her forehead as if it hurt. "I was worried about getting her hopes up, but Melodica seemed to understand it was an inquiry, not a promise."

Alma froze. Melodica? That was the east coast sable the Adjudicator wanted to ship her off too.

"She talked about how she wants a family and how she understands Alma is a hard case, not a lot of trust there, but she thinks she and Burton—I guess that's Tapman's first name. Who names their kid 'Burton'? But anyway, she thinks they could handle her—"

Panic spiked, and Alma stumbled back from the door, pulse pounding in her ears and drowning out all else. Activating her powers so she could hover a few inches off the floor and run without audible footsteps, she rushed back to the stairwell.

It was a lie. Everything about me having a choice, about not having to go with anyone I didn't want to, a lie. They're going to send me away so I never see Lupita again. What am I going to do?

Alma didn't stop air-running until she reached her bedroom. Once there she collapsed onto her bed. Her hand strayed under her pillow where she'd hidden her picture of herself and Lupita. She didn't pull it out, just rested with her hand against the cool, glossy paper and remembered what it felt like that day when they were together and happy before the system had separated them.

Her eyes watered. Alma had never been able to count on other people to protect or help her. Why should now be any different? How stupid had she been, thinking this time everything would somehow be all right?

No, if anyone was going to save Lupita, it would have to be her.

She needed a plan. One where she didn't have to

depend on anyone but herself.

Chapter Seventeen

Alma sat in the entertainment room, staring blankly at the TV. Keeper sat in the recliner, Yui on his lap, his attention on an animal documentary that Alma found easy to ignore.

Slipping her hand into her hoodie pocket, Alma clutched the list Handler had given her. Whatever she did, it would be a good idea to grab the stuff he wanted in case things went south. It might grant her some bargaining power.

Keeper laughed, and Alma looked up sharply. The older man focused on his cat, stroking her dark ears. "Ach. These documentary dobbers always get the little details wrong, don't they, my wee girl?"

Yui gave a chirping meow in response. Keeper laughed and reached for the remote.

"Aye, if I'm gonna watch this haverin', I'm gonna need something to sustain me." He gently picked up the cat, stood, and placed her back on the chair before turning towards Alma. "Want anything while I'm up, lass?"

Alma shook her head. As soon as Keeper left, she slouched deeper into her chair.

Yui narrowed her eyes at Alma.

"Stop looking at me, you judgy cat," Alma grumped. "What do you know about anything?"

Even if Yui's disapproval was all in Alma's imagination, she felt a little better for telling her off. Not as better as she would've felt being able to get out of the mess she was in, but it helped.

Her head ached. She hadn't slept much the night before. While Handler hadn't given her a deadline to complete his required tasks, she knew from experience that he wasn't the most patient man. She only had so long to come up with a plan to get her and Lupita to safety while freeing her from both Handler's influence and any attempts DOSA might make to relocate her. If she went after Lupita, she might be able to overcome Jabz and get her sister out of there—but Lupita couldn't fly and there was only so long Alma could carry her. Eventually they'd have to land, and Handler would find them. Now that he knew about Lupita, it was only a matter of him using Jackson's mapping powers to trace their route wherever they went. He'd find them eventually. As long as Handler was free, Lupita wouldn't be safe.

However, if she went after Handler, Jabz would find out and he'd hurt Lupita.

I need a way to take them both down at the same time, but assuming Jabz is in Encinitas watching over Lupita and Handler's near Oceanside, waiting for me to bring the goods —I need to be in two places at the same time—or I need help, but I have no one I can trust. Not really.

Footsteps and voices echoed down the hall before Prism and Fade entered the room, hand in hand and looking gut-churningly cheesy together.

In spite of her foul mood, or maybe because of it, Alma took a moment to make direct eye contact with Fade before sticking her finger into her mouth with a gagging face.

He didn't balk. "Hey, kid. What are you up to?"

"Nothing." She focused on the TV again.

Prism settled onto the couch, pulling Fade to sit beside her.

"Has Tanvi talked to you today?" she asked, searching Alma's face.

Alma brought her knees against her chest, doubling her efforts to only look at the TV—which was paused on a flight of birds over the ocean, pretty but kind of boring. "She said hi before she went out on her run. I think she's back, but she hasn't come in here."

"Ah, okay." Prism pulled her phone out of her pocket and texted. "Letting her know we're back. She mentioned something about having plans for the afternoon with me. She was being intentionally vague, so I want to see what she's up to."

Alma's stomach twisted. Maybe telling Prism what was going on was the only way to keep both herself and Lupita safe—but Alma didn't want to be safe if it meant losing Lupita again. Her gaze fell on Fade. Perhaps Fade was the one she should go to. After all, he'd been in the system. He knew what it was like—but would he understand her need to keep Lupita out of it? He didn't have a little sister, or any family outside of the team for that matter.

The intercom buzzed causing Alma to jump.

Prism paused mid-text. "I wonder who that could be. We're not expecting any deliveries, are we?"

"Maybe Tanvi signed up for another subscription box. I think she's running like three of them, right now." Fade leaned back more comfortably in his seat.

Prism moaned. "She needs to stop watching those unboxing videos. I'll go see who it is."

Alma hopped up from her chair. The last unexpected delivery had been a message from Handler. If he were trying that again, she needed to get in front of it. Otherwise, even someone as naive as Prism might catch on.

"I want to see what it is too." She started out of the room before Prism could object.

The two reached the lobby at the same time and stopped short. There, already inside, stood a tall man in a silver jumpsuit with a forest green cape. He flashed Prism a confident smile.

Alma furrowed her brow. Who was this clown?

"Glint, I wasn't expecting you." Prism offered him her hand.

"Why not? You sent a request for backup to my team." His smile stayed pasted on his face, possibly held in place by the same super-hold gel that was smeared through his perfectly styled hair.

"Yes, but I assumed you'd send, I don't know, Fleet or Scope or anyone but yourself."

"I needed the vacation. Good to get out of the chaos that is LA for a few days and enjoy quiet little Oceanside."

Alma arched an eyebrow, and Prism frowned.

"You do realize that the reason we asked for help is because we were recently attacked by a supervillain?" Prism pointed out. "We didn't send for backup because we needed company during R and R."

"Jabz isn't a particular worry for me." Glint rolled his shoulders so his cape fell better. Alma immediately decided that she didn't like the caped look after all. "If he shows up, I'll knock him down."

The tightness in Prism's posture loosened slightly. "Well, thank you. We do need the help. If you need a place to sleep tonight—"

"Pris! Is that you?" Tanvi jogged into the room. Her eyebrows shot up when she saw Glint. "What's Shiny-Boy doing here?"

A barking laugh escaped Alma.

Glint's lower lip went slack, then he chuckled uncomfortably. "Hey, Forte, it's good to see you again. We never got a chance to have that sparring match you suggested we have."

Tanvi's expression clouded. "Sparring match? That I suggested?"

"Yes, when we bumped into each other at your exo-armor flight training—"

A look of realization crossed Tanvi's face followed by a wry smile. "Me saying that I could kick your butt if you weren't zipping around like a panicked seagull does not equate to me offering to spar with you, but nice try, bud."

Glint's cheeks reddened, but Tanvi ignored him and turned towards Prism. "So, you ready to go?"

"Maybe." Prism folded her arms. "You still haven't told me *where*?"

"I booked us an appointment at a bridal boutique!" Tanvi clapped her hands. "They promised champagne and a chance to try on their best dresses."

Prism blinked. "A bridal boutique?"

Alma glanced behind her, wondering if she could sneak off now that the interesting part of the conversation had happened.

"You've been engaged for almost a month, and you haven't even cracked open a bridal magazine." Tanvi scoffed. "I'm seriously starting to wonder if you're actually a girl."

"I started a Pinterest board," Prism said defensively.

"So you're engaged?" Glint inserted himself into the conversation. "Congratulations! Curran's the lucky man, I assume?"

"He doesn't go by that name anymore," Prism corrected.

"By anymore you mean for over a decade." Fade emerged from the hallway followed by Keeper. "Hey, Glint."

Alma glanced at the gathered team. The urge to tell them about Handler's threat grew within her, but she didn't know this Glint character, so she stayed quiet and watched.

Prism glanced at Fade. "Tanvi apparently made an appointment for us to look at wedding dresses."

His face fell. "Now?"

"Yes, is that a problem?" Prism asked.

"I guess not. It's just that I asked Keeper if he wanted to go get a beer. If you and Tanvi are out shopping and me and Keeper are at a bar—" He glanced at Alma then back to

Prism. "Keeper and I can reschedule."

"No need." Glint stuck out his chest. "I can hold down the fort on my own. That's why I'm here, after all, to let you all have a break."

Prism bit her bottom lip. "Alma, if you want you can come with me and Tanvi. It might be fun—"

"No, I've got some stuff I want to do on my own," Alma said quickly. "I'm not really into shopping and dresses and all that junk."

"Are you sure?" Prism pressed.

Alma shifted from foot to foot.

Just tell them. Tell them and ask for help ... they can protect Lupita—

"Don't worry about the kid. I'll keep an eye on her," Glint interrupted.

"I would feel more comfortable if she had a phone," Prism explained.

"She can use mine." Keeper reached into the pocket of his Carhartt pants and pulled out a smartphone. "I only ever use it for work, and if I'm with Fade, I'll get any messages related to that through him." He passed it to Alma. "Passcode's one, two, three, four because I'm a simple man like that." He winked. "All the team's here." He tapped the contacts icon as she took it.

Sure enough, the top three contacts were Luce, Tanvi, and Fade. The wheels in Alma's head started to turn. She might be able to work with this.

"Thanks." She stepped away from the group. "I'll be in my room, reading. See you guys at dinner, okay?"

"Where do you control the security cameras from?" Glint asked as Alma fled the room. She ran up the stairs towards her bedroom, thoughts still spinning. The phone felt heavy in her hand, but it might be her salvation. A way to get exactly what she needed without having to give anything up in turn.

It had to work because if it didn't, she was out of options.

Chapter Eighteen

"Here you go, gentlemen." The waiter placed two coasters on the table and set a pint of beer in front of Fade and a tumbler of whiskey before Keeper.

"Thanks, man." Fade nodded his appreciation.

"Your Fries Quatro Queso Dos Fritos will be a few more minutes." The waiter bustled away.

Keeper picked up his drink and passed it beneath his nose. A faint smile crossed his face before he sipped. "Not bad for the price." He gazed at Fade over his glass. "I was surprised by your invite. We don't do much without the girls."

"Yeah, well, you're the only married man I really know, so I figured if I'm going to do this right with Luce, I should butter you up in case I need advice someday." Fade smiled. "Besides, thinking of her and Tanvi out looking at dresses ..." He gave a low whistle. "I got to admit, it makes the whole thing feel a lot more real."

"Just the trappings." Keeper shrugged. "Gettin' cold feet?"

"No, not really." Fade ghosted his fingers through the tabletop. "If anything, I'm anxious to get moving on it. We've had two premarital counseling sessions so far, and they've gone well. I mean, she cries a lot—lot a lot—but we're actually more in sync as far as values and goals go than I thought we were, which was a nice surprise." A smile flitted across his face. "No, definitely not getting cold feet. I think proposing to her was probably the second best decision of my life, right after accepting my place on the team, and that's only higher because if I hadn't done that, I wouldn't have met her to propose."

"Good." Keeper leaned back against the vinyl cushions of their booth. "And feel free to come to me for that advice, though I'm not sure I'll be much good at it. My own marriage is … let's say unconventional."

"I fully expect mine to be too. Maybe not to the 'wife is a cat ninety percent of the time' extent, but you know. Sables." Fade lifted his glass in a mock toast.

"To sables." Keeper clinked his own drink against Fade's.

Fade savored the bitter, citrusy notes of the cold IPA. If he could speak to his twenty-year-old self, younger Fade probably wouldn't believe that his future involved a quiet drink while talking about any relationship, let alone matrimony, with a middle-aged superhero. He especially wouldn't believe that Fade would ever enjoy that sort of thing. Weird how time could change things—and people.

Of course, he did have a few things he wanted to talk over beyond just casual conversation with Keeper.

"One thing that kind of surprised me is when the subject of children came up, I kind of felt excited," he continued between sips. "Even though I have no idea what it takes to be a good father—it's not like I had a lot of positive role models in that regard—I really want a chance to make up for what I didn't get with my own childhood, if that makes sense."

"It does." Keeper nodded. "Are you thinking sooner rather than later?"

"Yeah, I'm pushing forty, and I'd rather not be parenting into my sixties." Fade winced. "Prism has a little more time to work with than I do, but she seemed really happy when I said I'd like to have our first within two years. Apparently already has names picked out."

Keeper laughed. "Aye, that doesn't surprise me."

Fade cleared his throat. "I get that it's a really personal question, and you don't have to answer it if you don't want to, but is there a reason you and Yui decided not to have kids?"

The wrinkles around Keeper's eyes deepened. "It's not so much a decision as something that wasn't an option for us medically. Also, with Yui's agoraphobia, putting her through the scrutiny we'd need to go through to qualify for adoption didn't appeal to me."

"Sorry, didn't mean to—I guess I'm just looking for any potential pitfalls in our future." Fade brushed some foam off his upper lip. "The counseling is good, but it's got me thinking about all the things that could go wrong and how to sidestep them, you know?"

"Sometimes you can't. You got to plow through and hold fast to each other until you reach the other side." A sad smile quirked Keeper's mouth. "Especially in our line of work."

Fade's phone vibrated in his jeans pocket. He pulled it out and glanced at the screen. *New text from Bob/Keeper.* He blinked.

"Apparently you're texting me." He frowned.

"Gave my phone to Alma, remember?" Keeper arched his eyebrows.

"Oh, duh." Fade unlocked the screen.

Fade, I need help, but you can't tell anyone.

His brow furrowed. He glanced at Keeper, but the older man was focused on his whiskey, swirling it gently in his tumbler.

Before Fade could decide how to respond another text popped up: *Please, this is serious. I'll explain later, but I need your help now, and you can't tell anyone.*

Fade tapped the letters. *That's a big ask. I can't keep things from the team. What's going on?*

Please, I know you don't have a reason to trust me, but you're the only one who might understand. You know what the system is like. I need you to help me help someone stay out of it.

Fade's chest tightened. He didn't like being emotionally manipulated. If that was what she was trying, he'd have to come down hard on her—but if she were serious, if she were really in trouble, then he couldn't risk turning on her right now.

"Something wrong?" Keeper asked.

"Not sure yet." Fade stood. "Give me five minutes?"

"Let me know if you need backup." Keeper nodded.

Fade slid out of the booth and ambled towards the lobby area.

I'm with Keeper. It'll be hard to get away, and I don't want to go in blind. What can you tell me?

It's Jabz. He's going after my sister. I need someone to get to her and keep her safe, but if DOSA finds out where she is, they'll take her away from me again. You have to keep her safe, but don't tell anyone else where she is.

Fade's jaw clenched. Alma having a sister in hiding illuminated her attitude over her time with the team. Caution screamed at him, though. How did he know this was her? What if someone else had the phone and was trying to draw him away from the team for an ambush?

How do I know this is you? How do I know I can trust what you're saying?

The little dots that signified someone was replying pulsed for what felt like forever.

You told me that Prism and the team gave you a family and that I could be part of that family, but they're going to send me away.

Yeah, it was Alma. No one else had been around for that talk, but what did she mean? He knew Tanvi had talked about finding the girl's family, but could that have been misinterpreted as sending her away?

A new text popped up.

I can't get separated from Lupita again. She's all I have.

You have to protect her without letting her go back into the system. Please, Fade. You're the only one on the team who might understand.

Something within him gave out.

I'll do my best, but think about it. If your choices are your sister in the system or your sister getting hurt because I can't bring the team in on it, what would you choose?

For a moment the text conversation stayed achingly still. The dots started then stopped three times. He glanced back into the seating area. The waiter had just delivered their appetizer, and Keeper was picking at it, apparently not too worried about Fade.

The phone buzzed in his hand, and he glanced down at the screen.

Please, Fade. Please.

He shut his eyes. The pastor during their counseling sessions had said a few things about prayer. It wasn't Fade's natural inclination—though he was theistic, he tended to trust his own common sense and instincts far beyond any faith he had in God—but right now it couldn't hurt. *Please, don't let me mess this up, God. My brain and my gut are pulling me in different directions right now, and I need a tie breaking vote. What should I do?*

No lightning strike moment of revelation followed, but somehow he still knew.

He drew a deep breath, opened his eyes, and typed out, *Where is your sister?*

A link to an online map popped up on the phone. Fade glanced one more time at Keeper. The backup would be handy, and Fade knew from experience that Keeper had contacts well off DOSA's radar. He'd understand the need to keep this quiet.

Fade returned to the table but didn't sit down. "You up for an off the books mission for a good cause?"

Keeper pushed aside his now empty whiskey glass and

stood. "Aye. Always."
　　"Let's go. I'll explain on the way."

Chapter Nineteen

Alma's grasp on the phone tightened. Lupita's safety was in Fade's hands now, but for the next part of the plan to work, the timing had to be just right. If Alma got to Handler before Fade got to Lupita, Jabz might hurt Lupita. If Fade got to Lupita before Alma got to Handler, Handler might catch on and escape—meaning he could pop back into Alma's life in the future.

No, Jabz and Handler had to go down within minutes of each other. Once that was accomplished, she could focus on escaping DOSA and helping Lupita disappear again. Maybe Handler would even have some cash stashed away she could take with her to give them a head start.

She stuck the phone into the side pocket of her backpack and zipped it up before doing one last check to see if there was anything left in the room worth taking with her. Nothing. Everything she owned and cared about could be carried on her back. That wasn't likely to change any time soon. Still, this room had come to feel safe, like hers. She remembered Tanvi's offer to help her decorate it, and a pang of regret cut through her. For a short while she'd almost had a home.

Hardening herself she left the room, slamming the door behind her.

As she walked down the hall, she passed room 510. She paused. A "Do Not Disturb, Genius at Work" sign hung from the handle. She wrinkled her nose. It wasn't any of the team members' doors. She knew where all those were, and while there were a lot of empty rooms on the hall, this one looked as if it had been inhabited at some point.

An uneasy suspicion rose within her.

Getting that laptop might give me some bargaining power. If things go wrong, I'll regret not having it.

Jaw clenched, she tried the door handle, hoping that it would be locked. The door swung open.

Dim, stripey light passed through the window blinds to illuminate a sparsely furnished space with a futon bed, a work desk, and a stuffed bookshelf. A katana blade hung to the wall next to a poster of anime looking dudes with the word *Bleach* across the top as well as some sort of framed, professional certificate—maybe a diploma. She paused. Not a lot of personal items. While she suspected who the room belonged to—or had belonged to—she couldn't be sure, and maybe she didn't want to know. She turned to the desk where a closed laptop conspicuously sat. Behind it, a corkboard hung on the wall with some notes pinned to it along with a handful of takeout menus and a single photograph.

She flipped on the desk light and paused. In the photo Prism and Tanvi grinned at the camera, between them a thin, blond-haired man who looked a lot like a dude version of Prism. A beleaguered smile on his face, he seemed almost as if he were tolerating the two boisterous women literally hanging off him.

"To Aiden, the best annoying little brother ever, love Luce" was scrawled across the bottom of the picture in silver gel-pen.

Fears confirmed, Alma took a step back. This was a dead man's room—worse, a dead man who meant everything to the team, who they were still mourning. The laptop seemed to grow bigger, as if it were swelling with the guilt she felt over her plan to take it. She swallowed.

I need it, though. If I don't take it, I might not be able to save Lupita. He's already dead. Me taking his laptop won't make him any deader ...

Her hand extended towards the laptop. The images from the photograph eyed her and though their expressions didn't change, they somehow now seemed to accuse her, especially Aiden's calm, discerning smirk.

Alma jerked her hand away, shuddering. She remembered the pain she'd seen in both Tanvi and Prism's faces when Aiden was mentioned, a stark contrast to their happy smiles and laughing eyes in the picture.

I'm already hurting them enough. Whatever they are planning to do with me, they took me in, gave me a chance. No, I can't hurt them this way. I'll make things work with Handler.

Exhaling, she exited the room and hurried down the hall. She quickly detoured into the second floor where she knew there was a supply room filled with stuff the team used on missions.

She tapped Prism's two most common keycodes—5555 and 4242—each in turn. Both brought her only a disappointing "buzz" followed by a flashing red light. She grunted. Three incorrect inputs might trigger an alarm, and she still wouldn't be any closer to getting what she wanted. Well, being sneaky wasn't her only superpower.

Cocking her arm back, she sent her fist hurtling through the door. Her hand cracked pleasingly through the wood, not so much as scraping her knuckles. Apparently they didn't see this closet as worthy of reinforcing. Hopefully that meant it also didn't have any alarms she'd just triggered. Either way, best to hurry. She felt around for the inside handle and opened the door from the inside.

There was one thing on Handler's "shopping list" that Alma wanted even if she wasn't going to bend to his demands. Now she scanned the shelves looking for it. It only took her a few seconds. A stack of disruptors, both the anklet size version she'd worn when she'd first joined the team and the larger ones meant to wrap around a person's chest and arms and keep them restrained while dampening their superpowers, sat on a shelf, along with the remote controls used to activate and deactivate them. Slipping off her backpack, Alma snatched up several and shoved them into the main pocket of her pack. She then placed a handful of remotes in her hoodie pocket.

Okay, ready to go.

She pulled out Keeper's phone. It had been about fifteen minutes since she'd texted Fade. Assuming traffic was good, Oceanside to Encinitas was roughly twenty minutes by car. Yeah, she needed to get moving.

She exited the supply closet and stopped dead.

Yui glared at her.

"You again?" Alma snapped. "Don't you have mice to chase or something?"

The cat gave a strident, "Meow."

"Look, whatever, I have to go."

She started to walk, but the cat looped around her ankles, pushing her back against the wall.

"Cut it out!" Alma growled. She picked up Yui and lightly tossed her towards the end of the hall. "I'm leaving, and you can't stop me, all right?"

The cat hissed at her.

Alma snorted. "Whatever, puss. Kitty cats just aren't scary."

The cat went rigid then shivered then vibrated like a taut wire.

Alma's eyes widened. "What the—"

The cat shot up ten times its size, all a black blur which stabilized to reveal a bulky, toothy black panther. It gave a screaming growl.

Alma shrieked. Her powers kicked in by instinct. She shot upward, smashing into the ceiling, before bouncing over the panther and zipping down the hall.

What the frick, what the frick, what the frick, her brain screamed as she made the end of the hallway. She crashed through a window into the open air beyond. Hopefully whatever Yui was, it couldn't fly.

Heart still in her throat, she risked spinning around to look back at headquarters. No sign of feline pursuit. A bird darted through the broken window, however, and circled Alma, chirping madly.

Alma gulped. "Are you ... I'm going crazy." She tried to get her bearings. Before she could, though, a streak of green and silver shot from the building's roof and hurtled towards her. Her powers pulsed in front of her as a shield. The streak stopped short, hovering a few feet from her.

Glint's brow furrowed. He glanced from her, to the broken window, and back to her again.

"What are you doing?" he then scowled. "I thought HQ was under attack."

Alma swallowed. "I ... got spooked."

"Huh." His gaze fell on her backpack. "You going somewhere?"

She stiffened. "Yeah, I have something I need to do."

He glided around her, cape flapping behind him like a flag. "No, you don't. For multiple reasons. First, you're technically still under probation as an SVR subject. Second, there's a villain on the loose, and I can't let you go roaming around on your own. You might get hurt. I'm in charge right now, so if you did get in trouble it would be on me." He wagged a finger at her. "Finally, you're just a kid. There is nowhere you have to be important enough for you to zip around breaking windows and flying off without adult supervision. I don't have time to babysit you right now, so you need to get back inside."

Alma's stomach clenched. This was not going how she hoped. Stupid weird cat monster. Her mind raced. Could she pretend to go along with it, go inside, and then escape when he turned his back? No, that would take too long. Fade could reach Jabz at any minute, and if Handler found out Jabz had been attacked, he'd spook. She'd never be able to find him. She needed to go now.

Arguing probably wouldn't help here. Nothing she'd seen from Glint suggested he'd be likely to agree with her, and he was far too shiny a DOSA hero to not report Lupita to the proper authorities.

"Come on, kid." Glint gave her a condescending smile. "I don't want to do this the hard way, but if we did, you wouldn't have a chance against me. I know Prism and her band of misfit toys have been training you, but trust me: I'm one of DOSA's top heroes for a reason. You either do what I say or you're going to get dragged back to HQ and clapped in disruptor cuffs until the team returns. Up to you."

Alma's jaw clenched.

Oh, he is going down.

Alma threw her hands forward. Her power blasted from her like water from a fire hose. Glint yelped in pain as it hit him. The shiny sable did a mid-air cartwheel. He hit the ground in the soccer field a stone's throw from headquarters, tearing up grass as he skidded to a halt. Alma whooped.

Good luck getting those grass stains out of that slick jumpsuit.

With a guttural cry, Glint shot back into the air, hurtling right for Alma's chest. She gasped and let herself drop to the ground. He whooshed overhead, spun around, and came charging for her. She threw out another blast of energy, but he swerved around it. He slammed into her, knocking her across the parking lot. She yelped in pain as the pavement scraped through her sweatshirt and tore the skin on her arm. She sat up to find Glint hovering over her, arms crossed.

"No more games," Glint spat. "Get inside now. Last warning."

Heart pounding, Alma glared at him. "No, this is your last warning. I have something I need to do, and you're in my way. Move it."

His expression softened. "You're bleeding, kid." He nodded towards her arm. The scrapes weren't deep, but they stung. He landed before her. "I don't want to hurt you any more than I already have. Come on. Be reasonable."

Alma braced her palms against the pavement beneath her. Her power vibrated within her, and an idea formed in her head. She breathed in, then exhaled, imagining her power rushing down and out, through the ground beneath her. A burst of energy obeyed her will. The parking lot heaved then cracked open beneath Glint. He dropped into a crevice with a shriek. Alma moved her hands apart then slammed them together. An energy wave from either side rippled through the earth before her. The crevice snapped shut around Glint, leaving only his head and shoulders exposed, the rest of him wedged in the ground.

He strained and twisted. The pavement around him groaned.

Panicking, Alma yanked one of the disruptors out of her backpack and slapped it around his neck. He went limp. The color went out of his face as he squirmed futilely against the heavy earth.

Alma tossed her head so that her ponytail flopped from one side to the other. "Stay still. I don't want to hurt you any more than I already have."

"Let me go!" he growled.

A bird fluttered down and perched on his now much less carefully styled hair. It cocked its head to one side and chirped at Alma. Unease seeped through her. She'd already been delayed more than she wanted.

"You're in so much trouble," Glint continued to rant.

Alma swallowed. "Tell Prism and Tanvi I'm sorry, but I had to do this. You'll be fine, Glint." She dropped one of the remotes that controlled the disruptors just out of his reach. "Someone will find you and let you out eventually."

With that she zipped into the air. Hopefully she wasn't too late.

Chapter Twenty

"What about this one?" Tanvi held up a tulle and bling monstrosity that looked like it had to weigh about fifty pounds.

Prism fidgeted with the silk dressing robe the bridal shop had given her. "I don't know. It's a bit much."

"It's your wedding. It's supposed to be a bit much." Tanvi waved the dress, swishing the full skirts to make a point. She then put it back on the rack and picked up her champagne flute.

"What matters is what you want, my dear. It's your day." The middle-aged shop owner smiled kindly. "What exactly are you thinking?"

Prism closed her eyes, trying to imagine herself in anything that looked even remotely bridal. "Something light, not a lot of volume. I don't want to get lost in it. Maybe sleeveless but not strapless. Lace would be all right if it's not overwhelming."

"I have a few things that might be perfect." The owner nodded. "I'll be right back with some options."

Prism's shoulders relaxed. At first the experience had overwhelmed her, so many choices that didn't feel right and Tanvi all energy and ideas. Now, though, with the smooth cloth of the robe against her skin and the sweet champagne taking the edge off her anxiety, she was starting to have a little fun. She might even try on a few of the huge parade-float-looking things Tanvi seemed to like, just for laughs.

The owner returned and beckoned her into the changing room. A lovely ivory lace gown hung from the hooks. Something in Prism lightened.

"Oh, this is beautiful."

"Sleeveless, a lace illusion neckline that gives you the elegance of the deep v while still allowing you some classic modesty." The owner took it off the hook and exhibited the back. "Also, these pearl buttons? Aren't they to die for?" She beamed. "Ready to try it on?"

Prism managed to nod.

A few minutes later, she emerged from the dressing room, holding the flowing skirts up over her toes for fear of stepping on the hem and ripping the expensive garment.

Tanvi gasped. "Oh, Pris, you look ... oh, gosh, girl." She dabbed at her eyes with a napkin. "You're a bride! So beautiful."

Prism faced the mirror, and her throat tightened. This was real. This was her, in a wedding dress, ready to marry the man of her dreams. Her fingers caressed the lace at her neckline.

"I think this is the dress," she said firmly.

Tanvi came up behind her. "You can't pick the first one you try on. How do you know there isn't something better out there?"

"Sometimes you just know." Prism continued to admire the way the skirt flowed like falling water. "Even if it's your first, even if there might be other things out there that you could try, you just know and that's the one you want because it's everything you've always dreamed and you don't need to look for anything better." She sighed happily and toyed with her engagement ring.

Tanvi snickered. "Are you talking about the dress or the groom?"

"Maybe both."

"Unlike guys, dresses can be set aside while you try on one or two more without hurting their feelings all that much." Tanvi picked one of the big, full-skirted ballroom dresses off the rack again. "Humor me?"

Prism laughed. "I guess it wouldn't be much of a girls' day out if I called it now. Also, do you want to look at bridesmaid dresses? I think you'll be my only one, so you can wear whatever you want."

Tanvi clapped her hands. "I'm going to try on *all* the dresses, girl!"

The owner smiled. "We have plenty of time left in the appointment. I can add in a princess style ball gown, if you'd like to try something very different, but I also have a mermaid—"

"Prism, Tanvi!" Both women spun as a petite middle-aged woman rushed into the room. Prism blinked.

"Um, yes, and you are?"

"It doesn't matter." The woman hugged herself. Her dark eyes darted around the room, refusing to settle on anyone's face for more than a half second. "You have to come now. Alma is in trouble."

Prism and Tanvi exchanged a glance.

"What do you mean, in trouble?" Prism pressed. "And again, who are you?"

"It doesn't matter," the woman repeated. "You must come with me. Now."

"Yeah, it does kind of matter." Tanvi put her hands on her hips. "You're kind of familiar. Are you with DOSA?"

"No. Not DOSA. No." The stranger shook her head. "Please, I do not like to be here, but the girl is in trouble so I came. You have to come with me."

Prism's chest tightened. Was Alma really in trouble? Still, she knew better than to go rushing off with a complete stranger.

"Who are you?" Prism persisted. "It won't take you more than a moment to tell us, and then we can get going."

The woman shut her eyes and moaned quietly before mumbling under her breath in a language that might've been Japanese. She then opened her eyes and said in a pained voice, "I am Keeper's wife."

Tanvi coughed. "Really?"

"Yes, and you must come now."

Prism hesitated. Keeper sometimes mentioned his wife in passing, but the woman had never introduced herself to the team, and his evasiveness when talking about her had led to Prism wondering if the woman existed at all. Now this odd, secretive woman popped up, wanting them to follow. She needed to double check this.

"Can I call Keeper to ask him about you?" She reached into her pocket.

"No time! She fought Glint and ran away. She is in trouble. You must come now," the woman's tone grew more frantic, her whole body shaking. "Please. I do not like to be here in this form. I want to leave. I would not come at all if there was not a great need. You must believe me."

"No, we must not," Tanvi scowled. "Look, lady, maybe you are Keeper's wife and maybe you're not but I don't know you from Adam, and I'm not going to follow you into what could very well be a trap without—"

"*Mattaku mou*! I show you!" the woman barked. Her whole body shimmered before shrinking into a small, sleek, furry animal.

The shop owner screamed.

Prism's breath caught in her chest. "Yui?"

The cat meowed, shook herself off, then vibrated back into a human form. "Yes, Yui. That is me. Now will you come?"

Prism glanced at Tanvi.

"Actually, this explains a whole lot of stuff I've always wondered about Keeper," Tanvi whispered.

"Let's go." Prism took a step forward, but Tanvi's hand clamped down on her arm.

"In that?" She eyed the dress meaningfully.

Prism's face heated. "Give me a minute to change." She

entered the dressing room. "Do we have time to go back to headquarters to get our gear?" she called through the door as she shimmied out of the dress.

"I brought my exo-armor," Tanvi called. "It's in my purse."

"Of course it is." Prism sniffed. She couldn't really judge. Her laser wristlets were in the car's glove box. She pulled on her jeans, T-shirt, and favorite bomber jacket. Not quite dressed for work, but better than trying to fight supervillains in a bridal gown. By the time she emerged, feline Yui was lounging in Tanvi's arms as Tanvi awkwardly stroked her furry ears.

"This is really weird," Tanvi mumbled.

"Is she going to stay like that?" Prism eyed the cat.

Yui meowed and hid her face in the crook of Tanvi's arm.

"Yeah, she seems to be more comfortable like this. She gave me a bit of a run down. Apparently Alma turned on Glint and took off saying there was something she needed to do, but she wasn't very specific." Tanvi's mouth tightened into a firm line. "What are we going to do?"

Prism pulled her phone out of her jacket pocket. "If she still has Keeper's phone with her, I should be able to find her." While Prism didn't appreciate that DOSA kept such a close eye on the sables they employed, she'd bit the bullet and downloaded their tracking app, just in case something like this happened. "Got it. She's not far from here, heading north ... or at least the phone is. I hope she's with it." She pressed her hand into her suddenly aching forehead. "I'm going to text Fade and Keeper to let them know what's going on ... dang it, how are we going to catch up with her?"

"My exo-armor can handle me carrying you. It'll slow me down a little, but I can do it." Tanvi shrugged. "As for Yui—"

The cat opened her eyes and hopped out of Tanvi's

arms. A moment later, a bird sat on the floor in her place.

Tanvi let out a whistling breath. "I guess Yui's flying."

"All right. Let's go."

Nerves on edge, Prism started out of the bridal shop.

Oh, dear Lord, let that kid be all right.

Chapter Twenty-One

Fade parked the car a few blocks from the location Alma had linked to.

Keeper, who had been filled in on the drive over, scanned their surroundings. "Ach, I don't like this. Too many places where that tosser Jabz could be lurking." He glanced at Fade's phone which sat in the center console. "Sure you don't want to text the lassies?"

"Want to? Yeah." Fade scratched at the back of his neck. "Going to? No. I have to do my best to keep my promise to Alma. If it's just Jabz, I've got this." He slipped out of the car then leaned down to look in at Keeper. "Look, we don't have earpieces, and you don't even have a phone with you right now." He passed Keeper his phone. "Do you think you can figure out a way to signal me if you see Jabz? Or any other sign of trouble?"

"Aye, I have methods." Keeper nodded. "Be careful, lad. I don't like this."

"Neither do I." Keeping his powers at ready, Fade strolled down the sidewalk towards the house. He hadn't seen Jabz in over a decade, and he wasn't sure if Jabz knew about his current status as a hero rather than a villain. Unfortunately, the area didn't offer much cover even if he had wanted to hide his approach. He'd just have to hope Jabz didn't recognize him.

When he was one house away from the address with still no sign of Jabz, he paused, checked to see if anyone was looking, then ghosted through the stucco wall dividing the yard from the street. A brown chihuahua ran at him, yipping frantically. It nipped at Fade's ankles, only to have its teeth click when it tasted only air. It hopped back, yapping. Fade ghosted through the next wall into the yard outside of his destination.

He glanced through the window, and his muscles tensed.

A young girl and an older woman sat upon a couch, watching TV. Behind them, though, a figure lurked in the kitchen, a figure in a familiar hat and bandana.

Fade focused on the pair on the couch. The girl trembled, her hands tight on the old woman's arm. Tears ran down the woman's face.

Fade's jaw clenched. If Jabz was already holding the two hostage, they didn't have much time.

Before Fade could move, Jabz looked up, and his eyes narrowed. Keeping his powers active, Fade stepped through the sliding glass door into the small house. The girl whimpered, and the old woman threw her body over the child, as if to shelter her.

"Easy!" Fade held up his hands.

Jabz scowled for a moment before recognition flooded his eyes. He pulled down his bandana. "Well, well, well. Fade, isn't it? Long time no see."

"Over a decade." Fade crossed his arms. "What are you doing here, Jabz? Even back when we were beginners, you only ever hit high yield targets. What do you want with an old woman and a kid?"

"That's my own business." Jabz flicked his fingers. Metal spikes jutted out of his palm then retracted again. "So it's true that you're working on the side of the angels now? You used to be one of the best in the business, Curran. Kind of sad that you've gone soft."

"Even when I was in the business, I never targeted kids." Fade stood between the two hostages and the villain. "Come on, Jabz. Is this the reputation you want? You're a master thief, not a bully who goes after people who can't protect themselves."

"That's where you're wrong." Jabz scratched his chin with the edge of one of his blades. "I go where the money is, and right now, it's in helping my friend keep control over his brats. I have nothing against you personally, though. If you move out of the way, I won't hurt you. You never were much for fighting, if I remember. Sneak in, sneak out like a coward, never risking the loss of your own blood."

"And that's where *you're* wrong." Fade smiled. "Trust me, if you try to harm any innocent people today, you're going down, and you're going down hard. Maybe I'm on the side of the angels, but that doesn't mean I won't make you hurt like hell."

"Take your best shot!" Jabz snarled. A metal spike flew from his hand, hurtling towards Fade's chest. Fade's heart jumped into his throat as the projectile cut harmlessly through him. What if it hit the pair on the couch behind him? The hostages shrieked, and he whirled around to see the spikes slam into the TV. Sparks flew. Fade dove over the couch and threw his body on top of the girl and the woman, extending his fade into them.

"I've got you, but you need to move fast," he hissed. "Come on."

The old woman curled up into herself.

The girl shook her arm. "Tia Maria, please, we need to go."

Jabz strode forward.

"Get down!" Fade pushed them both into the couch. With a muffled whimper, they sank through the cushions.

"So you're gonna play it that way? All vapor and no muscle?" Jabz bared his teeth. "Come on, Fade. Take a hit."

Fade snapped up, allowed his powers to exit his hand, and swung. His now solid fist clipped Jabz in the chin. The supervillain recoiled. He stumbled back a step, cradling his face. Fade bent down, snatched up Tia Maria in his arms and shouted to the girl, "Hold onto me and you'll be safe.

Come on. We need to move."

Fully faded, Fade kept one hand clenched about the girl's wrist while he clutched the quivering woman to his chest. He burst through the wall and out into the street. He released them. "Look, there's a blue sedan parked down the street. Get to it and tell the driver to get you both out of here. Quick." The pair gaped at him for a moment before he released the woman with a gentle push. "Quick!" he repeated.

He darted back into the house. Jabz charged him only to crash against the wall. Fade solidified and aimed a kick at Jabz's crotch. Jabz dodged and swiped towards Fade's extended leg. Unable to fade quickly enough, Fade snarled as Jabz's spikes grazed his calf. Searing pain shot through him. Jaw clenched, he faded through Jabz, came up behind him and grabbed a kitchen chair. He swung with all his might. The chair shattered across Jabz's shoulders, but mostly hit his jetpack. The force of the blow sent the villain stumbling into the kitchen island.

Pushing off the island, Jabz spun and swiped. His spikes whiffed through the now ghosted Fade. Growing in frustration, he dove right through the sliding glass door. Glass shattered. Jabz landed in the middle of the yard and faced Fade.

"Good luck catching me." He sneered. The rockets on his jetpack roared to life, and he burst off the ground. Fade dove for one of the decorative stones edging the flower beds, snatched it up, and flung it with all his might after the retreating Jabz. The stone smashed against Jabz's head with a pleasing crack. The villain crashed first into the roof then dropped into the flower bed.

Fade snatched up another rock and cautiously approached the now still Jabz. The villain didn't move.

Cool relief trickling through him, Fade looked around for something to bind his prisoner.

I need to start traveling with disruptor cuffs. Oh well, next best thing. He unbuckled his belt and took a step closer.

Jabz shot up, hand spikes extended. Fade's heart jumped into his throat, and he ghosted.

With a hiss, a snake sprang from the flowerbeds and locked onto Jabz's wrist.

Jabz shrieked. He flailed, desperately trying to shake the reptile loose.

"Ach, I'd lie still if I were you, lad." Keeper sprang over the wall and approached. "My wee friend there doesn't like to be jerked around like that. He'll only pump more venom into you if you don't stop."

Jabz fell back, groaning. Veins bulged in his neck.

"Are you all right, Fade?" Keeper asked.

Fade gave a breathless nod. "Thanks for the assist."

"Happy to oblige."

The snake released Jabz and slithered into the bushes again. Jabz clutched at his wounded wrist, his face contorted in pain.

"I'd lie still. I already called in for DOSA back up. They'll be here any minute and can get you the medical help you need, but the more you move, the further the venom will spread." Keeper glanced at Fade's leg and raised his eyebrows. "You sure you're all right?"

Fade shrugged. "It's not deep."

Keeper passed him a large handkerchief. "Don't worry, it's clean."

"Thanks." Fade tied the cloth over his still bleeding calf then turned to Keeper and murmured, "Where's Alma's sister and the old woman?"

"Still in the car. Make a break with them. I'll stay here and wait for the response team. They don't need to know about the hostages," Keeper whispered back. "Here, you might need this." He passed Fade his phone.

Fade nodded and took off at a run. He'd honored his promise to Alma. He'd kept her sister safe and away from DOSA. Now he had his own questions to ask the girl, though. He needed to figure out what the hell was going on.

Chapter Twenty-Two

Prism squeezed her eyes shut against the wind battering her face, wishing she'd worn a warmer jacket. She clung to Tanvi's back like an awkward kid getting a piggyback ride and prayed her friend didn't let her fall.

"How much farther?" Tanvi called out over the roar of her thrusters.

Prying one eye open, Prism glanced at her phone which she'd attached to an armband so she could use it during the flight without dropping it.

"It's right up ahead," she yelled back. "We should probably land before we get there so they don't sight us coming in."

"Roger." Tanvi aimed towards the ground, and Prism's heart fell into her feet.

They landed in a dingy alley outside a rundown warehouse. A chain-link fence surrounded a small shipping yard, but sections of it had been bent in so that a grown man could easily slip through. Prism heart quickened as she glanced around the shady looking area.

"Oh, Alma, what have you gotten yourself into?" Tanvi breathed.

The hair on Prism's neck prickled. This didn't feel right. "We need to be careful. Stay close to me." She accessed her powers and projected an image of herself and Tanvi slightly ahead of their actual location.

A bird fluttered down from the nearest rooftop.

"Is that you, Yui?" Prism asked.

The bird shifted into a cat and gave a nod. Prism wondered how many times Yui had been hanging around in some form or another without them knowing. She was going to have to have a long talk with Keeper when this was over.

The women ducked under the broken fence. It jangled as Tanvi's shoulder brushed against it. Prism's shoulders hitched. So much for stealth.

A metal door was rolled halfway open revealing a dark interior lit by sporadic beams of light from upper windows. The women entered, trying to keep their footsteps quiet in the empty, echoing space.

Prism squinted. A large collection of crates against the far wall could potentially hide an ambush, but other than that, the space was empty. She glanced down at her watch again. The tracking app said Keeper's phone was within twenty feet. With one hand over her eyes, she scanned the interior. Yui meowed and rushed up a metal staircase onto a walkway that circled the second level. Following her trajectory, Prism found what she was looking for.

Alma perched on the catwalk, half hidden behind a support beam. She stared at the projections of Tanvi and Prism.

Prism tapped Tanvi's arm and jerked her head towards the girl.

"Don't let her know—" Prism started to whisper.

"Alma!" Tanvi shouted. Her thrusters went off and she rocketed up to the girl, the sudden movement shattering Prism's projection.

Prism winced. She drew her power into her hands, ready to set off a stun blast if the situation called for it. The power tingled in her fingertips like effervescent bubbles in her bloodstream.

Alma jumped off the catwalk to hover mid-air. "Tanvi, what are you doing here?"

"What am I doing here?" Tanvi gasped. "Alma, I don't know what's going on, but you need to get back to HQ. If DOSA finds out you're—"

"No, you don't understand. You need to go now! You'll ruin everything." Alma shoved her.

"Alma calm down." Prism started up the stairs.

Alma glared at her. "No, I will not! You two shouldn't be here."

"We're here because we care about you." Tanvi flew closer, reaching for Alma's arm.

"No you don't!" The girl wrenched away. "If you did you wouldn't—look out!"

Prism whirled but too late. A blast of electricity shot through her then arched up the stairs like a striking snake. Yui yowled and leaped, fur on end, onto the beams of the ceiling. Prism collapsed, her whole body throbbing.

"Pris!" Tanvi yelped. She dove towards her friend.

Prism's arms jerked in front of her. She stared in horror as a blast of light shot from her own hands into her friend's face. Tanvi fell back, stunned, landing hard on the concrete floor.

Prism wrenched her hands back to her own control and staggered to her feet.

"Shaina, no, don't hurt them!" Alma wailed, diving between Prism and the open door.

Another wave of lightning blanketed the warehouse's interior. It jolted into all three sables. Prism collapsed, the world swimming, Alma gasping for breath beside her.

"I'm sorry," a young voice choked out. "He's making me, Alma—I can't—"

"Shut up," a harsh, masculine voice snarled.

Heavy footsteps stamped into the empty space. A pair of muddy work boots at the end of an equally dirty—and hairy—set of legs came into Prism's shaky field of vision. She tried to pick herself up, but Tanvi grabbed her by the hair, yanking hard. Prism screamed out a mix of rage, confusion, and pain. The man bent down and pulled Prism's wristlets off her arms, disarming her.

"Pris! Sorry," Tanvi wheezed. "I'm not doing that. I swear."

"You were supposed to come alone." The man jerked the backpack from Alma's shoulders.

She whimpered. "I tried. They followed me somehow."

"Whatever. Did you at least bring the goods?"

The contents of the backpack hit the floor next to Alma. Clothes, shoes, and ... disruptor cuffs?

"Apparently not everything, but I'm glad to see these." The man picked up two disruptors.

Prism scrambled to a sitting position and tried to scoot away but too late. He snapped a coiled disruptor cuff like a whip against her chest. It clicked in place around her, fixing her arms to her sides and sending her powers retreating into her core. A second hit Tanvi an instant later.

"Let them go, Handler!" Alma wept.

"And Ramos makes three," the man mocked.

Alma jumped into the air, but the man waved his hand towards the ground. She dropped to the earth and stood, stock-still, staring at him in helpless horror.

Like a puppet on a string, Prism realized. *He has some sort of compulsion powers. That's how he got me and Tanvi to attack each other.*

Handler engaged the last disruptor around Alma's chest and arms then shoved her so she fell next to Prism. "Useless girl. Couldn't even do one simple task right," he spat.

Two other teens, a black girl and a red-headed boy, emerged from the shadows. Fear etched both their faces.

Handler kicked Alma. Her jaw clenched, but she didn't cry out.

"Hey, cut that out, you creep!" Tanvi growled.

Handler ignored her, cold eyes drilling into the shivering Alma. "You do realize this means my friend is going to hurt your little sister?"

Prism's heart stilled. *Little sister?*

A light of defiance kindled in Alma's eyes. "No, he won't. I told Fade where to find her. If your Jabz isn't in cuffs already, he will be long before he can hurt Lupita. You lost that one, Handler."

Hope filled Prism. Whatever was going on, if Fade was involved, they had a chance.

Handler's face paled then reddened. He pulled a phone out of his pocket and furiously texted. After a moment, his eyes darkened. He texted again then hit call. The unanswered ringing serenaded the group for half a minute before an electronic voice stated, "We're sorry but the person you contacted does not have a voicemail that has been set up."

Handler cursed and shoved the phone back in his pocket.

Alma's muscles relaxed. "Thank you, Fade," she whispered under her breath.

Prism silently echoed Alma's gratitude. A pang of worry cut through her. What had she gotten herself into? What if she never saw Fade again?

Hardening her expression, she faced the villain, holding herself as proudly as she could with her arms strapped to her side and every inch of her body aching from having just endured repeated jolts of electricity.

"You need to let us go. DOSA agents will be swarming this place in minutes, and whatever your powers, you're no match for the full force of multiple DOSA sables."

The two kids came up behind the villain, quivering.

"Maybe she's right," the boy said in a shaking voice. "We can't fight DOSA, Handler. There's too many of them—"

"Shut up." Handler shoved the kid then faced Prism, eyes glinting. "They won't dare attack us. Not when I could put a bullet between your pretty eyes." He pulled a handgun out of his waistband.

Prism's pulse pounded. Even with full access to her

powers, she wasn't bullet proof.

He chuckled. "Thank you, Ramos. Maybe you didn't get me the loot I wanted, but these two DOSA beauties will be worth far more than that crap ever would've fetched me. If DOSA wants you back, or if your friends and family want to see you alive again for that matter, they'll have to pay."

Chapter Twenty-Three

Fade let out a long breath as he surveyed the hotel room. Bringing Alma's sister and aunt back to headquarters would bring them under DOSA scrutiny. Until he'd figured out exactly what he was going to do about Lupita, he needed to keep them hidden but safe. Besides, after the day they'd had, the pair could use a worry-free night watching basic cable and eating takeout. The older woman already snored on one of the two twin beds while Lupita munched on orange chicken and watched *Spongebob*.

He nodded towards the landline. "You know how to use one of those?"

The girl eyed it dubiously for a moment then nodded. "Seen it on TV."

"I wrote my cellphone number on the pad next to it. Only use it if it's an emergency. The less contact there is between us, the safer you'll be. I'll come back tonight after I've talked to your sister, all right?"

"Okay." The girl took a sip of her soft drink.

Fade left the room, checking to be sure the door locked behind him.

He reached the parking lot and did a double take. Keeper leaned up against their car.

"How'd you find me?" Fade asked.

"I've got friends in high places." Keeper nodded towards some nearby power lines where a flock of birds rested.

Fade laughed. "Bird's eye view, huh? Handy skill to have." He unlocked the car and slid behind the driver's seat. Keeper got in beside him. "DOSA take Jabz in hand?"

"Aye. The tosser clammed up about whatever mission

211

he was on, but I suppose that's to our benefit if you don't want DOSA to know about the kid." Keeper eyed the hotel. "What's your plan there?"

"I don't know yet." Fade rubbed his forehead. "I need to talk it over with Alma—and Prism. On one hand, I get the kid wanting to keep her sister out of the system, but in just the short time I spent with them, I could tell her aunt isn't capable of caring for anyone—barely herself. She kept getting confused, forgetting where we were. Five minutes after we got to the hotel, it was clear she didn't even remember Jabz's attack."

"A pity." Keeper shook his head.

Fade put the key into the ignition. "Let's get back to headquarters. Hopefully talking it over with the team will give us some clarity. The foster system isn't set up to protect a kid who is already drawing supervillain attacks, so Alma's right: that's not an option here."

Before he could put the car in reverse, his phone vibrated in his pocket. Pulling out the device, he glanced down.

The screen read, *Keeper/Bob.*

He turned off the engine before hitting talk. "Hey, Alma, your sister's safe, but we need to talk."

"This isn't Alma," a menacing voice answered.

Fade's blood ran cold. "My mistake. Who are you then?"

"You can call me Handler. I'm an old friend of Alma's— and you? I have a feeling you're the one who is responsible for me losing a colleague tonight."

"If you mean the ill-tempered jackass with the questionable taste in sable handles, yeah, he's not going to be joining you any time soon—though if you want to come down here, you could join him." Fade switched the phone to speaker and held it between himself and Keeper. "Always room in the holding cells for one more."

"I don't think that'll be happening." The phone buzzed

in Fade's hand. "I sent you a little photo for your personal enjoyment."

Something in Fade twisted, but he tapped the notification. His heart leaped into his throat.

Prism, Tanvi, and Alma sat bound in what appeared to be the bed of a truck, disruptor cuffs holding their arms in place, all three with anger in their eyes.

"You, son of a—" Fade clamped his mouth shut. No, shouting over the phone at this jerk wouldn't do any good. "What do you want?"

Keeper's eyes widened as he stared at the image on the phone. "Ach! What are you doing with the lassies?"

"Oh, so you're not alone? Or did you just decide to change your voice to sound like a leprechaun for some reason?"

Keeper's face contorted in disgust. "Leprechauns are *Irish*, you tosser."

"Whatever. You're all basically English."

Keeper's face reddened, and he nearly hit the car roof. "You want to say that—"

"Bob!" Fade snapped. "Matter at hand?"

Keeper subsided, but there was murder in his eyes.

"I repeat," Fade said, keeping his voice calm. "What do you want?"

"It's hard to put a price on people, you know? To DOSA, I figure they're worth a basic salary and maybe a bonus at Christmas time." An irritating chuckle flavored Handler's voice. "To you, though? I can tell you care a lot for these pretty little things. You're in this phone as Fade. That's a familiar name to me. Used to be a bit of a thief didn't you?"

"A bit," Fade said guardedly.

"So I figure you might have the ability to quickly acquire resources, eh? I know this is short notice, and I want to clear out of town quickly, so I'll go easy on you. Bring me a quarter million per girl within the next two hours, and you can have them all back. If you can only work up the funds for one or two, that's fine with me. You just tell me which I get to keep."

Fade's hold on the phone tightened. His powers flickered in and out as if some illogical part of him wanted to go through the screen to wring Handler's neck.

Man, would that be satisfying.

"Let me give you a fair warning," Fade said through clenched teeth. "I'm already ready to break every bone in your freaking body, but if you hurt any of them in any way, I will definitely do it—and slowly. Unless you enjoy pain, I would let them go now."

Handler scoffed. "Sorry, but heroes don't scare me. You have your rules, your procedures, your ethics. I'm surrounded by children. You aren't going to risk blasting your way into my lair. Just pay the ransom like a good boy, and you'll see your friends again."

"You seem to think you're dealing with Prism." Fade laughed darkly. "You're not. Prism's a hero. She won't hurt you unless she absolutely has to. Me? I've walked the villain path for most of my life. I have no qualms about squishing you under my foot like the pile of crap you are, and if my wife isn't returned to me in exactly the state I last saw her in, I will kill you. Gleefully."

Handler hissed like a cornered snake. "Just get me my damn money." The line went dead.

Fade shoved his phone into his jacket pocket. "New plan. We're leaving now."

He turned and found Keeper smirking at him.

"What?" He scowled.

"You just called Lucia your wife," the older man pointed out.

Fade hesitated. He had? Damn. He had. He shrugged it off. "Felt right at the time."

Maybe he'd simply misspoke, but if this Handler idiot

prevented Fade from having a chance to make that miss-speaking a reality, Fade would do a lot more than just kill the bastard.

"You say we're moving out, but to where?" Keeper pressed. "What's the plan?"

Fade swallowed. "We need to find them first, I guess."

He withdrew the phone again. Stomach clenching he hovered his finger over the messages icon. He didn't want to look again, to see Prism tied up and helpless, too far away for him to rescue or comfort her. Pushing past it, he opened the image file once more and searched for any clues as to where the picture had been taken. Well, he could think and drive at the same time.

"Let's regroup at HQ. Maybe we can find something there to help us." He put the car into drive and pulled out of the parking lot.

"What are our options?" Keeper kept his eyes on the road in front of them.

"Two, basically. One is we pay the ransom and hope this Handler is at least an honest scumbag. If not, we have to find out where he's holding them and get them free the old fashioned way." Fade's grip tightened on the steering wheel.

"Prism has a tracking app on all the team phones, doesn't she?" Keeper asked.

"I'm not that clearance level yet." Irritation flooded Fade. "I barely rate a phone at all at this point."

DOSA could have their location in moments, presuming Handler held onto the phone, which he supposed was a big if. Once they did know, though, what would they do?

"What's DOSA's official policy on ransom demands?" Fade asked.

"They don't pay. Say it only encourages the behavior," Keeper murmured. "If they find out he's holding our folks hostage, they're going to go in guns blazing. That's just their way."

Traffic stopped for a red light, and Fade rested against the steering wheel, trying to think. "Even if I managed to hit a few banks without catching DOSA's attention, most of the branches around here are going to have less than 50k on hand. No way I can find a target for the full amount in less than two hours. I only have a few hundred in my checking account, and while Prism is probably the only millennial I know who actually has a six month emergency fund—it's not going to cut it here. Do you think we can get a hold of Tanvi's family? They're well-off, aren't they?"

Keeper gave a low whistle. "How much do we need again?"

"He said a quarter of a million each." Fade massaged his fingers into his aching forehead.

"Think he'll be all right with a wire transfer?"

"Probably—" Keeper's words sank in, and Fade's gaze shot up to stare at his friend. "Why are you asking?"

Keeper shrugged. "I played the stock market a bit back in the 80s. Hit a good run then shoved it into a couple of money market accounts for a rainy day. Never had a reason to skim off more than a little interest now and then, but last I checked it was all still there." He glanced at the sky. "I'm not a weatherman, but I think we may be looking at a rainy day."

A horn honked behind Fade, alerting him to the fact that the light had changed. He eased off the brake and through the intersection. "You'd do that?"

"I'd give all my money for any one of those girls and think I was getting a bargain. A portion of it for all three? That's a deal." Keeper smiled.

"Thanks." With that particular anxiety soothed, Fade's mind churned, going back over the image of Prism tied up. Anger stirred deep in his gut, boiling up until he was fuming. "Do we want to pay it, though? I don't know about you, but I have a feeling Prism at least wouldn't want this guy profiting off our attachment to her."

"Same with Tanvi, but I'd rather have both of them mad at me for paying than I would not having either of them, if you know what I mean?" Keeper pointed out.

"Agreed, but just saying, maybe paying should be our back up plan, not our go to." Fade ghosted one hand in and out of the steering wheel, fidgeting with his powers to try and gain some clarity. "We also don't have any real guarantee that once he gets the money, this Handler won't go back on his word. Have you ever heard of this guy? Handler's not a name that was on the scene when I was active?"

"No."

Fade sorted through scenarios. As someone who had lived in that world for many years, he knew that supervillains came in many different forms. While all were happy to subvert at least the letter of the law, some had their own rules. They saw crime as a business, and a business must be conducted with some semblance of structure in order to see a profit. If a ransom were paid, the hostages would be released, otherwise the next time such a demand was made, the loved ones of the hostage would have little reason to put down the money. Others, however, tended to be wild cards, just as likely to take the money and burn their bridges leaving a grief stricken family to mourn. Handler could be one sort or the other. Fade simply didn't know, and the uncertainty ate at him.

As they pulled off the freeway and into the line of cars waiting to get through the gate onto Camp Pendleton, Keeper went stiff in his seat.

"What?" Fade frowned.

"It's Yui. She's close by. Pull into the parking lot next to the sandwich shop, towards the back where no one will see us."

Fade's brow furrowed, but he nodded. "I didn't realize you and Yui were telepathic."

"We're not, not exactly." Keeper craned his head to look out the window towards the sky. "However, I have an ability to sense animals and communicate with them over a short distance, and when Yui is shifted, I can interact with her in the way I would any other non-human creature. Not in words but with ideas, feelings, and images." He closed his eyes. "Ach, my poor wee lass is frantic."

"She probably knows about the rest of the team then."

As they swung into the parking lot, Keeper pointed towards the roof of the restaurant. "There she is."

Fade parked at the far corner of the lot and hopped out of the car. A seagull glided down from the sky and onto the pavement. With a smile, Keeper held open the car's back door. The seagull hopped in and immediately transformed into Yui.

The shivering woman shrank into herself. Keeper took off his jacket and wrapped it around her.

"I got you, my wee lass. I've got you," he murmured. "You're safe here."

Fade shifted from foot to foot, not wanting to interrupt their reunion but needing to know if Yui knew anything that could help him get to Prism. He walked around the car to stand outside as Keeper slid next to Yui and cradled her on the backseat.

"The others are in trouble," Yui stammered.

"We know. We got a call asking for ransom for them." Keeper brushed his wife's dark hair away from her face. "Are you all right?"

She nodded, eyes pinched shut. "He didn't know I was human."

"Do you know where they are?" Fade asked, unable to contain himself any longer.

"Yes. I followed as a bird until they stopped. Once I was

sure they weren't leaving again, I came here, to find you."

"Can you take us to them?" Fade gripped the edge of the car door.

Keeper shot him a warning glance. "Give her a moment."

"No. I am all right." Yui pushed Keeper's arm away. "I can. I ... I know how to get there as a bird, but I think I can make the journey by roads. I need to picture it from above."

"How about this?" Fade pulled out his phone and switched the map app to satellite. He passed the device to Yui who spent about a minute swiping and zooming in and out.

"Here." She handed the phone back to Fade.

He considered the image. It looked like a trailer park. He tapped the screen.

"We can be there in forty minutes." He glanced at Keeper. "Is there anything you need from HQ?"

"No, I've got everything I need right here." Keeper placed his hand on Yui's back.

A pang of longing cut through Fade. He needed to get Prism back. Pushing down his anxiety, he took out the car keys.

"Let's go."

Chapter Twenty-Four

Prism wrinkled her nose in annoyance as Tanvi's squirming jostled her again. "Lie still," she hissed. "We're crammed in too tight for you to wriggle around like that."

Tanvi stopped moving but moaned. "How can you stand it? It's like having my whole body asleep. I feel weak and sluggish and ... ugh!" She shuddered. Somewhere in the darkness beyond Tanvi, Alma gave a commiserating whimper.

"I've been in disruptor cuffs before," Prism pointed out. It wasn't a pleasant memory. She'd almost lost Fade that day. "I think my powers are more on demand than either of yours, if that makes sense. Like I only really feel or sense them when I call them up."

Her arm, pressed against the plywood floor of the shed Handler had deposited them in, ached and prickled then started to go numb. She grunted. "Look, I know I was just giving you a hard time about this, but if I don't shift my weight, my arm's going to go to sleep."

"Go for it."

Prism rocked from her side to her back only to find her left side crammed up against the wall while her right side pressed into Tanvi. A faint trace of light slid around the doors beyond her feet but didn't quite reach the section of the small shed where her head, and therefore her eyes, were.

The dry air, tainted with dust, sawdust, and the acrid scent of motor oil irritated her nose, making her long to itch it, and she didn't want to think too hard about what sorts of spiders or scorpions might be lurking nearby. She'd once seen a tarantula the size of a grown man's hand inside a

Camp Pendleton outbuilding. If one of those happened to crawl across her face with her unable to flee or slap at it, she'd die. She'd just give up and die.

Tanvi groaned again and banged her feet into the floor, causing vibrations to enter Prism's skull.

"Cut it out!" Prism snapped.

"How can you be so passive?" Tanvi growled. "We need to do something to get out of here."

Prism indulged in an eye roll. "I'm up for suggestions. I spent the first hour or so after he locked us in here trying to come up with a plan, but without our powers—or even our arms for that matter—what are we going to do? I'm still thinking—and praying—but honestly, as much as I hate it, our best chance right now is waiting for a rescue ... or for someone to pay our ransom, I guess, though it would irk to see Handler rewarded for his crimes."

"He always has been. It's not like this time will be any different," Alma's sulky voice rose from the darkness.

Prism hesitated. She'd been so focused on getting out of the situation she hadn't stopped to think about how they'd gotten into it, but with nothing practical she could do to better her situation, maybe it was time to bring that up. Besides, there might be something useful she could learn about their captor from Alma.

"Alma, I need you to tell me everything you know about Handler and his team."

"He's got compulsion powers. He can make people do things, but you probably already figured that out."

"I had my suspicions." Prism winced at the memory of having her powers used against her friends.

"Sorry about the hair," Tanvi said.

"I've had worse," Prism said, which was true but didn't make her scalp ache any less. "What are his limits? Any weaknesses?"

"No weaknesses that he's ever let on, but he needs to be

able to see the person he's controlling and he can't keep the control up for very long. Maybe a minute or two at the most, depending on the person." Alma let out a staggered breath, as if she were trying not to cry. "He can make you do an awful lot of bad things in that time, though."

Pity crept into Prism. "How long did you work with him before you came to us?"

For a moment it was quiet. Then Alma spoke. "What makes you think—"

"Cut it out, Alma!" Prism snapped. "This is not the time to hang onto secrets. You need to trust us if you want to get out of here, all right?"

"Trusting you has worked out so great in the past." Alma snorted.

Prism's jaw clenched. "I'd say it worked out a lot better than running off on your own to deal with Handler apparently did."

"I had it under control until you two showed up. You weren't supposed to be here!" From the rawness in her voice, Alma was now undoubtedly crying. Prism's conscience balked. She hadn't meant to upset her.

No, upsetting her is not what you should feel bad about, a voice in her head that sounded a little like Fade chided her. *You gave that girl every chance, more freedom than she merited, and in return she turned on you. Maybe she had her reasons, but dang it, Prism, it's time for you to be the adult here. Not her friend. Not her confidant. A damn adult.*

"No, we should've been there. We should've known exactly what you were doing so that we'd be able to face it with you rather than stumbling into it blind," Prism forced her tone as stern as she could make it.

I'm a superhero team leader. What does it say about me that I can't even control one wayward teen? All right, focus. This isn't the place to doubt myself, or to bargain. Dang it, why wasn't I firmer with her from the start?

"Maybe it's partially my fault. I trusted you too much. Gave you too long a leash, but I'm used to dealing with adults who can be trusted with that sort of freedom, not kids who aren't ready for it—"

"I'm ready—"

"No, you're not," Prism barked. "The very fact that you flew off to face a dangerous supervillain on your own without warning your team what was going on makes that undeniable. Like I said, partially my mistake, but this isn't the time to go over who mishandled what. It's time to work together, trust each other, and get the heck out of here. So now, I repeat, how long did you work for Handler?"

"Almost two years," Alma mumbled.

"What did he do to you during that time?" Worry tinged Tanvi's voice.

"Mostly just made me steal stuff. That's all he's really interested in. Money. I guess there are worse sorts of creeps out there, but I still never liked him much."

"Me either." Tanvi cringed.

"He said something about your sister—and you said something about Fade knowing." Prism sickened at the thought that Fade might've been hiding something that momentous from her. "Is Fade in danger?"

"I hope not." Prism could hear the boards creak as Alma changed positions. "I didn't want to get him involved, but I didn't know what else to do. I couldn't be in two places at once, and I needed to take care of Handler but also get Jabz away from Lupita. I only texted him right before I came here. He doesn't know anything about Handler, and I think the fact that Handler can't get a hold of Jabz means Fade got to him and … and maybe Lupita is safe." The girl's voice cracked.

At least Fade hadn't kept a secret from Prism for very long.

"Why didn't you tell us about your sister?" Tanvi

squirmed to angle herself towards the girl, jostling Prism again as she did so.

"Because if DOSA finds out where she's hiding, they'll take her away from me. Are you guys going to adopt her? She doesn't have superpowers, so you won't have any use for her." Bitterness laced Alma's words.

"Use for her?" Tanvi's pitch rose. "What does that matter? She's your sister and you should be with her."

"That's never mattered before. It especially won't matter when you ship me off to the east coast to be with that stupid couple. They're sables. They won't want my non-sable sister."

Prism blinked. "You're talking about Melodica and Tapman?"

"I heard you last night. You're going to send me away." Alma's speech turned to full on blubbering. "But it doesn't matter now. Handler will never let me get away. Even if they pay the ransom, he won't let me go. He never lets go, and as long as he's got his claws in me, I can't be with Lupita. It's too dangerous."

"Oh, Alma, we won't let them separate you two!" Tanvi said. "You don't have to go with Melodica if you don't want to. We were only considering it because this is dangerous. It's bad enough to lose an adult friend to the hero life." Tanvi choked on a sob. "If something happened to you, though, it wouldn't just be sad, it would be my fault, and I can't ... you need a chance to grow up. Once you do, if you want to fight at my side, I'd be honored, but until then, we need to find a solution that lets you be safe ... and now that I know about her, we need your sister to be safe with you."

Prism gave a firm nod, in spite of the fact that no one could see it in the darkness. "She's right. We'll stick up for you in this, but first, let's focus on getting out of here." She dropped her voice lower. "You told me about Handler, what about his team? I saw two kids, a boy and a girl."

"That's all he's got unless he's found somebody new since I left." Alma sniffled. "Dang it, I need a tissue."

"The girl—"

"Shaina," Alma added.

"She's the one with the electricity powers?"

"Yeah, they can stun and hurt a lot, but mostly Handler uses her to overload alarms and security systems when we're on a mission."

"What about the boy? I didn't see him use any powers?"

"Jackson, and it's hard to explain. He calls it 'mapping' but he can trace people's routes in his head or tell a building's floor plan from looking at the outside. Mostly he cases potential targets and keeps track of police patrols for Handler, but he also probably used it to mark my approach so Handler was ready when I got here." Alma sighed. "I knew he would. I just hoped if he thought I was bringing him what he wanted, his guard would be down."

Prism frowned, remembering the way Handler had searched through Alma's belongings.

"What exactly did he—"

The door to the shed creaked open, letting in pink evening light. Prism blinked as dots danced before her eyes.

Shaina entered, a camping lantern in one hand, a large bottle of water in the other. "Handler said I could bring you something to drink."

"Thank you." Prism gave the girl her best smile. "It'll be hard to drink with my arms like this." She indicated her cuffs with her chin.

Shaina scowled. "I'm not stupid. You'll just have to figure it out."

Prism grimaced and wriggled into a sitting position. Alma and Tanvi followed her example. Shaina held the bottle up to each of their mouths in turn.

"Don't suppose there's a chance at getting some food

too?" Tanvi tilted her head to one side like a hungry puppy anticipating a treat.

"Sorry," Shaina mumbled. "It was hard enough convincing him that you needed to drink something to stay alive long enough for him to get his money."

"Why are you working for him?" Prism asked. "I saw your powers. They're incredible. You could get away from him. DOSA would love to have a sable with your ability someday."

Shaina's gaze dropped to her feet. "It's not that easy. I … if DOSA finds me, my mom and stepdad will know where I am. They'll get custody again, and I can't … I can't go back there."

Pain rippled through Prism. "I'm sorry. Let me help you. The SVR—"

"DOSA doesn't want kids," Shaina jerked back. "And you're stupid if you think any of us are getting out of this. He won't risk letting you go. He'll kill you once this is over, and then who will help me? No one." She stomped out, slamming the door behind her but thankfully leaving the lantern.

Prism's chest deflated. So many hurt kids. These ones had only come onto her radar because they were superpowered, but there had to be countless others. It ached to think about it.

The SVR can't help kids. It's not equipped for it, as we've learned with Alma, but there needs to be something.

Something rustled nearby, and Alma cringed. "What's that?" With her head, she indicated a small shadow crossing through the lantern light.

Tanvi pushed herself further away. "Oh, please, don't be a scorpion."

"I think it's just a mouse," Prism said.

"Just a mouse!" Alma squeaked. "Those things carry diseases. What if it bites me?"

"You'll scare it away with the noise you're making." Prism forced a laugh.

However, the mouse didn't spook. It sat beside the lantern, watching the trio of prisoners, its tiny ears twitching. The shed fell silent.

The mouse vibrated and expanded. Alma sucked in a breath as Yui formed before them.

"Oh, thank God it's you." Prism allowed her muscles to relax. "I wasn't sure what had happened to you in the warehouse."

"I followed you," Yui explained.

Alma frowned at her. "You're that weird cat, aren't you?"

"I am a normal cat." Yui bristled. A slow smile crept across her face. "But I am a weird person."

"We need to get out of here," Prism said. "Handler has the remotes for these disruptors somewhere. Do you think you can find them? Or get a message to Fade and Keeper so they know where we are?"

"Fade and Keeper are near," Yui said, glancing anxiously back at the door. "They asked me to make sure you were all right."

"You can tell them we're fine—"

Yui tensed. "Someone's coming!" She shrank immediately into a large, hairy spider.

Prism's skin crawled, and Tanvi moaned, "Seriously?" as the now eight-legged Yui skittered across the floor and up the nearest wall.

The door burst open. Handler's gaze shot around the interior before resting on Alma. "Come with me." He reached down and yanked her up by the disruptor cuff across her chest. Her eyes went wide with fear.

Prism's chest tightened.

"Let her go!" Tanvi snarled. She kicked out at him, but he hopped out of the way, forcing Alma's body between himself and the other two captives.

"Quiet." A slow smile spread across his face. "Your friends are apparently coming through with the ransom money, so you two at least will be out of here soon. Alma, though, I have another use for."

Alma dragged her feet as he pulled her out of the shed. In response, he twitched a finger at her. She stiffened then fell in step walking quietly beside him. Her jerky movements and furious eyes spoke to her frustration.

Prism gritted her teeth as the door shut again. "Dang it."

Yui skittered off the wall and reformed in her human form, face drawn. "What should I do?"

"See if you can get me the remotes for the disruptors to get us out of here," Prism said. "We need to hurry. We can't let him hurt her."

Chapter Twenty Five

Alma's muscles relaxed as Handler's hold on her faded and her limbs returned to her own control. Handler's beat up trailer sat a stone's throw from the shed. A fire crackled in a metal firepit in front of it. Around this, Shaina and Jackson sat in two ancient folding chairs, both hiding in hoodies. They focused on their feet when Alma passed them.

Handler jerked open the door to the trailer and motioned for Alma to get in.

She drew back. "Why?"

He raised his hand. "You've never been able to resist my powers for long, and with that disruptor on you, I'd bet you're even more susceptible to them. Don't make me do this the hard way, Ramos. We need to talk."

In spite of her rage and fear, curiosity chewed at Alma. What could he want to talk about? She stomped into the trailer and slouched on the bench seat on one side of the collapsible table.

Handler slid onto the bench on the other side and stared her down. "Jabz told me you foiled his attack on the DOSA HQ."

"He was an easy take down," Alma shrugged. "A couple hits and he ran like a loser."

"That's what we need to talk about." Handler leaned across the table. "Jabz is *not* an easy take down. He's stayed out of DOSA's grasp for longer than you've been alive and has a reputation for crushing anyone who gets in his way. How did a fourteen-year-old kid beat him in a one-on-one fight?"

Alma glowered at him rather than answering.

"I want to make you a proposition, Ramos." Handler

reached into his pocket and pulled out one of the disruptor remotes.

Alma tried not to look at it, but it called to her, promising freedom and the ability to access her powers again.

Dios Mio, I feel like I've run a marathon wearing concrete boots. How do normal people put up with feeling so weak and sluggish?

"The DOSA sables out there, they're too hard to control, too eager to turn me in, but you, you're not the hero type. Even before I got a hold of you, you were committing petty theft, trespassing, even the occasional B and E."

"To survive!" she snarled at him. "Not because I liked it."

"There are plenty of ways to survive that don't involve crime. People like us, we don't go into the villain life because we have to. We do it because we want to. Because it gives us the power to live by our own rules, if by any, to take what we want and leave what we want and never look back." He fiddled with the remote. "After I made the ransom demands, I got to thinking: sure, I'll take a quarter of a million a piece for those two, but you? You're worth way more to me than that, not as a hostage but as a partner."

Alma's eyebrows shot up. "A partner? To you?"

"Think about it!" He sat up straighter, eyes glinting. "Nothing could stop us. We could have our own criminal empire. Between your powers and my strategic mind, we'd leave DOSA in the dust."

"How about you go shove your criminal empire up your butt?" Alma snapped. "You think I'm an idiot? You think I believe for one second that I'd be a partner rather than your slave?"

A rustling noise drew her attention away from Handler's face to the open window behind him. Her jaw dropped as she watched a tarantula the size of her hand wriggling through a rip in the screen.

Got to be Yui. Looking for the remotes probably.

The tarantula skittered out of sight behind Handler's head. Alma wished she could send telepathic messages to the spider. The backpack containing Alma's belongings, and probably also everything she'd brought with her from HQ including any spare disruptors or remotes, rested on the couch at the far end of the trailer.

A thought struck Alma. She forced her voice to steady and tried to keep her eyes off the remote. "Okay, maybe I'm being unreasonable. You're right. I'm not really the hero sort. I was planning to bug out of DOSA as soon as possible anyway. Maybe working with you wouldn't be so bad."

His fingers caressed the remote. Her throat tightened. The tarantula appeared again, climbing up the front of the couch towards the backpack. Sweat broke out across Alma's forehead.

Just let me go. Let me free.

"Good. We'll talk about it after we've unloaded the DOSA bimbos." He started to stand.

"Wait!" Alma gasped. The tarantula scurried the last several inches and hid inside the backpack. Alma tried to push her heart out of her mouth. "Aren't you going to free me?" She glanced down at the disruptor cuff.

Handler laughed. "What kind of idiot do you take me for, Ramos? Why would I do that? So you can fly off? No, you are keeping that on until I am sure you aren't going to try anything stupid."

Alma's face darkened. Anger sparked within her, and her powers bubbled and fizzed in response, like a soda bottle that had been shaken up. The energy pushed against the disruptor, fighting to get out of her. The disruptor shoved it down, foiled it, prevented her from using it to lash out at Handler. She wanted to scream.

If she wasn't going to be able to get out of this by

pretending to go along with him, she might as well give him a piece of her mind.

"I'd sooner die than work with you. No, wait, I'd sooner kill you! All my life, I thought I had no choice but to go along with creeps like you, people who might use me, but at least they'd keep me safe, give me a chance to survive, but I'm done with that. I want more than survival. I want to be cared for. I want to have people who care about me—"

His lip curled in contempt. "You're not worth caring about, you worthless—"

"That's where you're wrong." Alma squared her shoulders. "I found people who do care about me. My team cares about me. They think I'm important and have potential. They want to keep me safe without taking anything from me in return. They're good people, and you put me in a position to hurt them. I'll never forgive you for that. You're right to not take me out of these cuffs because the moment I get out, I'm going to punch you so hard your teeth will end up in a different state."

"Don't you talk to me like that, you brat," Handler snarled.

"I'll talk to you however I want because I'm not worthless. You are! You are because no one would ever want to be with you if you didn't force them to, if you didn't threaten and intimidate them, bully them into staying. You can't understand what it's like to have people you care about because no one will ever care about you, you garbage person—"

Handler shot across the trailer and slapped her face.

Alma recoiled, her eyes watering from the sting.

He raised his hand again but stopped. An evil smile blossomed on his face, the grin of a shark about to chomp down on a baby seal. "Maybe I'm wrong. Maybe you're not worthless. You're my insurance policy in case this goes south." He walked over to the cabinet where he kept his private stash, unlocked it with a key from his pocket, and pulled out a bulky looking belt with exposed wires. "I bought this off an acquaintance with an unhealthy fascination with explosives." He stomped over and strapped it around Alma then exhibited a remote with a fingerprint scanner. "This is a deadman's switch, but rather than going off if I let go of a button, this one will go off if it doesn't get an input with my fingerprint on it within a certain time frame. I think I'll set it to once every five minutes." He twisted a dial.

Alma's pulse spiked. "What good will that do you?"

"If your DOSA pals decide to take me out instead of paying the ransom, you'll go up in itty bitty pieces." He cackled. "Maybe I'll be standing close enough for it to take me out too, but I'd rather get vaporized than for DOSA to take me in. I've never been one to stay in one place for more than a few weeks, as you know, so a holding cell— well, it would probably kill me anyway."

A glint of madness crept into his eyes, and Alma's heart hammered until it hurt. He was serious. This was real. Was she going to die today?

"You can't do this. Please. Just let them give you the ransom money for all three of us and let us go." She choked on her own fear. The world blurred, and her powers buzzed within her until she could hardly hear or see let alone think straight.

"Easy, Ramos." He tapped her on the nose with his remote. "I'm not sure how well this thing is engineered. You shake too much, it might just set that bomb off. Don't try to wiggle out of it. Wire comes loose, and you won't be seeing fifteen." He winked, spun on his heels, and exited the trailer, slamming the door behind him so hard the whole trailer shook.

Alma sat, stiff and still, tears that she couldn't wipe away trickling from her eyes.

Yui sprang up in her human form and crossed to her. "Can I get it off?" She reached for it, but Alma leaned away.

"No! What if he's right and it goes off?" she hissed.

Yui's lips pursed. "I will get the team. Tell them what's going on. We'll bring you help." She returned to the backpack and pocketed the remotes for the disruptors as well as Tanvi's portable armor, and Prism's wrist lasers before giving Alma a faint smile. "Hold on. I'll be right back."

"Please, hurry," Alma whimpered.

Yui shrank into her spider form again and scurried out the window. In spite of her terror, Alma had to wonder what happened to the things in her pockets—like the remotes—when she shifted like that.

Her chest ached from the pounding of her heart. She didn't want to die like this. She had to get out of here.

Oh, please, Yui, hurry.

Chapter Twenty-Six

Fade pressed himself against the concrete wall that surrounded the trailer park. He concentrated his powers in his right hand, fading it in and out of the wall, trying not to think about Prism being in danger or about potentially never seeing her again ... but somehow only being able to think about exactly that.

Keeper stood a little ways from him, watching the road that led up to the gate. From what they'd observed, most of the lot was empty. The few trailers and RVs parked there looked derelict and abandoned. At least that meant they wouldn't have to deal with potential civilian involvement when it came time to make their move.

"What's taking Yui so long?" Fade hissed.

"It's a lot slower traveling as a mouse," Keeper reminded him. "She needs to be something a wee bit smaller than usual to avoid being seen. Wouldn't do to have a cheetah streaking through a San Clemente trailer park, now would it?"

Fade subsided, but anxiety still chewed at him. "Can you check in on her telepathically?"

"Out of range."

Fade shut his eyes. Once this was over, he wasn't letting Prism out of his sight for a week. His phone buzzed. He jerked to attention.

"It's him again." He scowled at the screen. He hit answer and flipped it to speaker. "What is it now, Handler?"

"My friend with the tracking powers says you're close," the villain answered. "I'm hoping that means you've got my money."

Fade and Keeper exchanged a glance. Fade hadn't

anticipated dealing with tracking powers.

He cleared his throat. "We do, but not in cash. We need to figure out how to do a wire transfer to you."

For a moment the line was silent.

"If you are planning to do a wire transfer, then why are you here? Also, how did you find me in the first place?"

"First off, we're here because we're not transferring the money until we have eyes on our friends," Fade said through clenched teeth. "Second, you're not the only sable with access to tracking powers, and our methods are our business. Do you have Prism, Tanvi, and Alma or not?"

"I'll let you have your two DOSA friends, but Alma's staying, an insurance policy that you won't turn on me the moment the other two are safe."

Keeper's fists clenched, and Fade's jaw tightened until it hurt.

"That wasn't the deal."

"The girl was mine to start with. You stole her from me. I'm simply taking back what I own. Also, don't come any closer if you want to keep her in one piece. I've got her strapped to explode. If something happens to me, or if I see you trying to save the hostages like an idiot, the bomb goes off. Understand?"

"Perfectly," Fade growled. "I'm warning you, though, if that's how you want to play it, you're signing your death warrant. If you take Alma, we'll come after her, and we won't stop until you're caught. Trust me. I don't do gentle takedowns when someone is threatening my family."

Handler scoffed. "I'm trembling, but I'll get over it. Come to the front gate. I'll send you a text message with a link to an online account I set up for just such an occasion. Once you've seen that your girls are safe, you hit transfer, I let them walk to you. Deal?"

"See you there." Fade hit the hang up button then glanced at Keeper. "We can't let him take Alma. This guy has to go down now."

"Sounds like he's got some sort of dead man's switch on her, though." Keeper's brows melted together. "How do we take him down without also taking down the lass?"

Fade blew out a long breath. "We need Prism and Tanvi. Come on. Let's get closer and you can try and communicate with Yui."

Fade's head ached.

Easy, he told himself. *Lucia isn't going to be sitting on her hands. If there's a way out from her end, she'll be working towards it, and Yui and Tanvi are competent too. We'll get through this. We have to get through this.*

***

Prism's shoulders slumped in relief as Yui shot up to full size in front of her. The minutes since Handler had dragged Alma out of the shed had passed like hours. Tanvi was still shaking with rage and distress.

"How's Alma?" Tanvi burst out before Prism could speak.

Yui's face pinched. "Not good. He has her strapped to explosives, and he's got the deadman's switch."

Prism's blood went cold.

"That bastard," Tanvi hissed.

"Can you get us out of these?" Prism nodded towards her cuffs.

Yui pulled remotes out of her pocket and clicked the buttons. The cuffs retracted and clattered to the ground. Crowing in delight, Tanvi popped to her feet.

"Shh," Prism cautioned. She extinguished the lantern and walked to the door. Pressing her eye to the crack, she squinted out. A fire crackled a little ways away and she thought she saw the glow of streetlights against the twilight. Her fingers twitched. "I can't see very well, but I doubt Handler is far. If he sees us break out of here, he might hurt Alma." She turned to face her companions, now hidden in the darkness towards the back of the shed. "Tanvi, do you think you can get through the back of this shed without making too much noise?"

"Sure. It's just cheap plywood." After a small crash, a beam of faint light pierced the back wall close to the floor. Tanvi pulled at the hole's edges, slowly but surely widening it. "If I weren't afraid of making noise this would be quicker," she grumbled.

"We can't risk it, sorry." Prism knelt beside her. "I think I can make it through that."

"Let me go first." Yui shivered and shrunk into a spider again.

"Oh gah!" Tanvi shied back. "Couldn't you do something less creepy? A butterfly maybe?"

The tarantula waved her front legs like an irritated teacher wagging a finger. She skittered through the opening then returned a second later and waved again.

"I'm guessing that means the coast is clear." Prism pocketed the disruptor cuffs which had coiled into tight springs. "Let's go."

Squeezing through the gap, she found herself in an empty section of the park, lit by a single streetlamp. The shed itself blocked their view of Handler's camp—and hopefully also his view of them.

Tanvi rubbed her bare arms against the chill night air. "I wish I had my armor."

Yui shot up to human size again and reached under her jacket. "I forgot. I found this." She passed Tanvi the armor belt. "Oh, and also these." She presented Prism with her laser wristlets.

Annoyance rippled through Prism, and she almost snapped that if Yui had given her those right away she could've cut their way out of the shed rather than have Tanvi punch through the wall, but she kept quiet.

Tanvi beamed, slapped the travel armor around her

waist, and activated it. The plates of light, flexible metal slid to cover her body.

Yui's eyes lit up. "I know where Bob is. I can take you to him. Follow me." She transformed into a bird and fluttered towards the wall surrounding the park.

Tanvi eyed Prism. "This means I'm carrying you again, doesn't it?"

"Well, in a figurative sense, haven't I been carrying the team for a long time?" Prism winked.

Tanvi groaned. "We better hurry. Keeper's weird wife is getting away."

"Here, let me project us." Accessing her powers, Prism pushed their images away from them, hopefully still out of Handler's view. "We need to go fast, before he figures out we're gone and does something to Alma."

Tanvi lifted Prism into the sky, this time only a short hop over the nearby wall. They landed in the street on the other side, and Prism's heart skipped a beat. Fade and Keeper stood a little ways down the road, talking with the now human again Yui.

Instinctively she dropped her projection. "Fade!" she gasped.

He turned, and his eyes widened before a broad smile spread across his face. He sprinted towards her. Prism took several steps before she even realized she was running. They collided into each other. Her feet left the ground as her arms surrounded his neck, holding on with all her might. His hands tightened into her rib cage, and he pressed his mouth into hers in a firm kiss.

Tears filled her eyes. Her suppressed fear of never seeing him again, of not living long enough to experience a life as his spouse, welled through her. She clung to him.

He pulled away. "You're all right?"

She managed to nod. His hand brushed across her face and up into her hair.

"I thought ... when I found out you'd been captured—" He swallowed and dropped to his knees.

Her breath hitched. "Fade, are you all right?"

"Will you marry me?" He gazed up at her earnestly.

Fear turned to confusion. "I ... already said yes?"

"No, I mean as soon as we've taken down this Handler jackass and saved Alma. You, me, Vegas? It's like a five hour drive. We could be there in no time."

She stared at his fingers entwined with hers, remembering the way she'd felt in that dress what felt like forever before and how much she'd longed for him during her captivity. Her resolve hardened, and she kissed his forehead. "Yes, definitely yes, but first we have work to do."

She looked up and found Tanvi, Keeper, and Yui all smiling at her. She blushed then crossed her arms.

Fade coughed and got up from the ground. "Uh ... yeah. Let's get to work."

Prism glanced at the wall. "Handler doesn't know we're gone yet, but it won't take him long."

"He's expecting Keeper and me to meet him at the entrance in a few minutes with his ransom," Fade put in. "He's got Alma strapped to a bomb, though Luce."

"I know. Yui told me." Prism bit her bottom lip. "There's no way around it. Once he finds out Tanvi and I have escaped, we have no assurance he won't kill Alma—or the other kids for that matter. We've got to call his bluff. If he hurts Alma, we hurt him. He has nothing to gain by turning on her and everything to lose." She glanced at Tanvi. "Get around to the other side of his trailer in case he tries to escape out the back. Don't let him see you."

"Roger." Tanvi nodded and sprang into the air. "I'll take the long way around." She zipped off down the street, keeping below the level of the wall.

"Keeper, Fade, you need to head to the entrance as if you're really bringing the ransom." Prism pointed at Yui.

"Try to get into the camp in whatever form you think is best. I'm going to shadow Fade and Keeper in case something goes wrong."

Yui gave a curt nod, shimmered into a bird, and flapped back over the wall.

"Let's go," Prism said to her remaining team.

Prism stayed a few feet behind as Keeper and Fade approached the entrance to the trailer park, a metal gate with a keypad code. Projecting herself so she could stay hidden, she moved to stand directly behind the men, allowing her a clear view through the gate and into the mostly empty trailer park.

Handler's trailer was in line of sight from the gate. The two kids still sat in front of the fire. Handler looked up at the men's approach. "Code's 1234. They aren't too bright around here." He entered the trailer only to emerge a few seconds later dragging a red-eyed, shaking Alma. Prism's heart twisted. Luckily Tanvi wasn't there. The sight probably would've sent her into a rage.

"You okay, Alma?" Fade called out.

Alma shook her head, her shoulders hitching in a sob.

Handler thrust her to the side and held up his hand to exhibit the deadman's switch. "So you don't think I'm playing." He nodded to Alma. "One false move and I vaporize the brat."

Alma stood taller, staring directly forward.

"Shaina, Jackson, get the hostages," Handler ordered.

Prism's stomach flipped. This was it.

The two kids hurried to obey. She eased closer to Fade. His energy flickered in and out, tangible even from a foot away. She scanned the camp but couldn't see any sign of Yui. Of course, for all she knew the woman might be a flea at the moment. She brushed her hand against Fade to let him know she was close then crept forward. Any moment now—

"Handler!" the boy shouted. "They're gone."

Handler jolted. He whirled around snarling. "What the hell? What do you mean they're gone?"

Shaina and Jackson returned, both quivering.

"There's a hole in the back of the shed, and they're—they're just gone," Shaina stammered.

Handler's gaze darted from Fade to Keeper. He pointed the hand holding the deadman's switch at them. "What did you do?"

"Nothing. Our girls can take care of themselves," Fade said calmly.

Prism eased to stand directly beside Alma. Maybe she wouldn't be able to protect the girl from a blast, but she needed to be close enough to try … something. She considered the device strapped to Alma. Of their team, only Aiden had ever gone through EOD training, and obviously that didn't do her much good now. Dang it, she needed to put that on her to-do list.

"So I guess you don't care if the girl dies then?" Handler growled.

Alma shuddered.

"Think before you do anything," Fade said. "With Prism and Tanvi free, that girl is the last card you have to play. Sending her up in smoke? That's just bad business, isn't it?"

The veins in Handler's neck bulged. "Maybe I want to see your face when she turns into a fine red mist. Maybe that would be worth a little bad business."

Prism's mouth went dry. If they took Handler down, how long would they have before the bomb went off? Would it be immediate?

Keeper stepped closer. "Ach, don't be a fool. Let the lass go, and we'll let you go. It's that simple."

Handler's gaze darted from Fade to Keeper to Alma then back again. Then his face hardened. "I'll see you all in hell. Shaina!" He jabbed his finger at the girl. She cried out in pain as her hands shot out in front of her. Jackson yelped and hit the ground, covering his head. A wave or crackling electricity shot from the girl straight at Fade and Keeper.

"Look out!" Fade ghosted but the power still surrounded him. He winced and staggered back a step, his face contorting. Keeper hit the ground, screaming.

"Bob!" Yui flashed to her full form right beside Handler. Handler spun to face her. "What the—?"

Yui punched him. He staggered back, gripping his nose and cursing. She shimmered into cat form and bounded towards her husband.

Handler pulled his hands from his face. Blood streamed from his nostrils onto his mustache. "That's it! You're all going down even if I go with you!" His hand holding the deadman's switch shook.

Desperate, Prism activated her lasers, dropping the projection.

Handler's gaze shot to her. "You! You're going to fry!"

He directed his hands at Shaina again. A thought struck Prism.

Electricity makes light. I bend light.

Shaina whimpered as her powers exploded again. Acting on sheer instinct, Prism projected a burst of blinding light. The energy waves collided. The electricity bounced off Prism's light blast and washed back over both Shaina and Jackson. The two kids screamed in pain and hit the ground.

Handler shrieked. "I'll take you down myself!" He drew a gun from behind his back. He aimed it at Prism then pushed past her to grab Alma. He backed towards the front of the trailer where a beat up truck was parked. He shoved his weapon against Alma's neck. "I'm getting out of here and if you want the girl to keep breathing, you'll stay back and let me go."

Prism's muscles tensed. Could she move fast enough to

disarm him before he hurt Alma?

With a huge crash, Handler's trailer left the ground and hurtled over everyone's heads. It slammed into the concrete wall surrounding the park. All heads whipped around to see Tanvi glaring at Handler from where the trailer had previously sat.

"Let Alma go!" she bellowed.

Keeper jerked to his feet, gripping Yui the cat against his body. Fade, looking shaken but overall no worse for wear, put his hand on the older man's arm, trying to help him stand.

"Ach, I'm fine. Just a wee shock." Keeper shook him off.

Handler pulled Alma against his chest, jabbing the barrel of his handgun hard into her neck. "I'll do it! I'll kill her!"

The group surrounded him, Tanvi gliding in from one side, while Prism, Fade, and Keeper closed in from the others. Shaina and Jackson melted into the shadows, not seeming eager to come to Handler's aid.

The man's hand shook, and Prism froze. Her gaze darted to each team member in turn, wishing she could telepathically tell them to be careful.

"What do you even want her for? She's nothing, a nobody I plucked off the streets!" Handler spat. "You DOSA lackeys won't want her for long. For now she's a shiny new toy, but I know the truth. She's a nobody and good for nothing."

Rage rippled across Alma's face, chasing away the fear. Her whole body shone. The disruptor around her chest sparked.

"I'm not nobody," Alma hissed.

"Shut up!" Handler shouted.

"No, I won't shut up."

The disruptor gave a loud whirring whine, as if it was struggling to hold a great weight in place. Everyone stared.

"I'm not nobody!" Alma shrieked. "I'm Soulbird!"

A blast of energy shot from the girl. The disruptor flew into pieces and the explosive belt disintegrated. A shock wave crashed into Prism, knocking her back on her butt. She sat up, head spinning to see her team similarly laid low —but not hurt. Handler crashed into the ground several feet behind Prism.

Then all was quiet.

Alma stood, glowing from the inside, eyes alight.

Tanvi picked herself out of the dirt. "Girl, what the crap?"

Chapter Twenty-Seven

Alma stared at her own hands. Light raced through her veins. She could feel her power in a way she'd never felt it before, alive, like a separate being within her. The team stared at her in a mix of awe and horror and the reality of what she'd just done hit her like a load of bricks. She collapsed to her knees, sobbing.

Prism hopped to her feet. "Fade, Keeper, secure Handler and the kids." She reached into her pocket and pulled out a disruptor. "Snap this on Handler and don't be gentle." She tossed the disruptor to Fade.

"My pleasure." Fade scowled.

Tanvi rushed to Alma and grabbed her by the arms. "Are you all right? You just … exploded or something."

Alma managed a shaky nod. "I'm … I'm fine."

"You don't look fine." Tanvi brushed her hand over Alma's forehead, pushing back stray locks of dark hair that had fallen out of her ponytail and into her face.

The tenderness after a night of trauma was the last drop of emotion Alma could take. Alma collapsed against Tanvi and wept. "I'm so sorry. I'm sorry. I didn't mean to get you hurt. I didn't mean for him to … I'm sorry."

Prism came up to them and touched Alma's shoulder. "It's all right. Let's get you back to headquarters."

Even with Yui back as a cat and Tanvi flying behind, the tiny compact sedan that Fade and Keeper had driven there in didn't fit everyone who needed to be transported. They ended up having to call in a DOSA team to take Handler into custody. Prism managed to get them not to take Jackson and Shaina. The kids huddled in the back seat next to Alma, still watching her as if she might explode again at any moment. Alma focused out the window, trying not to look at her former friends. Her last chance at being normal had slipped away from her. After what had happened tonight— whatever she was, it wasn't normal.

Prism got into the passenger seat and waited for Fade. Instead he passed the keys to Keeper.

"There's only room for one more in the car, and I have something I need to do. I'll see you all back at HQ, all right?" He leaned down and kissed his fiancé.

She furrowed her brow. "All right, but stay safe and hurry back. We have ... things we need to talk about."

"By 'things' I hope you mean travel plans to Las Vegas." He smirked.

Her cheeks reddened. "So you were serious about that?"

"Dead serious." He kissed her again.

"I'll pack a bag," she whispered.

Alma didn't speak the entire ride back to HQ. However, when they pulled into the parking lot, her face went numb. An exhausted looking Glint glared at them from where he was still wedged in a hole in the ground.

"Let me out!" he screamed the moment they got out of the car. Prism walked over and picked up the disruptor remote. She pushed the button.

With a sound somewhere between a sob and a growl, he shoved himself out of the hole. "You ... you ... you awful child!" He wagged his finger in Alma's face.

"Sorry, dude," Alma deadpanned.

He gaped at her.

The utter ridiculousness of it combined with her sheer exhaustion overcame Alma, and she doubled over giggling.

"Glint, I'm sorry, it looks like you've been through hell but ..." Prism paused. "What happened tonight is extremely complicated, and I'll have to fill you in later. All that matters is the team has two more supervillains in the bag than they did before this evening and also two new potential SVR recruits." She nodded towards Shaina and Jackson who stared at her. "All's well that ends well, right?"

Glint's mouth opened and closed but nothing came out. Alma snorted, laughing so hard her sides hurt.

Alma stumbled into the lobby, still cackling madly. Prism tried to steer her towards the elevator, probably to get her into bed, but Alma couldn't see straight. She leaned against the wall and laughed until she cried.

The sliding glass doors wooshed open again.

"Hey, Alma, I've got someone here for you," Fade's voice said.

Alma looked up, and her heart jumped into her mouth.

Lupita smiled at her. With a cry, the sisters ran into each other's arms and held on for dear life.

***

Alma's eyes fluttered open. She lay on her bed with Lupita beside her. Her vision was blurry, and she felt sleep dragging her down. Why had she woken up at all?

Tap, tap, tap.

Someone knocked on the door … again. She vaguely remembered that she'd heard someone knocking a moment before.

"Who is it?" she moaned.

"It's me, Tanvi. Can we talk?"

Alma sat up. "Just a minute." Not wanting to wake Lupita, she slid out of bed and tiptoed to the door. She still wore her grungy clothes from the day before. They smelled of sour sweat and had a stiffness to them she didn't like, but the evening before she'd been too tired to care.

She cracked open the door. Tanvi smiled hopefully at her from the other side.

"What is it?" Alma asked.

"Can we talk?" Tanvi asked.

Alma crept into the hallway and eased the door shut

behind her. "Make it quick."

Tanvi's face fell. "Hey, don't be like that. I'm missing a chance to be in Vegas with Pris and Fade-o to be here with you."

"Sorry. I'm just really tired." Alma rubbed her eyes. "Vegas?"

"Long story—well, short story. They got sick of waiting and decided to elope." Tanvi shrugged. "I wanted to go, but someone needed to be here with you, you know?"

"I guess." A thought struck Alma. "What about Tia Maria? Where is she?"

"Back home, with a nurse I called in. She really needs full-time care, Alma. You know that right? And I don't mean full-time care from your little sister. That's not going to work."

"I guess," Alma mumbled. "Is that what you wanted to talk to me about?"

"No. I mean, it's part of it, but mostly I thought we should clear the air about Melodica and all that." Tanvi searched Alma's face.

Alma's throat tightened. "I don't want to go with her."

"You don't have to, but Alma, you should give her a chance." Tanvi guided Alma down the hall and into the stairwell. "I talked with her on the phone this morning. She's not at all fazed by you having a little sister without powers. In fact, she was delighted at the idea that she could help keep you two together." She cleared her throat. "The fact that you're probably one of the most powerful sables on record was a little harder for her to get her head around, but she said that was even more reason for you to have a stable home life and a chance to grow up in a safe environment."

Alma blinked. "The most powerful? What are you talking about?" She kind of knew but didn't want to acknowledge it. What had happened with Handler was a one-off, driven by panic and necessity. It wouldn't happen again.

"Alma—or Soulbird, apparently." Tanvi beamed.

Alma averted her eyes.

"Hey, don't do that." Tanvi gripped Alma's arm. "Look, what you did was amazing. You stood up for yourself and all of us, and you knocked that monster on his butt. Still, I don't know a lot of sables who can overcome a disruptor cuff—in fact, I don't think I know any who can. Even Glint, as you no doubt saw, becomes a whiny baby when he's in one."

"I guess." Alma shifted from foot to foot. "I just ... Tanvi, I like it here. I want to stay with you."

"Oh, Alma. I wish you could." Tanvi hung her head.

Anger prickled within Alma. "Why can't I, though?"

"Because it's too dangerous! Since you've joined our team think about how many times you've almost gotten yourself killed." Agony creased Tanvi's face.

"Yeah, but almost all those times were because I did something stupid," Alma pointed out. "It's not like you were putting me in danger. I just made the wrong choices."

"No, but dang it, Alma, you deserve to be an environment where your temptations are things like being offered a beer at a friend's house or a chance to cheat on a history test, maybe sneak out past your curfew to talk to a really cute boy—not ones where you end up in knock-down-drag-out fights with supervillains." Tanvi's hold on Alma's wrist tightened to a painful degree, but Alma didn't pull away. "You need parents to keep you safe, to give you guidelines. I love you like a little sister, but I'm not sure I'm cut out to be your mother. I'm not ..." Tanvi's voice cracked. "I'm not brave enough to be a mother just yet."

They stood in silence for a moment.

"Look, if not for you, think about it for your little sister. She can't live being threatened by supervillains just because she's close to our team," Tanvi pointed out. "Maybe you two will never have a normal life, but I'm hoping that with Melodica you can at least have a safe one."

"But what if … but what if Melodica can't love me?" Alma whispered.

"I bet you anything she can because I fell in love with you so easily, and I didn't even know I wanted another family member. Melodica *wants* you, and so does her husband." Tanvi's hold on Alma tightened again. "And I promise, if anything goes wrong with Melodica, if she's awful to you, or even if you're having a bad day and need to talk, I'll only be a phone call away. The whole team will." Tears trickled down Tanvi's cheeks. "If you do leave, don't get me wrong. I'm going to miss you, girl. I'm going to miss you so much, but … but I can't be selfish about this. Please, at least give them a chance?"

Hope teased Alma. A chance to have a family, a normal family—at least as normal as someone as weird as she was could hope for—with Lupita. Could it be real? She wouldn't know unless she tried.

"All right, I'll give it a chance."

Chapter Twenty-Eight

Prism closed her eyes and massaged her fingers into Fade's back, savoring the weight of his body pressing down on hers, firm and undeniable yet gentle, leaving her cradled rather than crushed. He hid his face in her hair and let out a contented hum.

She tilted her head to look him in the eyes. A slight smile curled the corners of his full lips, a hazy, blissful look in his half-closed, beautiful brown eyes.

"You look happy," she whispered, trailing her fingers across his cheek to play with his ear.

"I am happy. More so than I can remember being in a long time." He kissed her then propped himself up on one elbow beside her, his gaze lingering on her with obvious appreciation. She blushed.

Deprived of the warmth of his embrace, her skin cooled quickly beneath the thin hotel blankets. She shivered and pulled them up around her bare shoulders.

"It doesn't feel real." She laughed quietly.

"What doesn't?" He arched an eyebrow.

"Finally being Mrs. Fade … Powell? Were you serious about taking my name?"

"It's not like I have one of my own to give you." He lay back on the pillows before slipping his arm around her waist and drawing her against his chest.

She rested her ear over his heart and listened to the gentle thrum of it beating. A memory of his pulse at a more frantic rate, beating in time with hers as she held onto him with all her might, fingers tightening into his shoulder muscles for fear of falling apart if she let him go, stirred a pleasant warmth through her. Her body melted into him, torn between desire prompting her to initiate more lovemaking and contented laziness that made lying still and quiet seem like the perfect choice. Maybe she'd just gently flirt with him and see what he chose.

His stomach grumbled.

She opened her eyes. "Are you hungry?"

"A little." He reached over to the nightstand and glanced at his phone. "It's almost nine. I kind of feel like a big breakfast. How about you?"

She tapped her fingers lightly against his chest. "I guess I could eat." Actually now that the idea had been introduced, her belly did feel hollow. "Order in or dine out?"

"Let's see what's available." He swung his legs out of bed and reached for his jeans. "Either way, I guess I should put on some pants, huh?"

"If you must." She gave an exaggerated sigh.

He chuckled as he pulled them on.

Prism sat up in bed. "Do you see my nightgown anywhere?"

He bent and retrieved it from the floor. She reached for it, but he backed a few steps away, allowing the garment to dangle from his fingertips.

Suppressing a grin, she rose from the bed, never breaking eye contact, and walked to him. His smile broadened. She took the nightgown before draping her arms around his neck.

"Thank you," she whispered. "I think I'm going to take a shower."

"You want company?" he murmured as he kissed her face and neck.

"I wouldn't say no to it." She winked, tossed her nightgown over her shoulder, and sashayed towards the bathroom.

Sometime later, Prism plucked a strawberry from the

top of her takeout french toast and dipped it in whipped cream. She took a bite. Juicy, sweet, and a little tart. Was it just her or did everything taste slightly better today?

She considered Fade who sat across the table, heartily enjoying a plate of eggs and bacon.

"We really didn't set aside time off for a honeymoon, and with everything that happened with Alma, Handler, and Jabz, when we do get back, there's going to be a lot of follow up. As much as I hate to say it, we probably need to go home soon."

Fade washed down a bite of eggs with a gulp of coffee. "Yeah, I know you're right. Truthfully, Vegas isn't my choice for honeymoon spots anyway. I'd rather go somewhere isolated, you know? Me and you in a cabin in the middle of nowhere?"

"Yeah, that sounds good, though I don't regret coming here just to get the legal stuff out of the way." She straightened her engagement ring. "Not exactly my dream wedding, but it got the job done."

"Nothing says we can't have a more traditional ceremony later." He reached across the table to squeeze her hand. "Speaking of legal stuff, though, what's going to happen to the other two kids Handler had in his clutches?"

"Well, if Alma and her sister do accept Melodica and Tapman's offer, it sets a precedent for sable couples adopting at risk sable kids. I'm not saying it will be easy to find a family for every kid who might be out there, but I feel two kids isn't too much to ask. The girl, Shaina I think, apparently has parents, but they're not anyone she wants to be with." Prism shook her head. "I can't imagine being that young and having the strength to be on my own. If her parents are as bad as she says, I think DOSA should help her stay away from them." She tapped her fingers on the paper to-go cup that contained her coffee. "We need some sort of safety net specifically for sable kids in the system.

It's not fair expecting foster parents to manage kids who can fly, shoot electricity from their hands, or knock down walls. Normal parenting is hard enough without introducing those sorts of complications."

"True." Fade took a bite of bacon and chewed slowly. "You do realize, though, that if Alma does accept leaving the team, then we're right back where we started with the Adjudicator wanting us to replace Aiden."

A pang of sadness interrupted Prism's well-being and the sweet, fluffy french toast lost all flavor. She pushed the last few bites around her plate. "I guess. I mean, having Alma as part of the team both helped me realize that I can move forward while making me aware of how much it was going to hurt. All the little reminders that I don't have him on the team anymore—but the long term plans for the SVR were to cycle through various villains. Looking back now, though, that was short sighted. It takes too long to rehabilitate a villain, and by the time the process is complete, they'll have integrated too deeply into the team to easily separate. Look what happened with you."

"I like to think I'm the exception and you won't feel the need to marry every villain you take on as a pet project." He dabbed at his mouth with a napkin in a failed attempt to hide his laughter.

"Well, then look at Alma. If not for her being a minor, do you really think we could've passed her off on another team once she learned to work with us?" Prism pointed at Fade with her fork. The argument renewed her appetite, and she eyed the last piece of bacon on his plate. "Are you going to eat that?"

"I was." He held it up. "What will you give me for it?"

"Whatever you want." She gave him her most seductive smile.

"Sold."

The salty bacon crunched in her mouth.

"You're right, though. If a sable bonds with a team, breaking that bond won't help their path towards rehabilitation. Those anchors are what keeps a sable on the hero path." Fade swigged the last of his coffee.

"Exactly. New spaces simply won't open up all that often. One SVR team isn't enough to meet the demand." She ran her fork through the whipped cream left on her plate. "I think what I need to do is start introducing more teams, training other team leaders to enter the program and take on their own projects."

"Makes sense, but can you sell it to the committee?"

"I think so." Her brain already churned through possible PowerPoint slides and talking points. "I'll start working on a presentation as soon as we're back at HQ."

"That's my girl." Fade chuckled.

Warmth spread through her. This could work. This could be the solution that moved the SVR, and her team, to the next stage. Excitement blossomed within her, and she beamed.

"I have a feeling something amazing is about to happen."

Epilogue

"Brink!"

Doctor Sherman Brink slowly turned his computer chair to face the door as the Adjudicator's angry voice echoed through his lab. He steepled his fingers beneath his chin and gazed pointedly at the doorway.

The Adjudicator stormed through but paused abruptly when his eyes met Brink's.

Brink indulged in a superior smile. "Really, Frank, why must you yell? You interrupted a chain of thought I'd been working on for a good two hours, and it will take me nearly that long to pick up the pieces." He stood and stretched. "Of course, I couldn't expect you to understand. I doubt you've ever had a thought chain longer than two or three links."

"Shut up, you arrogant idiot!" the Adjudicator snapped. He slammed the door shut behind him. The test tubes on the nearby table jangled. "I just found out that our investigatory team traced the payments made to Jabz back to an account under one of your shell companies. Thankfully no one other than me recognized the name, but we might not get that lucky next time. What were you thinking? What did you need from the SVR that was worth the risk of drawing attention to our project?"

"'Our project' meaning my late father's work which only I have the mental acuity to continue?" Brink arched an eyebrow. "That project? Does that mean you're volunteering to help, because I could use a lab assistant to sweep up."

"Don't blather," the Adjudicator grunted. "I'm already on thin enough ice with the other committee members for keeping you on staff at all. If they catch wind about *Osiris* it won't just be your career that's over." He crossed his arms. "I repeat, what did you want from the SVR so badly that it was worth drawing the attention of Powell's team, not to mention a DOSA investigation, to steal?"

Brink let out a long breath. "I have been worried for some time that Aiden Powell might have left behind electronic copies of the will we altered to allow us to take possession of his body. If his sister or team members were to discover it, they could start asking awkward questions."

"Then you should've come to me and let me assign an official DOSA team to collect his personal effects—"

"Which would also cause his team to ask similar, awkward questions." Brink sighed wearily. Would he ever be free of this man's density? "Does it really matter, Frank? You know as well as I they'll never trace the payment back to us. You only recognized the shell company because you've used it as often as I have. What are you really here about?"

The Adjudicator paced to the side of the lab where two isolation chambers, each with an unconscious subject on a table, sat behind walls of bulletproof glass. "Any progress with either subject?"

"No. If there had been, you would've been the first to hear." Brink faced his computer again.

The Adjudicator's shoulders rose and fell in a great breath. "Then pull the plugs."

Brink bolted to his feet, his chair spinning across the floor away from him. "What?"

"It's been months with no progress." The Adjudicator faced him, jaw clenched, voice tight. "The possibilities of a successful experiment were too good for me to give up on without proper diligence, but if it were going to work, we would've seen signs of sentience from at least one of them by now. I have no use for braindead shells, no matter what powers they might've had at one point." He took a step

towards the exit. "If you need help disposing of the bodies
—"

Brink grabbed the Adjudicator's arm. "You can't do this
to me! I'm so close. This project was my father's greatest
work, his lifelong obsession, and you're asking me to give
up after a trial of a few paltry months—"

"It's been over six." The Adjudicator shook himself free.
"With the other committee members breathing down my
neck and the SVR on edge because of the attempted theft, I
can't risk Talon or Shepherd checking in on you—"

"Then we move the lab to a remote location,
somewhere the rest of DOSA doesn't know about." Brink's
heart pounded. This couldn't be happening again. He was
so close this time.

The Adjudicator put up his hand. "Look, I'm not
shutting you down forever. It's too hot to continue with
these two, though, particularly him." He nodded towards
the second isolation room. "We close this down, set up a
new facility, and I'll get you new subjects in a few months.
Ones no one is looking for. Consider this set a learning
experience."

The Adjudicator turned away.

Brink's fists clenched and unclenched, but he pushed
down the rage building within him. Right now, the
Adjudicator had him in a corner. Brink needed his
resources and protection. However, he was so close to the
point where neither would be a factor. Where he could do
whatever he wanted and no one in DOSA—especially not
the Adjudicator—would be able to stop him.

Maybe, though, with a few adjustments, that point
could be sooner than he'd planned.

"All right. I'll take care of it," he said.

"Good to see you reasonable." The Adjudicator gave a
curt nod. "As soon as the evidence is destroyed, send me a
notification. I'll start looking for new locations where we'll

have more privacy as well as secondary subjects."

"Sounds good." Brink returned his computer chair to its previous location as the Adjudicator exited the lab. As soon as he was gone, Brink turned on the computer and switched to the surveillance program he'd set up to watch all exits. He kept his eyes on the screen until he witnessed the Adjudicator leave the building and get into a waiting SUV.

"Not ideal," he then murmured. He stood and walked to the metal table. From this he took to a syringe which he filled with a blue liquid. "Still, if I can push through this last stretch, accelerating the schedule, I can work with it."

Entering the isolation room, he glared down at the body lying there. The unnaturally pale young man with patchy beard and tousled blond hair frowned in his sleep, his chest rising and falling in shallow breaths. A metal band filled with sensors rested about his forehead like a halo.

Brink checked the power disruptor he'd placed around the man's neck. Still active. If only he'd put it on him right away, the subject might not have projected, might not have tried to get a message out. Thankfully, Brink's sensors had caught the spike in telepathic activity almost immediately.

"You're nearly perfect. The most powerful thing I've ever created, far better than anything my father built." He caressed the display screen next to the table, admiring the frenetic brain activity from the deceptively motionless body. "Kevin Powell and his team brought down my father at the height of his genius, reducing him to a DOSA slave when he had the mind power to rule the world." Brink gripped the sleeping man's arm. "And now? Kevin Powell's son will be the weapon I wield to bring down DOSA and all of its petty heroes." A smile spread across Brink's face.

He couldn't wait to get started.

THE END

The Supervillain Rehabilitation Project will return in Book 3: *Reborn.*

ABOUT H. L. Burke

Born in a small town in north central Oregon, H. L. Burke spent most of her childhood around trees and farm animals and always accompanied by a book. Growing up with epic heroes from Middle Earth and Narnia keeping her company, she also became an incurable romantic.

An addictive personality, she jumped from one fandom to another, being at times completely obsessed with various books, movies, or television series (Lord of the Rings, Star Wars, and Star Trek all took their turns), but she has grown to be what she considers a well-rounded connoisseur of geek culture.

Married to her high school crush who is now a US Marine, she has moved multiple times in her adult life but believes home is wherever her husband, two daughters, and pets are.

For information about H. L. Burke's latest novels, to sign up for the author's monthly newsletter, or to contact the writer, go to :

www.hlburkeauthor.com

Also by H. L. Burke

Supervillain Rehabilitation Project
Relapsed (a short story prequel)
Reformed
Redeemed
Reborn
Refined
Reunion

Supervillain Romance Project
Romantic Novellas Set in the SVR Universe:
Blind Date with a Supervillain
On the Run with a Supervillain
Captured by a Supervillain
Engaged to a Supervillain
Accidentally a Supervillain

Superhero Romance Project
Fun, Hallmark-esque Romantic Comedies set in the SVR Universe.:
A Superhero for Christmas
A Superhero Ever After

Supervillain Rescue Project: Young Adult Spin-Off
Power On
Power Play
Power Through
Power Up

For Middle Grade Readers
Thaddeus Whiskers and the Dragon
Cora and the Nurse Dragon
Spider Spell

For Young Adult Readers

An Ordinary Knight
Beggar Magic
Coiled
Spice Bringer
The Heart of the Curiosity
Ashen

The Nyssa Glass Steampunk Series:
Nyssa Glass and the Caper Crisis
Nyssa Glass and the House of Mirrors
Nyssa Glass and the Juliet Dilemma
Nyssa Glass and the Cutpurse Kid
Nyssa Glass's Clockwork Christmas
Nyssa Glass and the Electric Heart

The Elemental Realms Series
Book One: Lands of Ash
Book Two: Call of the Waters

The Dragon and the Scholar Saga (1-4)
A Fantasy Romance Series
Dragon's Curse
Dragon's Debt
Dragon's Rival
Dragon's Bride

The Green Princess: A Fantasy Romance Trilogy
Book One: Flower
Book Two: Fallow
Book Three: Flourish

Ice and Fate Duology
Daughter of Sun, Bride of Ice
Prince of Stars, Son of Fate

To Court a Queen

Spellsmith and Carver Series
Spellsmith & Carver: Magicians' Rivalry

Redeemed

Spellsmith & Carver: Magicians' Trial
Spellsmith & Carver: Magicians' Reckoning

Fellowship of Fantasy Anthologies
Fantastic Creatures
Hall of Heroes
Mythical Doorways
Tales of Ever After
Paws, Claws, and Magic Tales

Match Cats: Three Tails of Love

Made in the USA
Las Vegas, NV
25 November 2023

81506926R00157